DEAD ON COURSE

Glenis Wilson

severn House

This first world hardcover edition published 2015
in Great Britain and the USA by
SEVERN HOUSE PUBLISHERS LTD of
19 Cedar Road, Sutton, Surrey, England, SM2 5DA.
Trade paperback edition first published 2016
in Great Britain and the USA by
SEVERN HOUSE PUBLISHERS LTD.

British Library Cataloguing in Publication Data

Wilson, Glenis author.
  Dead on course.
  1. Horse racing–Fiction. 2. Murder–Investigation–
Fiction. 3. Suspense fiction.
  I. Title
  823.9'2-dc23

ISBN-13: 978-0-7278-8544-9 (cased)
ISBN-13: 978-1-84751-646-6 (trade paper)
ISBN-13: 978-1-78010-703-5 (e-book)

Typeset by Palimpses
Falkirk, Stirlingshire,

Printed digitally in the U

DEAD ON COURSE

Dedicated to my parents
Edna and Albert 'Tal' Wilson

And to my late sister, Heather, the
artist in the family, who loved horses,
supported the horse welfare charities
and helped design the cover of my
first racing novel, Blood on the Turf.

ACKNOWLEDGEMENTS

Mr Nick Sayers at Hodder & Stoughton. His belief in me and the manuscripts kept me going.

Mr David Grossman, my literary agent.

David Meykell, clerk of the course, Leicester Racecourse, for allowing me to 'do' a murder on his racecourse.

Roderick Duncan, clerk of the course, Southwell Racecourse.

Jean Hedley, clerk of the course, Nottingham Racecourse.

Mark McGrath, former manager, Best Western North Shore Hotel and Golf Course, Skegness.

Bill Hutchinson, present manager, and all the lovely staff at the above hotel with special thanks to Gavin Disney, Dan, Nikki, Mariusz and Katie for all their help.

Sarah at Sarah's Flowershop.

All the library staff at Bingham, Radcliffe-on-Trent and Nottingham Central, with special thanks to Steve and to Rosie for her expertise on computers.

David and Anne Brown, printers and friends for bailing me out – twice – and finding just where chapters twelve and thirteen had disappeared to!

Lois Brough, a savvy lady from Crime Readers' Group.

The police at Skegness and the staff at Nottingham Prison for checking facts.

Management at The Dirty Duck at Woolsthorpe.

Kirsty at The Unicorn Hotel at Gunthorpe.

Vickie Litchfield at The Royal Oak, Radcliffe-on-Trent.

Sue, Alison and Martin, the chef at the White Lion, Bingham.

And for all the people who have helped me in whatever way during the course of writing the 'Harry' novels, may I say a very big thank you and have a great read.

ONE

I knew I was a target when I opened the cottage door that morning and found, sitting on the doorstep, a pair of false teeth. I stared down at them, they grinned back at me. A twinge of guilt, unexpected, unpleasant and unwarranted, made itself felt. They weren't real, as in made of porcelain; these were plaster. But they were real enough to me and I knew the message they conveyed.

A finger of apprehension ran down my spine. I was prepared to bet Harlequin Cottage they were replicas of the original false teeth belonging to Carl Smith, jump jockey. Now deceased. Or – more accurately – murdered. We shared unpleasant history.

The whole business was over in physical terms, but obviously not emotionally and mentally with some other person – or persons.

Picking up my morning bottle of milk – and the teeth – I backed into the cottage and nudged the door closed behind me. Leo, my ginger tomcat, fired up his personal pneumatic drill at the sight of the milk and purred loudly. I poured him out a generous saucer before tipping some into my waiting mug of tea. Then I hooked a foot around the chair leg and sat down at the kitchen table.

Placing the teeth on the tabletop, I scrutinized them at close quarters. Lifting the upper set, I delicately placed it squarely above the bottom one. Carl had used a good dentist. The dentures fitted together perfectly. But the reason he had needed to visit the dentist was entirely my fault. However, Carl didn't need them any more; he was dead.

So, the question remained: who had benefited from his demise and inherited his estate, after payments out, of course, of all outstanding debts and testamentary expenses?

I had no idea and I was going to have to find out. Before whoever it was found me. I sighed deeply. *Too late, mate*, I told myself – they already had me pegged and in their sights. The very act of leaving the teeth on my doorstep said, in clear tones, *all your fault*. And, undoubtedly, repercussions would be coming my way very soon.

So, what was new?

For the last three or four months, trouble and personal danger had dogged me. Unfortunate accidents, occasioning actual bodily harm, had befallen me with sickening frequency. But they hadn't been accidents. I'd been a target. However, I'd thought that at last the hellish time was behind me. Now, I was being targeted again.

Sudden anger blazed high inside me. This time I was going to stamp down on whoever was threatening me – very hard.

A ginger paw, complete with grappling irons for claws, reached across the table, batted the dentures and sent them clattering. That was what Leo thought of them. My anger died instantly. He had a very balancing effect on tense situations. I grinned and tickled him behind the ears to deflect him whilst I rescued the teeth from further indignity.

Scooping them up into a plastic freezer bag, I took them through to the office and slid them into one of my desk drawers. I needed them perfect and unbroken. They were crucial to discovering just who was gunning for me.

Leaving them on the cottage doorstep may have been a declaration of war, but as far as I was concerned, the dentures were going to lead me right into the enemy camp.

TWO

I left the dimness of the weighing room and walked across to the parade ring, bathed in late-summer sunshine, to meet two friends. One, long-standing – Mike Grantley, racehorse trainer – and one, very recent – Samuel Simpson, racehorse owner. The man whose racing silks – purple and green – I was wearing, and whose horse – Online – I was about to ride in a three-mile steeplechase over the course at Market Rasen.

I hoped like hell I didn't make a complete horlicks of it and betray their trust. Today was the first time in six months I was race riding. It wasn't my first time in the saddle, of course. Riding out every morning for the last five or six weeks, for Mike on his gallops situated on the Leicestershire/Nottinghamshire border had, thankfully, put paid to my fear. Prior to this, yes, I had doubted myself, felt I'd never ride again.

But gentle hacking, followed by riding out in the morning string and finally riding work, akin to simulated race riding, had sheered up my very real insecurity and wobbly self-belief.

A shattered patella, following a fall over a brushwood jump whilst travelling at possibly thirty miles an hour, was not guaranteed to give any jump jockey confidence in a comeback to race riding.

'Hello, Mike, Samuel,' I greeted them.

Samuel stepped forward and clapped me on the shoulder. 'Good to see you, lad.'

His hand landed on my left shoulder and I was relieved to find it gave me no pain. For one disloyal moment, I wondered if he had deliberately chosen the left one to see if I felt any resulting discomfort. Well, after all, I was riding his horse and he was paying Mike for its upkeep. Samuel needed a jockey who was fully fit.

He knew, only too well, I'd suffered a smashing blow to that shoulder from a criminal intent upon murder and, just days later, taken a bullet in the same place. It could have left my shoulder significantly weakened. Thankfully, it hadn't.

And on a very personal level, it was also entirely my fault that his daughter was struggling to cope with overwhelming heartache and the shame associated with it.

But looking at his open smiling face, I chided myself for the uncharitable thought.

It was a good job I was getting back to normal, going back to work racing. I was in danger of getting paranoid.

I hated to admit it, but finding the false teeth waiting on my doorstep had brought back all the unpleasant and deeply hurtful memories of the last few months. I had found it necessary, then, to be deeply suspicious of just about everybody, with the exception of Mike. And, of course, Annabel.

Annabel, my darling wife. My darling, *estranged* wife who I still desperately wanted back. At that point, I reined in my thoughts. It did no good whatsoever letting myself think of her. I found it deeply enervating.

I needed to concentrate on the imminent race.

'Leg you up?' Mike's enquiry was what I needed. He was smiling and nodding. He knew better than anyone my anguished soul-searching regarding my racing future. Mike was a glass-half-full type of chap. His belief in me had never wavered. I was very lucky I could call him a friend – had been doing for the last twenty-five years or more since we were kids at school together.

Now, he was my boss, and a very successful racehorse trainer – amongst the top ten in the country. Before the ride on Gold Sovereign earlier in the year that resulted in the smashing fall, literally, I'd been his retained jockey. It was a satisfying partnership for both of us, financially and as friends. When you found your back against the wall, there was no finer person to have on your side. I'd trust him with my life. Of course, the reverse was also true, as he knew very well.

I bent a knee and Mike flipped me up into the saddle.

He gave me a light, friendly punch on the thigh. 'No instructions. Ride like you always do.'

'And I've every confidence in you, too, lad.'

'Thanks, Samuel. Glad you could make it today,' I said and meant it. 'Do my best.'

He beamed widely. 'I know you will. And it's not just me, Harry; Chloe's arrived – look.' He nodded towards the crowd packed tightly against the parade ring rails.

A delectable young woman of about thirty, wearing a red belted suit and black ankle boots, topped by a black beret set at a brave, jaunty angle, made her way through the throng and entered the parade ring. She waved and came over to us.

'Darling,' Samuel said and gave her a quick peck on the cheek, 'you look delightful.'

'Thank you, Dad. You know how to bolster a girl's confidence.' She gave him a quick, fierce hug. For a sliver of a second, her veneer of self-belief slipped a fraction. If you hadn't been watching carefully, you wouldn't have noticed. But I was watching and I did. It was going to take time for her to pull up out of the hole into which she'd been pitched head first.

Again, I experienced a twinge of guilt, unexpected, unpleasant and unwarranted.

THREE

Online and I shared previous history. I knew he was a very genuine horse. A bright bay, deep-chested and big-hearted. Always gave of his best and never gave up trying until the post was passed. Owned by Samuel Simpson, I'd ridden him whilst he was being trained by Elspeth Maudsley. When Elspeth had, literally, retired from the scene, Samuel had transferred most of his horses to Mike's yard.

Online was the horse I'd ridden many times on Mike's gallops during the last few weeks. I'd got to know him pretty well. He was one of those horses who didn't respond to the whip. In any case, there was no need to use one: his eagerness to run was gratifying, matched only by my own enthusiasm. We were striving after the same goal.

I cantered him down to the start and walked him in circles with the other horses and jockeys until the starter called us to order.

When the tape went up, we set off at a steady pace consistent with a race of three miles in front of us. Eighteen horses were entered for the race and I settled him into midfield. We lobbed along, holding a nice line close to the rails. Online wasn't favourite – that distinction was held by Dark Duke who was odds-on – but at seven-to-one, fourth in the betting after Silver Charm, he was certainly in with a chance.

However, it wasn't the horse's ability that was in question – he'd won three times, come second several times and was consistently in the frame, especially when the field of horses numbered sixteen and above. For more than fifteen in a race, fourth place counted and was paid out on. With his record, I hoped we could manage fourth.

But it was my own riding that would determine the outcome. Race riding brought its own level of fitness. I'd been sidelined for months, of necessity, with no riding whatsoever. Just how fit I was, I would soon find out. And you certainly needed to be fit to ride a three-mile race and then have energy in spades to push for home

and ride a finish. If Online failed to come in the frame, it wouldn't
be his fault, it would be mine – no question.

And I desperately wanted to make a good fist of this first race.
Not only was fitness necessary for a racing jockey, he needed
confidence – and I knew right now I hadn't got it. A good result
here would be worth far more to me than the prize money it would
bring.

But the other reason I badly wanted to get a result was for Samuel
himself. It was unforgivable of me to have entertained such a low
thought of his intention earlier. But the constant stress I'd been
under for months, together with having to be suspicious of everybody, had left me with my trust in other people considerably shaken.
The end had proved my suspicions justified. But it had made me
less able to trust my judgement – not a pleasant feeling.

It was because of me that Samuel's family had been rocked to
the core. They could have gone the other way and blamed me, and
I wouldn't have blamed them, whereas all I'd received from them
was consideration for the part I'd played – been forced to play. In
the midst of their own pain, they had spared sympathy and compas-
sion for my own grievous loss. If Online could run a good race, I
would feel I was making amends for a situation that had gone way
beyond my control and inflicted such dreadful consequences on
them, especially Samuel's daughter, Chloe. It said a great deal for
Samuel that he had specifically asked Mike to put me up as jockey
today.

But riding Online, with the wind blowing against my cheeks and
the emerald turf flashing away beneath his hooves, my spirits rose
like a released bird. The pure pleasure of simply riding a good horse
that loved his racing was like a drug in my system.

I felt a surge of joy as we met the twelfth fence perfectly placed
and Online flew it with inches to spare and gained three lengths'
advantage, putting him now into sixth place behind the leaders. This
was the real reason I was a jockey. I was doing the only thing I
wanted to do on God's earth. Nothing else compared with the elation
that coursed through me as I galloped for home on a willing, eager
horse who exulted in doing what he'd been born to do – race.

Three fences from home found two of the horses in front running
out of petrol and falling back. I knew how they were feeling. By
now, my own fuel was getting pretty low, but the adrenalin rush in

my bloodstream was overriding my lack of fitness. I set Online at the next brushwood jump and he took it smoothly.

With four horses in front – two fighting it out in first and second place, and third and fourth nose to nose two lengths behind – and only two jumps left before the run-in for home, I knew Online had reserves I could ask of him.

We cleared the last safely, and as the other jockeys were now making use of whips to urge their horses on, I simply lay forward along Online's neck and forcibly threw the reins forward, rhythmically matching his reaching, ground-eating stride, and kicked for home.

The great-hearted animal responded magnificently, found that extra drop of petrol and stretched for the post.

Vaguely, I heard the crowd roaring on the stands, but the winning post was coming up fast and, with a horse on either side of me, the three of us flashed past perfectly in line. It was going to take a photo finish to decide the one, two, three.

I was as high as a jet plane, the weeks lying in a hospital bed a long, long way behind me now. I was back. If Online hadn't won, I knew *I* had.

We pulled up, both sweating and blowing, but filled with the intoxicating joy of living life at full tilt, as it should be.

We walked back towards the winner's enclosure as the tannoy broke in above the shouts of the crowd. It was a dead heat between Dark Duke and Online, with the other horse, Silver Charm, in third place.

I patted the horse's sweating neck, pulling his ears gently and telling him what a great fella he was. He in turn shook his head, making the bit jingle, and arched his solid, well-muscled neck proudly. Horses know when they have done well and he deserved my gratitude for his gallant effort.

There was a concerted burst of clapping as we entered the winners' enclosure. I dismounted and undid the girth, letting the saddle slide down over my arm. I needed to take it into the weighing room with me to weigh in, check that it tallied.

'Well done, Harry.' Samuel grabbed my hand and pumped it. 'A superb race. Knew you could do it.'

'Thanks for the support. It certainly helped. Just glad I didn't let you down.'

'You could never let us down.' Chloe appeared at her father's side, her silky hair blowing in the breeze from beneath the black beret. 'You did great.' She stood on tiptoe and gave me a quick kiss on the cheek. 'What a marvellous comeback. Bet you're wired.'

I grinned and looked across at Mike standing with the stable lad beside the horse. Online was very pleased with himself, tossing his head, still full of it. 'You could say that.'

Mike, courteously allowing Samuel to speak first, said, 'Told you so. Should have put you on several more.'

I raised a palm. 'Uh-huh, one's enough today.'

His smile spread wider. He knew what I knew and what the others did not: right now my legs were feeling like chewed string. It was true. Nothing but race riding could get you fit. And I certainly wasn't – not yet. But I would be, very soon. Nothing was going to stop me from accepting rides now. Suddenly, my life was back on course. It was a very sweet feeling.

They were all three waiting for me in the owners and trainers' bar after I'd changed out of the green-and-purple silks into normal clothes.

I threaded my way through little groups of laughing, chattering owners and their trainers, many of whom raised an acknowledging hand to me or called out a quick greeting on the lines of good to see you back. It reminded me of the old saying: nothing succeeds like success. And in the world of horse racing, a jockey was only as successful as his last winning ride. I smiled acknowledgements back and made my way over to where Chloe's red suit added a bright splash of colour amongst the more muted and suited men.

Mike pushed a cup of unsweetened coffee into my hand. 'Grab a seat.'

My euphoria had calmed and all I felt now was a contented weariness, coupled, unfortunately, with an all-over aching, but especially in my left leg, the one that had suffered the broken kneecap. However, I was glad to be alive, to feel the aches; the man I'd landed on top of back in the spring of the year was dead. He was murdered before he could spill the beans to me about who was trying to kill my disabled half-sister.

I pushed the dark thoughts away. Today was for celebrating, for coming through and triumphing against the odds.

Chloe, nibbling a sandwich, pushed the loaded plate in my direction. 'Are you allowed to indulge?' she asked coquettishly. And if I hadn't known better, I'd have thought she was flirting with me. But she wasn't: it was all a very brave front to hide the gaping wound inside. My admiration for her rose even higher than it was already.

'I'll join you in one, thanks.' I sipped the welcome coffee and started on the food.

Samuel lowered the level in his glass of lager. 'Business before pleasure, lad. Will you ride Lucifer for me next week at Huntingdon?'

I looked at Mike who inclined his head in agreement – best not to argue with owners' requests was a good maxim for a trainer to remember. It would be the first time I'd returned to Huntingdon, scene of the debacle in the spring that had left me flat on my back, first on top of Carl Smith and then in a hospital bed for weeks. Mike didn't say anything, which actually said a lot. He was leaving the choice up to me, knew there would be some mental fences I'd have to jump, as well as big brushwood ones. We held each other's gaze for a moment.

'Yes, thanks, Samuel, I will.'

'Good, good.' He took another pull of his lager. 'That takes care of the business. So, how about a bit of pleasure, eh? Will you both join me in a round of golf, then dinner at North Shore Hotel?'

'I'm up for that.' Mike's eyes lit up.

'Me too,' I said.

'What say we make it a foursome – ask Victor Maudsley?' Samuel looked at us enquiringly.

'That would be very kind of you,' I said. 'I'm pretty sure he'll accept.'

Maudsley was Elspeth's ex-husband. He was also, before he retired, a trainer – one I'd worked for in my younger days.

'Settled, then,' Samuel said with satisfaction.

'Better make it a day when we're not racing, though,' Mike said. 'I sure will.'

'When you chaps have finished,' Chloe said, pointing her finger at the massive television screen high on the wall, 'they're just about to go off in the next race . . . and my horse is running in it.'

'Sorry, my darling.' Samuel switched his gaze to watch the coverage.

White Lace, a pretty grey mare, was circling round with the other seven runners, waiting for the starter's orders. She had yet to win a race but had been in the frame once before. Samuel had very recently purchased her as a present for Chloe. 'Give her another interest,' he'd confided in me. 'Well, sort of consolation prize, I suppose.' As a parent, seeing Chloe's misery and pain had caused him suffering, too.

We all settled to watch as the race got underway – a much shorter one of two miles. Joey Godaling was riding, an up-and-coming apprentice. It should prove an interesting race.

And it did. With an early charge, the leaders went away far too fast, but Joey, already wise to tactics, held White Lace steady just one in front of the back marker. For three-quarters of the race, the three leading horses galloped away, leaving the rest of the field behind by a good eight to ten lengths. But at the next jump, the first horse stood off, made a complete mess of it and pitched forward on the far side. It brought down the other two in a melee of thrashing legs and rolling jockeys.

With only four horses left in the race, Joey cannily made up ground on the rails and chased the leading pair home. White Lace came in third.

Chloe was elated, cheeks pink with pleasure and excitement. We cheered and clapped, downed our drinks and hastened from the bar, downstairs and across to the winners' enclosure.

The horses walked in, nostrils flaring, flanks steaming, to a loud burst of applause. The jockeys dismounted, slid saddles off and left the stable lads to flick over the coolers to prevent the horses getting chilled. I watched as Samuel and Chloe congratulated Joey and patted White Lace. Chloe clutched her father's arm, thanking him for giving her such a marvellous present. Samuel looked smug. For a little while at least, all Chloe's heartache had been banished. That, for him, was reward enough.

The horses were led away and we left the winners' enclosure and rejoined the crowd. Unexpectedly, I felt a tap on my shoulder, looked round and came face to face with a total stranger, thin-faced, wearing a hooded jacket.

'Got something for you.' He thrust an envelope into my hand and turned away.

'Hey, wait a minute . . .' But he had melted into the crowd. I opened the envelope, read the message and a wave of cold shock ran through me.

I legged it after him. Dodging in and out round the milling race-goers, I finally caught sight of him near the entrance to the stands. Totally unaware I was following, he'd stopped now and was attempting to light a cigarette. The stiff breeze kept on blowing out the flame on his lighter.

I came up behind him and dug my fingers deep into his arm.

'What the—' He spun round.

'OK,' I panted. 'You've given me the note. So, who sent you?'

'I don't know what it says – sealed, innit?'

Forcing him against the wall, I read it to him.

It was very short: a telephone number at the top followed by the words, *You and I are going to meet. Ring after the twenty-sixth of September. If you don't, I'll be forced to meet Chloe.* The note was unsigned.

I waved the paper in front of his face.

'So, who wrote it?'

He shrugged and said sullenly, 'Jake. He's inside right now but he gets let out on the twenty-sixth.'

'In prison, you mean?'

'Yeah, s'right. Got caught. He's doing time for GBH – maimed a security guard.'

'Why does he want to see me?'

The man looked at me slyly. 'Don't you know? That murdered guy, Carl Smith – Jake's his brother.'

FOUR

I watched the black beret being repositioned on the raven locks; the angle was even more jaunty than when I'd first seen Chloe in the parade ring. We were all at Mike's house helping Chloe celebrate her horse coming in the frame. Generously poured glasses of bubbly had raised her spirits even higher.

She gave a last peek in the hall mirror to adjust the little hat before swinging round, still on cloud nine, still enthusing about

White Lace two hours after seeing her horse hosed down, driven home in the horsebox and comfortably stabled up.

'When the racing bug bites, it really sinks its teeth in, doesn't it?' She beamed at me. 'What a buzz! I can't wait to go racing again now.'

I smiled at her flushed, excited face. 'It doesn't always go the way you'd wish it.'

'Dear Harry, if it did, there wouldn't be a buzz, would there?'

'True.'

'Come along,' Samuel chuckled, 'these two chaps have work to do.'

He ushered his daughter over the doorstep and into his BMW. She climbed in and ran the passenger window down.

'Thanks again, Mike. I'll see you soon, shan't be able to keep away.'

We waved them off and went back indoors.

'One happy lady,' Mike said.

'Samuel's preening. He's reversed her mental state in one move.'

'Yes, a gamble buying the horse, but it's come off.'

'And she's tough. She'll take the knock-backs along with the glory days. A new life-long love affair with racing,' I agreed.

'Can't be bad.' Mike grinned. 'She's using me as her trainer – it's great for business.'

'Go on, your cynical act doesn't wash – this is me, remember? With animals and pretty females, you're a pushover.'

'Nah. Hard as a horseshoe, I am.'

'In that case,' I said and put a hand into my pocket and drew out the note I'd been given earlier, 'could you tell me what I should do with this?'

He read it and the grin faded. 'Not something you'd want to be given. Where did you get it?'

'At the races, this afternoon.'

His male protectiveness asserted itself. 'You'll have to ring. I mean, it's a threat to Chloe.'

I sighed. 'Yeah, but you don't know who wrote it.'

'So?'

'Jake Smith. Currently in clink for GBH.'

'Phew. Still, he can't do any damage if he's inside. You'll have to do a prison visit.'

'Due out in two days' time.'

He whistled. 'I take your point. Not the sort of company you'd want to cultivate, eh?'

'Exactly.'

He looked sideways at me. 'But you're going to.'

It wasn't a question.

'As you've pointed out, there's Chloe to consider. At least if I ring, it will deflect him from her.'

'Any ideas why this guy *wants* to see you?'

'Oh, yes. Jake is – or, rather, *was* – Carl Smith's brother.'

'Found dead in a lavatory at Leicester races.'

'Too right.'

'And he blames you?'

'Your guess is as good as. But it's the only reason I can think of.'

I filled Mike in about finding the false teeth on the cottage door-step that morning.

'Bloody hell! You've just got out of one tough situation, now you're feet first into another.'

I inclined my head. 'Pretty much my own assessment, Mike.'

'Samuel knows, does he?'

'No, just you and me – and the also-ran who gave me the note.'

'Just a bit player?'

'Reckon so. It didn't take much to get Jake's name out of him.'

'Well, you're not ringing this Jake tonight, mate. You and me are down the pub. We may have done the necessary and celebrated with Chloe and Samuel, but that was basically trainer's obligations. No, I'm talking a real celebration – just us. I'm sorry that bloody note arrived when it did, but don't let it spoil things. You've come back, Harry, back to race riding – and winning. After six months of not knowing if you even would, it's got to be marked. OK, you can name the pub, but you're definitely going.' He slapped a hand on my shoulder. 'It's great to have you as my retained jockey again.' He hesitated, raised a questioning eyebrow. 'You *do* want to throw your hand in with my stable?'

I slapped him back. 'Don't be so soft, it's all I've wanted for months.'

He lowered the eyebrow and grinned. 'That's OK, then. So, which pub?'

'Horseshoes will do me fine.'

He nodded. 'Do me, too. But after evening stables.'

'Count me in. Carrying water buckets will help the biceps no end.'

Happy hour at the Horseshoes had come and gone, but the majority of stable lads were still lounging along the bench seats and chatting three-deep up at the bar. They were all familiar faces. Several of them worked for Mike.

A rippled cheer greeted our arrival through the heavy wooden door.

'Keep 'em comin', Harry.'

'Good on yer, mate.'

'. . . should have had a bit more on.'

'. . . great to see you back on board.'

A few of the snatches of dialogue I picked up; the rest was swallowed up in the general racket, but the bonhomie was practically tangible. I raised a hand in recognition of their bantering good wishes.

'How about a free round?' Mike said the words out the corner of his mouth.

I cast a quick glance round at the good-natured crowd; the pub was crowded. 'Phew . . .'

'We'll go halves with the tab.'

'I can't say no to that.'

'Drinks all round on us.' Mike had to raise his voice to make himself heard, but the erupting bellow of appreciation was deafening.

Bill, the publican behind the bar, smiled widely and began lining up the glasses.

'You, too, Bill,' I said.

'God bless Online, I say.' He filled a glass and passed it over.

'Amen to that,' I replied, accepting the pint of beer and raising it in acknowledgement.

'So, when's your next ride?'

'Better ask Mike.'

Bill turned an enquiring glance in Mike's direction.

'We've runners on Tuesday at Huntingdon and some declared at Cheltenham on Friday and Saturday. Nothing's definite, but Harry's got the shout which horses he'd rather ride.'

'I'll be keeping an eye out for your next, and that's for sure. We had a bit on you today, lad. We're all glad you're back racing.'

'Thanks, Bill. Nobody's more pleased than me, I can tell you.'

'You've had a rough time. Everybody's real sorry about your sister.'

'Thanks, I appreciate your support.' I took a long pull of my beer. I used it as a good excuse to avoid looking into his sympathetic face. I could take any amount of abuse, but it was always people's kindness that got under my guard.

Darren appeared at my side and accepted a free pint from Bill. He'd swapped stables when Elspeth retired and was the stable lad in charge of Online and three other jumpers.

'No problem with the new whip rules, eh, Harry?'

'Darren.' I nodded. 'No, Online's a gift in the present situation.'

'Pity they're not all like him; you wouldn't have to bother counting the eight slaps.'

'Harry always uses the minimum to get the job done anyway,' Mike agreed. He'd happily set Darren on when his string had increased overnight with all Samuel's horses being withdrawn from Elspeth's stables.

'A.P. and Ruby aren't happy about the ruling – well, most of the lads aren't. What's your take, Harry?'

'I'll be glad when they've finished gnawing on the bone at the BHA. The present rules aren't workable, so they'll get tweaked. Let's face it, whips are made differently these days and they're needed for steering as well as encouragement.'

There were rumbles of agreement from the lads close enough to the bar to hear.

'Your leg holding up OK?' Mike inquired.

'Yes, guv'nor, thanks. No probs.' Darren had been hospitalized for weeks following the car crash he and I had been involved in.

'Glad to hear that,' I said. I'd got away lightly, but he had suffered a fractured leg. I'd been consumed with guilt following the crash, quite irrationally blaming myself. Darren had been behind the wheel of the car taking me home that day. To hear him saying he had no lingering problems was a big relief.

'There were some tasty nurses in that hospital,' Darren said, a faraway look on his face and a smile lifting his lips.

'Got in there, did you?' one of the other lads shouted.

Darren turned pink, his face clashing horribly with his carrotty-red hair. A gale of laughter rang out.

'Here, have another pint on me,' I said as he emptied his first beer, trying to hide his embarrassment.

'Thanks, Harry.' He lowered his voice. 'I'm seeing Annette regular. She's a nurse.'

'Is she nice?' I gently kidded.

'Yeah,' he said and his chest swelled, 'she's great.'

'Treat her right. Good ones are hard to find.'

'Oh, I do, I'd never hurt her . . .'

'Whey-hey, Darren's in luuuuurve,' someone catcalled.

The banter carried on.

'You know what they say about nurses.'

'Has she got a friend?'

'Better still, tell her to bring all the girls from the nurses' home. There's enough lads in here to keep them going . . . or *get* them going.'

'Satisfaction guaranteed.'

Roars of raucous laughter filled the pub and Darren's face turned from pink to crimson.

'Aw, shut up,' he said, 'you're just plain jealous.'

The outer door opened and two women walked into the pub. The blast of noise was enough to have knocked them back. They stood hesitantly, scanning the packed, boisterous crowd. Heads turned as they do when strangers enter a bar and there were a couple of catcalls.

But as the laughter slowly diminished in volume and Darren's face returned to normal, Mike turned and saw the two women. He let out a whoop of delight. I looked at him in surprise; it was not his style.

'Hey,' he waved vigorously, 'over here.'

The two women spotted him and wide smiles spread across their faces. One was a middle-aged woman, a good-looking blonde. The other . . . the other was also blonde, younger, much younger, early twenties and quite stunningly beautiful.

I, along with most of the lads in the pub, stared in overt admiration. If Mike hadn't claimed them from the off, I've no doubt several of the lads would have made a move on them. But Mike represented their bread and butter, was one of the boss-men, and like all pack animals, the young males watched enviously from a distance.

The women wove their way between tables and drinkers, and Mike, spreading arms wide, engulfed them both in a massive bear hug.

'Wonderful to see you both.'

'Mike, darling, so good to be back.'

'Hi, Uncle Mike.'

Uncle Mike? I looked at the younger one. Was it possible? How long ago was it I'd met his niece? Ten, twelve years, maybe more – probably was. I had a mental picture of a plump child with hair ribbons and bunches astride a grey pony who proudly sported a red rosette in its brow band. Had the caterpillar really metamorphosed into this imago, this gorgeous creature?

She drew away slightly from the encircling arms and our eyes met. Apart from Leo's, she had the most incredible green eyes I'd ever seen.

'We've been up to your house,' the older woman was saying. 'When there was no reply, we knocked up the head lad's wife. She took our bags in and pointed us over here. She also said she didn't know what condition you'd be in as this was a celebration.'

Mike threw back his head and roared with laughter. 'But you weren't expected for another couple of days.'

'Well, we could always push off if you're not ready for us,' the young woman teased.

'Don't you dare!' Mike suddenly became aware he hadn't introduced me. 'Harry, I want you to meet my sister, Maria Chantry.' We smiled and shook hands. 'And this is Fleur, my niece, Maria's daughter.' I held out my hand and she took it in a cool, firm grip.

'Very pleased to meet you,' she murmured.

'Actually, I think we have already met, some twelve years back, though. And you have . . . changed.'

She gave a gurgling laugh. 'Less puppy fat, more curves, yes?'

I grinned. 'You're spot on.'

Mike stood, his arm around his sister's shoulders, watching us, a satisfied smirk on his face. I shot him an I-know-what-your-game-is look, but he was unabashed.

'Now then, what will you ladies have to drink?'

With glasses charged, we found a table away from the congested bar area.

'I'd better explain.' Mike took a quick pull of beer. 'Maria's sold up abroad. She lived in Italy and she's looking to buy a property in England. She lost her husband three years ago.' He looked across the table at her, but apart from momentarily dropping her gaze, she didn't appear to find his frankness distressing.

'I'm sorry,' I said automatically.

'Thank you. I've assembled all my pieces again – well, almost.'

Fleur covered her mother's hand with her own. The deep bond between them was obvious.

'You can't change change,' she said. 'You have to ride it and go on.' She directed her words at me.

I inclined my head. 'Yes. But saying it's one thing; doing it – that's the tricky bit, I find.'

My thoughts went back to the last but one time I'd seen Annabel, my estranged wife. I was now daily expecting to hear from her that she wanted a divorce. She'd told me she was pregnant with another man's child. The news had rocked my already shaky foundations. That was a few weeks ago. The emotional pain had been mind-numbing. Still was. My success this afternoon suddenly didn't matter any more. Some things were so much more important. I gulped my beer.

'So true,' Fleur replied, 'but if life was easy, the emotions that make it worth being alive wouldn't be deep and enduring; they'd be shallow. I'd say the other side of the coin of love is pain.'

I raised my eyes and met hers. 'Profound . . .'

'Yes.'

We held each other's gaze and there was chemistry between us. It shook me. I knew I was still in love with Annabel – would always love Annabel – but this woman in front of me was touching some place deep within. The touch was as light as a cobweb but, God help me, it had power.

And inside me something was responding.

FIVE

F ive thirty a.m. Still dark, but dawn quivered on the horizon. A working day, thank God. I'd spent too many days lying in bed instead of sitting in the saddle. I slapped a hand down on the alarm clock beside my bed and a few seconds later cut off the shrill back-up alarm on my mobile.

After a quick hot shower followed by an even quicker cold one, I was dressed and down in the warm kitchen with Leo weaving his beguiling, sinuous body in and out of my legs. No chance of getting any sustenance for myself until he'd been fed. I poured boiling water on to a teabag and ice-cold milk on to cereal. Then, contentedly, we munched away – he on the floor, me at the table – and I let the coming day spool through my mind.

Drive over to Mike's stables, ride out, probably three lots, no runners at any tracks today, so muck in with the lads – or, more accurately, muck out – then a light lunch down the Horseshoes . . . My thoughts stalled. Today Maria and Fleur would be staying at Mike's. Not an ordinary day, then.

I gulped scalding tea and let the picture of Fleur fill my mind. No doubt about it, she had made an impression on me.

Mike's delight in seeing his sister and niece had been heartening. He had been my source of support for many months and I was pleased that he was enjoying seeing his only remaining family after many years of living on his own. He deserved a bit of happiness. His wife, Monica – a red-hot live wire and extrovert – had carried Mike along in her slipstream. Indulgently, he'd allowed her a long lead – unfortunately, a bit too long for safety.

Total opposites, Mike as placid as a lily pond and Monica a raging weir, they'd attracted each other with a powerful magnetism. He had adored her.

Since her accidental death, he'd remained celibate, never even dated another woman. I doubted he ever would. Monica was an off-limits subject of conversation and I respected his need for silence. Despite the healing years, the wound was not yet fully knitted.

Conversely, he was always encouraging me to get back together with my estranged wife. Or had been until Annabel said the words that killed any hopeless hopes I myself had in that direction. I shook my head; I didn't want to think about Annabel. Mike's wound wasn't the only one that hadn't yet formed scar tissue. Scar tissue forming on me? I was kidding myself. Blood – hot and scarlet – was still running out.

I knew I owed a big debt to Annabel for her help in my speeded-up return to health. Even the world-weary hospital specialists had been surprised and impressed. As a qualified spiritual healer, she had given me amazing hands-on treatments. But she'd also gone the extra mile and spent a lot of her precious spare time after finishing her day job sending me absent healing. How many treatments I had no idea, but I would have guessed at daily ones. As this would, if successful, end in my return to race riding – something she could never come to accept because of the intrinsic pain and injuries the inevitable falls inflicted on me – it said everything about the depth of her unselfish care. She was a woman in a billion.

So why had I found Fleur attractive?

I finished my tea, turned on the tap and ran hot water over the empty mug.

The stable lights were on, bright patches illuminating a contained racing community that emphasized the surrounding countryside stretching away dark and empty. Small, highly active figures flitted to and fro between the individual stables, all committed to doing their own particular three, maybe four, racehorses, the welfare of each of utmost importance. The relationships built up between the stable lads and their horses were deep and emotionally fulfilling. The lads would never openly admit it, but they all loved 'their' horses and cosseted them like babies.

The horses, sensitive and intuitive, responded to the care being poured out upon them, giving of their best efforts in races and proudly accepting the accolades and adulation when they won.

I could say Mike was lucky to have stable staff who worked as a team, but it wasn't luck. It was Mike's leadership and positive personality which transmitted itself to each lad and resulted in a smooth-running, efficient workforce that achieved results.

I went to join them, breathing in the intoxicating smell of warm

horseflesh, combining with the reek of ammonia, hay, leather . . .
my world . . . and I was grateful beyond words to be there. Even
for Annabel, I wouldn't – couldn't – give it up. Yes, it was a
dangerous way to earn a living, the infrequent rewards of winning
races scarcely justifying risking a serious injury, even death, but
there was nothing else on God's green earth that I would choose to
spend my life doing.

I closed my mind to the inescapable fact that one day, not too
far into the future, I'd be too old to race ride. Until then, I was
doing what I'd been born to do. I'd live in the present and appreciate
every precious moment.

I went to collect a saddle and bridle for White Lace. I was riding
the mare first lot. The overpowering smell of saddle soap and leather
flowed over me as I stepped through the door of the tack room.

'Mornin', Harry. How're y'doin'?' Joe, the head lad, ducked
under the line of dangling bridles.

'Good, thanks. Seems I'm on White Lace.'

'Yep.' He lifted down the saddle from a tree, reached for a bridle,
looped up the reins and dropped it over the pommel. 'There y'go.
Can you ride back marker in the string? Let the others take the lead
and give her time to settle. She's been a bit spooky and restless.
Reckon she might be coming into season. Safer if she's at the back.'

'Sure.'

I took the tack out across the yard to the mare's stable. Speaking
soothingly, I tacked her up, but she seemed quiet enough and obediently followed me out the door. Whilst I waited for the other lads
to bring out their mounts, I checked the tightness of the mare's
girth. One of the other riders came up to me.

'Glad to see you again, Harry.'

I looked up – then did a double take. A girl stood in front of me,
dressed in riding gear, complete with crash cap sporting jaunty red-
and-black quartered silks. A tiny tendril of blonde hair had managed
to escape and helped to confirm my surprised recognition. It was
Fleur.

'Are you riding first lot?' I asked stupidly.

'That's right,' she grinned. 'But I think Uncle Mike's given me
the stable hack. He's very protective, isn't he?'

'Er . . . yes.'

'There's really no need,' she laughed softly.

'If he thinks you need looking after, I'm sure he's right,' I said diplomatically.

She sobered instantly. 'I do understand the reason why. It's because of Auntie Monica.'

I stared at her.

'Blames himself, doesn't he? Like, if he'd taken a pull, not allowed her to play wild, she might still be alive.'

'Do you always speak your mind?'

'Oh, yes. It cuts through the dross. Saves wasting time. Life's precious, isn't it?'

'Yes, it is indeed.'

Around the yard, other riders were all mounted now and our conversation ended as we, too, swung up into saddles.

White Lace snorted and skittered sideways, and I shortened the reins. Could be Joe was right. I circled her round the stable yard and gave the other horses time to string out in front before tacking myself on at the back.

Before we'd gone a couple of strides, I felt her muscles tense and knew what was coming. To a spectator, it probably resembled a child's rocking horse being ridden, but this was no game. White Lace bunched her powerful quarters and put in a massive buck. If I hadn't been anticipating it, she would have pitched me straight over her head. But feeling the propulsion from her back legs, I rose in the saddle and forced my weight down hard into the irons. All the same, it was spine-jarring and I fervently hoped my left knee would withstand the shock waves.

For a couple of minutes, it resulted in a test of will power between us as she continued to buck. Then, quite suddenly capitulating, White Lace stopped playing up, dropped back on to all four hooves and went into an extended trot, catching up with the rest of the string.

We trotted on in single file, reached the end of the stable drive and walked out on to the tarmac road, hugging tight to the left-hand side of the pavement edge. A short way further on, the pavement ceased altogether where a wide grass verge replaced it, and we trotted on smartly, leaving no chance for dropped heads reaching for a pick of grass.

Feeling the turf under her hooves, White Lace started to play up again, swinging her rump sideways and tossing her head around, and my whole attention was taken up with controlling the mare.

After a quarter of a mile, we swung off to the right on to the gallops. But the mare seemed to have got rid of the flies in her feet and, after a warm-up canter, moved into a beautifully smooth gallop upsides Lenny on Mud Pie. She was a delight to ride and I found her very responsive to hands and heels. Her hooves thudded rhythmically into the turf beneath me and I felt the chill wind whip my cheeks. With every minute in the saddle, my spirits rose. It was like a drug. Riding gave me a sense of complete freedom, yet, conversely, I was totally hooked for life.

Walking her round to cool down after the gallop, I was able to watch Fleur riding Pipsqueak, as she had said, the stable hack. But hack or not, under her control he turned in a pretty slick performance. No doubt of it, the girl could really ride. I found myself nodding in appreciation of her riding position and obvious expertise. She'd been quite right, and I'd have to have a quiet word with Mike. There was no need for him to be so over-protective; she could very ably take care of herself, at least in the saddle.

Mike himself, having allowed the string time to get up the gallops, had driven his vehicle after us to watch the morning workout. With binoculars trained on the horses, he was now intent on each one's performance over specific distances. The knowledge of what each was capable of was vital when it came to choosing which races to enter them in.

Finally, satisfied, he waved the string back to the stables and drove away. This was first lot; there would be two more trips up the gallops with different horses during the morning.

The horses reassembled into a single line. As before, I tacked on at the rear and we began the hack back. We'd covered perhaps half the distance to the stables when I heard the heavy drone of a tractor coming towards us. A bend in the lane and I could see the tractor was also pulling a trailer loaded with huge, round bales of hay. The tractor chugged steadily towards the horses and I felt White Lace begin to quiver and tremble. Taking a hand off the reins, I ran it soothingly down her neck and withers.

'Steady girl, steady; you're all right.'

But she most certainly wasn't. Her trembling increased as the tractor drew level.

She suddenly dropped a shoulder, catching me unawares, and I found myself out the side door and hitting the unforgiving tarmac with a hefty thump to my crash cap and right shoulder.

White Lace, free now of any restraint, reared up and whinnied loudly before coming down with a crash of steel-shod hooves. She took off as though she was entered for the Derby. The other horses, upset by her actions and the noise, were milling around, the lads trying to calm them down.

I scrambled to my feet, gritted my teeth against the vicious pain stabbing through my shoulder and ran after the frightened mare.

The lane led downwards, past the entrance to the stables. I hoped fervently that White Lace would have headed for safety and swung in off the tarmac towards the stable yard. No chance. Her flying hooves carried her past the entrance to the stables, past the church and lychgate, and on down the lane. I could only watch as she drew further and further away, until, reaching the bottom of the hill, she turned the corner of the churchyard and disappeared from sight.

I couldn't see what was happening, but I could hear it. With gut-curdling certainty, I heard the distant roar of an engine. A vehicle was driving up through the village main street. Going too fast and getting closer by the second.

The car, obviously driving now along the road towards the corner, suddenly changed gear and applied brakes. The sound of its slewing, screeching tyres carried clearly in the cold, still air.

Although I was braced for an impact, the sound still rocked me. Above the protesting tyres, there was a hellish crash and an ongoing battering of steel on steel.

A terrified horse gave a single, shrill, agonized scream of pain.

SIX

A drenalin coursed through me as I sprinted towards the scene of the accident. Gasping for breath, I rounded the corner of the churchyard wall, heard and saw the full horror. Saw the blood – scarlet – and spattered – and shocking. The car, a white Audi A4, had obviously struck White Lace, throwing her up and across the body of the vehicle. Half a ton of horseflesh was now sprawled over the bonnet.

The mare neighed wildly, her flailing, iron-shod hooves battering against metalwork and windscreen. Stirrups, thrown from side to side by the frenetic thrashing, added to the din as they clouted the body-work repeatedly. But the car was no longer pristine white. The front end had blood splashed all over with rivulets running down the wings and dripping on to the pavement.

I skidded to a halt. Rushing the mare would only exacerbate her fright. I needed to approach calmly, confidently, project the image I was in control of the situation, she'd be OK now.

The driver and his female passenger cowered low in their seats. The woman's left hand, her wedding ring glinting in the sunlight, was thrown up protectively in front of her face as the mare's hooves threatened the windscreen.

I walked cautiously forward towards the frightened animal, talking a soothing stream of reassurance, and managed to catch hold of a rein. I put my full weight behind it and pulled her head around away from the vehicle. Her shoulders, already sodden with sweat and blood, followed through and she slithered down the side of the driver's door, her hooves connecting with the solid pavement.

White Lace stood, shivering violently, shock preventing her from further wild exertion. I pulled on her ears whilst running my hand gently down the heated, sweaty neck, and murmured comforting words. Gradually, she began to relax, dropping her head down nearly to her knees with exhaustion.

A vehicle came round the corner and for a second she flung up her head, neck stiffening, fear flaring in her eyes, but Mike, who was driving, took in the disaster and immediately cut his engine. There were two men in the Land Rover. With relief, I saw the second man, now climbing out, was Desmond Bailey, our usual vet. I remembered Mike had said he'd be coming over first thing to check out one of the two-year-olds that had developed heat in a leg.

'Bloody thing to happen,' grunted Mike, his lips tightening to a thin line.

I handed the slippery reins over to him and left the vet to assess the damage and course of action.

Inclining my head towards the Audi, I said, 'I'll have a word?' Mike nodded absently, already focused on White Lace's injury.

The driver had lowered his window, and I went over and bent down.

'You both all right?'

'Just about. Christ it gave me . . . us . . . a fright. The horse came round the corner like a runaway train.'

'She was certainly a runaway,' I agreed ruefully, suddenly, strongly, aware now of an increasingly painful shoulder.

'You were riding her?' The white-faced woman in the passenger seat leaned forward and gave me a concerned look.

'Yeah, until a tractor spooked her higher up the lane.'

'Thank goodness we're both OK – well, shaken up, naturally, but basically OK. Did you know your nose is bleeding?'

I rubbed it inelegantly with the back of my hand. She was right.

'Goes with the territory. But let me give you our name and address. Whatever needs doing about repairs to the vehicle, we'll obviously sort out with your insurance company.'

The man produced a scrap of paper and ballpoint. 'Well, neither of us require repairs, thank God. We'll be fine, when the shock's worn off.'

'So, that's the humans sorted,' said the woman, her face now slowly regaining colour, 'but what about the horse?' She craned her neck out of the passenger window. 'Is it very bad? The poor thing's lost a lot of blood.'

'It was a good thing the vet happened to be up at the stables when the accident happened. I think there's only the one bad gash down the shoulder.'

'Let's hope so.' The man took the piece of paper from my hand, barely glancing at it. 'Mr Grantley's a sound chap; sure there won't be any problems.'

'You're locals?'

'That's right, we live in the old creamery – you know, last building on the east side of Boxton, the neighbouring village?'

'Uh-huh,' I nodded. It was a conspicuous property. At this point, Mike came over to offer apologies.

'Vet's loading White Lace into the box.' He flipped a hand towards the junction where the yard's smallest horsebox had appeared.

'Is it very bad or will she recover?'

Mike nodded to the woman and smiled. 'Nice of you to be concerned when it must have given you one hell of a shock.'

She looked up at him and gave him a sweet smile back. 'A car is a car is a car, isn't it? Doesn't have feelings, feels no pain. But an animal – well, that's different. And horses *are* pretty special, aren't they?'

'Yes, yes, they are.' Mike was holding her gaze. 'Do you own one?'

'No, but I love hacking out when I get chance.'

'You must pay us a visit, up at the stables. Show you round – least I can do. I apologize again for the shock – and the damage.' Mike cast a quick look at the car.

'Apologies accepted,' the man assured him. 'Don't think any more of it. After all, it was purely an accident. We all have them. Pep and I wouldn't like to make a big thing about it. We've not lived here very long. Last thing we'd want, to be at odds with anyone.'

Mike nodded. 'Very civil of you, Mr . . .?'

'Paul Wentworth.'

'And I'm Penelope. Pep to my friends. And I hope that will include yourself . . . and . . .?' She turned her gaze on me.

Mike said hastily, 'Harry Radcliffe.'

She frowned. 'Surely I've heard that name before?'

'He's champion jockey.'

'Oh, of course!'

It was starting to get embarrassing when Des Bailey came up. He nodded at the Wentworths.

'All OK?' They both nodded. 'I'm going back in the box, Mike. I've given White Lace a couple of jabs and strapped up the wound temporarily. We'll get her back to the stables and I'll stitch it. Looks considerably worse than it actually is. She should recover quite quickly.'

'Thanks, Des. Yes, you go back with Joe in the box and I'll bring Harry in the Land Rover.'

He walked off and we watched the horsebox as it negotiated the narrow lane and disappeared back to the stables.

'Such a pity to meet in dire circumstances,' Pep said, 'but it was nice to meet you.'

'Indeed,' Mike said. 'Just let me know when you'd like to come up to the stables. I look forward to it.'

At the end of morning stables, the three of us – myself, Mike and Fleur – took ourselves over to the house. Walking through the back door directly into the kitchen, I was reintroduced to Maria who had rustled up a deceptively simple-looking lunch which proved very tasty: Caesar salad with omelettes flavoured with chopped tomatoes and red peppers. She offered crusty bread rolls that Fleur declined.

'And for you, Harry?' Maria gestured towards the plate.

'Would love to, but I have to think of my riding weight.'

'Of course. I'm well used to it with Fleur's riding diet.'

I looked across the scrubbed pine table. 'Fill me in.'

'Modesty,' Mike cut in. 'Fleur won't tell you, but she's one of the best up-and-coming young women riders in Italy.'

'Really!'

'Oh, Uncle Mike does love exaggerating.'

'She doesn't ride like you, Harry,' Maria said. 'She rides on the flat.'

'Right.' I nodded and turned reproachfully to Mike. 'You never told me.'

Mike smiled lazily. 'You've had more than enough to think about this past year.'

'You mean, I've been too buried in my own woes to surface and look for stars?'

'Something like that.'

'Can't deny it.'

'The brain puts blinkers on all non-essential information when it's at full stretch coping with priorities.'

'Talking priorities, you were on the spot pretty quick earlier. Who told you White Lace had dropped me and had an accident?'

'I did,' Fleur said. 'Had my mobile with me, zipped in a pocket of my jacket whilst I was riding out first lot. Came in useful.'

'I'll say.' Mike helped himself to a roll, split and buttered it. 'She's a quick-thinking lass.'

'Yes, thanks. I appreciated you and the vet turning up so fast. Certainly shortened the mare's bleeding time.'

'How is the mare?' Maria reached for the glass jug and helped herself to a top-up of mineral water.

'Doing very well. Except she's still spooky. Could do with calming down.'

'Want me to ask Annabel to give her some healing?' I asked.

Two curious females, eating arrested, stared at me.

'Now that's a thought.' Mike was still chewing away on his roll. 'Yes, it would help.'

'Fair enough, I'll text her after lunch. See if she's free after work.'

'What are you talking about, Mike?' his sister asked.

'Sorry. Annabel – Harry's ex-wife – is a spiritual healer, works miracles.'

Two pairs of female eyes grew wide and round.

'Like you say, Fleur,' I murmured, flipping a dismissive hand, '*Uncle Mike* is given to exaggeration.'

'But, this woman . . . Annabel . . . actually does hands-on healing?'

Mike inclined his head. 'She sure does.'

'But she doesn't work miracles, Mike. Come on, Annabel wouldn't dream of saying such a thing. And mostly she works with hands off, not on.'

'OK, OK, maybe I was over-egging it a bit.'

'Does it work, though?' Fleur wrinkled up her nose. 'Or is it like . . . well . . . *faith* healing?'

I sighed. It was always difficult for me to describe. Annabel herself would have done a brilliant and accurate job of explaining what she did.

'First of all, she's not my *ex-wife*. She's still my wife.'

Mike groaned.

'Well, she is . . . legally,' I protested, dropping my gaze and concentrating on a delicate dissection of my remaining omelette. It was a very raw nerve and I didn't want to think about the all too real likelihood of Annabel approaching me to ask for a divorce. OK, she had left me over two years ago to live with Sir Jeffrey – a very sober, upright man, who was also very rich. But above all else, very *safe*. He didn't go hurtling down racecourses atop half a ton of pounding horseflesh at thirty miles an hour.

They lived in a beautiful country house on the outskirts of Melton Mowbray, where, incidentally, Annabel worked as a psychotherapist. She'd added spiritual healing to her list of accomplishments fairly recently. Also fairly recently, she had discovered she was pregnant.

I was still trying to come to terms with my feelings. I'd discovered in the last few months that despite Jeffrey being my successor and taking my beloved Annabel to his bed every night, I actually liked the fellow. Confusing – not to say very weird. But not so weird, I was insanely jealous that he was the father of Annabel's expected baby.

'Come on, Harry,' Fleur prompted, 'you haven't answered my question. Does it work?'

'It certainly worked in Harry's case,' Mike said.

'Yes, it works. Annabel did a great job in helping me to heal from a bad fall a few months back. I don't think I would have been riding White Lace last Saturday without having the spiritual healing. Apparently, it helped my bones to knit back together much quicker.'

'Wow!' Fleur's eyes were now as round as milk bottle tops. 'And you think she'll be able to help the mare?'

'Annabel prefers to see who she's healing, but she does also do absent healing if she's tied up and cannot get over personally.'

'Does that work, too?'

'Oh, yes, she did absent healing for me most days. I have to say I didn't know, but I'm so grateful for all the time she put in. My future was looking pretty grim at one point.'

'Hmmm . . . so interesting.'

'So committed, I would add to that,' Maria said and gave a knowing little smile. There were a few moments of awkward silence around the table.

'Yes,' I said to try to fill the gap, 'Annabel is totally dedicated . . . to her work.'

'Have we all finished lunch?' Maria pushed back her chair. 'I'll make coffee.'

'That would be nice.' Mike picked up his empty plate.

'I'll fill the dishwasher, Uncle Mike. Make myself useful.'

'I'm very glad you're here,' he said, beaming. 'Harry and I will be in the office, OK?'

We made ourselves scarce and headed down the hall.

'Now,' he said as we sprawled in comfortable, leather armchairs, 'what about sending that text?'

Annabel replied within minutes.

'Says she'll pop in on the way back from work. Be around four thirty.'

He nodded. 'And I'll pay her.'

'She probably won't accept anything,' I warned.

'I don't give a stuff. I've asked her for professional help – she's going to get paid.'

Laughing, I shook my head. 'Sooner you than me. She's her own woman.'

But even as I said the words, how I wished to God I could say she was mine.

SEVEN

'What about that other call – have you made it yet?' Before I had chance to answer Mike, Maria came in with two steaming mugs.

'Thanks very much – for the coffee and the lunch,' I said, taking the mug she held out.

'Well, Mike tells me you live alone. I expect it's a nice change to have someone prepare a meal for you.'

'How very true. But you and Fleur are here as Mike's guests, not as his cook and bottle-washer.'

'Piffle.' She smiled. 'It's never a one-way street, life. I find it nice to be wanted.'

'I certainly want you, Maria. You and Fleur. You're all the family I have. You're both a bit special.'

'Here,' she said and pushed a mug into his hand, 'shut up and have your coffee.' Turning as she reached the door, she said, 'You're making afternoon tea for us girls, right? When Fleur wakes up. She's gone upstairs for a sleep. Expect she'll be a couple of hours.'

'Sure thing.' Mike waved his coffee mug towards her, narrowly avoiding it slopping over the rim. 'Let me know when she surfaces.'

As the door closed behind her, he said, 'So? Have you rung this Jake Smith?'

I shook my head. 'No, not yet.'

'Don't you think you should do – like yesterday?'

'You're thinking about Chloe's safety, yes?'

'Too right I am. Well, that and her continuing to breathe and pay her horse's stabling and training costs.'

'Get away.' I slurped the hot, very strong coffee.

'No, let's be serious here, Harry. That girl's in danger if you don't make contact.'

I nodded. 'I was trying to decide the best place to meet an ex-con just out of gaol after a GBH sentence. You know, the place where I might just have a chance of carrying on breathing myself.'

'Sure, yes, I'm sorry, Harry. It's a bugger of a situation all round. Look, do you want me to ride shotgun?'

'Oh, no, certainly not. Anybody gets their heads knocked off, it's definitely going to be me. After all, it was me that set Carl up for the chop.'

'But you didn't know that,' he protested.

'Doesn't alter the fact he died.'

'Not your fault.'

'Tell that to his brother.'

'You tell him. As soon as you meet him. Get in first, before he has a go at you.'

I reached for my mobile. 'No, I'll tell him now.'

I didn't need to find that piece of paper. The telephone number was imprinted in my mind.

Mike retreated behind his mug of coffee.

I tapped in 141 followed by the number, and knew beyond doubt, once I'd done it, that running my own life would not be left in my own hands. I'd be handing over the reins. Jake would be the one calling the shots.

Other people had been running my life far too much in the last few months and I was heartily sick of it.

This call, setting up a meeting with him, was only the first thing. A resultant chain of action and reaction would be set in motion – none of it of my choosing. An unpleasant feeling.

Anger flared inside as I tapped the final digit and waited. Not long. Within seconds, a man answered.

'Jake Smith?'

'Naah, I'm his dad. Just get him for ya.'

I raised eyebrows towards Mike. 'Sounds like he's living with his dad.' Mike nodded.

'Who is this?' It was a much younger voice, tough, abrupt.

'Harry Radcliffe. Are you Jake Smith?'

'You got it. Took your time, didn't you? I was all set to do business with that doll, Chloe.'

'No need,' I said quickly. 'Any business to do, it's between me and you.'

He snorted. 'Don't you mean it will be *me* telling you?'

I didn't answer.

'Things need sorting. Get yourself to Southwell on Tuesday. Stand by the horses' walkway, near the entry on to the course. I'll find you.'

'What time?'

'Since you're not riding, don't matter, does it? I could've been real difficult – made it Huntingdon, this Sunday. But since you're riding in three races, and two of them for *Lord Edgware* . . .' He was openly sneering now.

A cold feeling filled my stomach. He was keeping tabs on my movements, *wanted* me to know.

I knew nothing about him, whilst he obviously knew quite a bit about me. How? Declarations weren't in yet stating I was down to ride. So, who had told him?

He laughed, but laugh wasn't the right word – the sound contained no humour. 'We'll make it just before the last race. Soon as they start to peel off from the parade ring. Got it?'

'Yes.'

'No cop out. You're not riding, so be there.' His voice dropped to a low hiss. 'And if I don't get the right answers, you won't ever be riding again.'

His voice held all the chilling menace of a king cobra.

A trickle of icy sweat ran down between my shoulder blades. I'd been denied my race riding for six months, been right down there in the pit, but then, by a miracle, had beaten the bleak forecast and ridden for the first time last Saturday.

I knew I couldn't survive if my livelihood and ability to race were snatched away a second time.

But I had definitely been threatened.

And Jake was a man who never made idle threats.

As the previous threatened man, who had ended up in a hospital bed, could certainly testify.

I scrubbed a fist across my forehead and found it came away damp with sweat.

'Well?'

I grimaced. 'Any more coffee going, Mike? I could do with another – a strong one, a very strong one.'

'With a splash of whisky?'

'Why not?'

He disappeared, leaving me to assimilate Jake Smith's words. At one level, I was incredibly relieved that he hadn't dictated our meeting take place in a dark alley in the middle of Nottingham. But on another, his threat had the power to rock me. Having tasted a future as a finished jockey, no way was I going down *that* alley again.

What the right answers he was seeking were, I'd no idea. But I had to meet Jake – I had little choice when Chloe's safety was seriously at risk. Whether Jake would actually harm her physically wasn't something I could even bring myself to consider. It wasn't going to come to that. I'd meet him as he'd dictated, at Southwell races on the fourth. After I'd ridden at the jumps meeting on Sunday the second. Three rides – as Jake had pointed out – one for Samuel, plus two for Lord Edgware who had booked my services following last Saturday's success.

Mike reappeared with the pungent coffee.

'Have you made the decs yet, Mike, for Huntingdon?'

'No, not yet.'

'Hmm, thought not.'

'Why?'

I accepted a mug from him and sipped cautiously. The drink delivered everything I needed, sweetened with honey, very strong and generously laced with whisky.

'Can you explain how Jake Smith has just managed to tell me I've got three rides there, two especially for Lord Edgware?'

He whistled softly. 'The devil you say . . . No, I've no idea.'

'Me, neither. But it must have taken some spadework to dig up that information. How long ago did His Lordship book me to ride his two fillies?'

Mike pursed his lips. 'I *think* it was last Sunday . . . yes, I remember. I was in the kitchen here, the girls were busy with Sunday lunch preparation and I was hindering more than helping – you know, getting in the way – when I took a call from him on the kitchen extension.'

'And who else knew?'

'We . . . e . . . ll,' he said and shrugged. 'I don't know off hand. I told Joe, of course. And I suppose he could have told the other lads. Oh, yes, and Samuel knew, because I was speaking to him later about you riding Online at the same meeting. He probably told Chloe.'

'And that's all?'

'Yes, I think so. But don't forget, Harry, His Lordship could very well have told other people we know nothing about.'

I sighed heavily. 'Yes, of course. I never considered that possibility. It's not going to be easy to pin down Jake's source of information.'

'If I were you, Harry, I'd just let it go. You'll turn yourself inside out trying. Strikes me from the whiter shade of pale you turned after the phone call, you've got enough on your plate already.'

I took another pull of the delicious coffee. 'He wants me to meet him at the Southwell flat meeting on the fourth.'

'Does he?' Mike rubbed his chin thoughtfully. 'Well, that's a bit safer than some other places I could think of.'

'My thoughts, too. Except, just at the end of the phone call, he left me with a threat to finish me for racing if I didn't produce the answers he wants to his questions.'

'Which are?'

'As yet, I've no idea. But I'll find out when I get to Southwell.'

We left it at that and followed our normal non-racing day routine. Mike put stocking-clad feet up on the coffee table, spread the *Racing Post* over his face and opted out.

I slid further down in the squashy, seductive comfort of my leather armchair and followed his excellent example. Over in the lads' quarters, they would all be in the same somnambulistic state – tradition in racing stables – an early start required a toes-up couple of hours in the afternoon before back on duty for evening stables.

The first thing I became aware of, sometime later, was a light floral scent teasing my nostrils. I came up from the depths and heard a feminine voice close to my ear.

'Mum told me we were getting our afternoon tea made for *us*, but I told her not to be silly.'

I opened an eye. Fleur, holding a steaming mug, was hunkered down beside me.

'Decent of you, thanks.'

I looked across at Mike. He was still hidden beneath the newspaper, gentle snores frilling and rippling the edges of the pages.

Beyond his head, the clock on the desk read four twenty-eight. I struggled upright.

'Don't fret. She's not here yet.' Amusement danced in Fleur's eyes. 'I'm dying to meet her.'

'Never mind Annabel,' said a voice, 'did you make me some tea as well?' The newspaper slowly slid down, revealing Mike's blue eyes.

'Not that you deserve any, but yes.'

A grin spread across his sleepy face. 'I owe you.'

Right then, we heard the muted sound of a vehicle pulling into the yard and a moment or two later a car door slammed.

Annabel had arrived.

Impassively, I stared down into the bottom of my mug of tea, whilst inside two conflicting feelings warred for victory. I felt like running for cover to avoid any further emotional pain and yet, simultaneously, Annabel's magnetism was a force field that inexorably drew me to her. Caught between the two opposing emotions, I was helplessly immobile.

Mike heaved himself out of the chair and went to let her in.

'Does she drink tea?' Fleur asked.

'Hmmm . . . no sugar.'

She disappeared after Mike, and a couple of minutes later Annabel came into the room. At the sight of her, self-preservation rolled over and died on the spot.

I stood up.

'Harry, darling.' Her face alive with pleasure, Annabel gave me a hug.

Bittersweet.

Her body, so familiar to me after years of marriage, for the first time felt strange, different. Pressed close to her, I could feel the swell of her coming baby. *But the baby wasn't mine.*

Bitter, bittersweet.

I had never in my life been a jealous man. Whatever anyone else had or achieved, I was pleased for them. Now, I was blown away by the destructive, enervating power of a swamping wave of jealousy. I was hideously jealous of Sir Jeffrey and it was a far from pleasant feeling.

Annabel, feeling the sudden tenseness I was unable to prevent, had immediately understood. She eased herself gently away from me.

'I'm so pleased you thought of calling me for some healing. How is the mare?'

'Better in physical shape than mental. Mind you, she was spooky to begin with this morning before the accident.'

'Well, we'll see how she responds. I'll go down to the stable, shall I?'

'Not until you've had some tea.' Fleur appeared.

'Oh, yes. Lovely, thanks.'

'You two haven't been introduced, have you?'

I did the honours.

'Harry says the healing really does work.' Fleur was regarding Annabel with interest. 'Could I watch you?'

Annabel smiled. 'I don't mind. Your watching won't affect it in any way.'

'Does it make a difference, your being pregnant?'

Annabel shook her head. 'It's never a one-way street. Other healers all seem to say the same thing. Giving healing also benefits the healer. So, if it benefits me, it will also benefit the baby.'

'How do you feel, you know, when you're actually doing it?'

'Very calm, centred – filled with awe, actually, because the healing energy always comes down when I ask. Not demand – you never, ever demand.'

'Wow!' Fleur's eyes grew wider. 'You say it comes down – isn't it inside you, then?'

Annabel gurgled with laughter. 'Every living thing in the universe is only alive because they're filled with energy or the life-force. But to *give* healing, well, you don't use your own energy. If you did that, you'd become depleted very quickly.'

'So what energy do you use? Where does it come from?'

'You could say *God* because that's correct, but some people feel more comfortable if I use the word *source*.'

'And it just . . . comes down?'

'Yes,' Annabel said gently, 'and, believe me, it's incredibly humbling to feel the power.'

'I bet!'

Mike stuck his head round the door. 'Just off down the stables. You coming, Harry? I could use another pair of hands. Buzzword's leg needs hosing for twenty minutes.'

I nodded. 'He's the one the vet called about this morning?'

'Yes. There's still heat in the near fore.'

'I'm right with you.'

We all trooped out across the yard and peeled off to our respective jobs, Fleur sticking as close to Annabel as a gun-dog to its master.

It would be interesting catching up with her later to get her impressions.

'Hey, hang on!' There was a shout behind us. 'Wait for me. I don't want to miss out.' And Maria came beetling across after us.

EIGHT

'You can't be serious, Harry.' Annabel's eyes were filled with horrified dismay. 'With this Jake Smith's track record, it's incredibly dangerous.'

'No choice.'

'Surely there's some other way. Why not tell Samuel? He could arrange some sort of protection for Chloe.'

We'd gone back to Annabel's house for supper. She'd invited me. I'd declined. She'd insisted. I'd given in. Mike, well, Mike had disapproved very strongly. Sir Jeffrey was away in London.

'You're having supper here, Harry, with the three of us.'

I'd spread my hands. I knew he was serious, wanted me to eat with his family, but I also knew he was concerned. It was a complete switch around from his former attitude of trying to throw us together again.

I understood his reason, of course – the baby. Since Annabel had conceived, everything had changed. Now he thought it was tempting fate for me to be having supper with Annabel, at her house, alone.

That thought had occurred to me, too. At the point when I'd been directing the hose down Buzzword's foreleg, taking the heat out and watching the cold water trickling down and dripping steadily off his hock, I realized I could do with turning the hose on myself. Cool my ardour down a bit. But long ago I'd realized there was no

hope of recovery. My feelings for Annabel were intrinsically part
of me; they ran through my veins like blood. It was a terminal
illness with no cure.

So, leaving Mike glowering, we had set off from his stables in
our two separate vehicles and I'd followed her along the Leicestershire
lanes.

The meal she prepared was a simple smoked salmon salad with
a side helping of brown rice. She knew I could indulge myself and
not have to worry about weight gain. Annabel was a thoughtful,
caring person.

I shook my head. 'I can't tell Samuel. He's a father, above all
else, a devoted father. He'd just go completely nuts, get overpro-
tective. And chew himself to bits because he couldn't provide
wraparound protection.'

Involuntarily, Annabel's hand strayed to her swelling belly. The
gesture said everything.

'You see?' I said softly.

'Yes.'

'So, I have to see Jake Smith.'

'But the false teeth, on your doorstep – he couldn't have left
them there, could he?'

Her words pulled me up with a jerk. Since receiving the note,
I'd automatically assumed he had.

'Harry, he was still in prison when the teeth were left.'

'You think someone else left them? As in someone not connected
with Jake?'

'I don't know. Maybe. Say, another member of Carl's family, or
a girlfriend, even someone Carl was involved with at work.'

Her words set me thinking. She certainly had a point.

'Could have been Carl's father. He was the one who answered
the phone to begin with.'

'There you are, then.'

'Well, when I get to Southwell, I'll ask Jake *before* I answer any
of his questions.'

'Promise me something, Harry . . .'

She reached across the table and put her hand over mine. I noticed
it was her left hand. Bizarrely, despite her living with Sir Jeffrey,
she was still wearing my wedding ring.

I stared down at her third finger and wondered just how much

longer she would go on wearing it. Until this baby was born? Until
she wanted to marry again? Until she asked me for a divorce?

I lifted my head and looked into her face, swallowed hard. Was
this what tonight's supper was all about? A prelude to asking for a
divorce?

'Promise,' she said urgently.

'What? What do you want me to do?'

'Ring me, as soon as you get back from Southwell. Ring to tell
me you're safe.'

Relief swamped me. 'You bet I will,' I said. 'Bank on it.'

I drove away down cold dark lanes to my lonely cottage and empty
bed – leaving Annabel to sleep alone in hers. What a bloody waste.

But there was a slight compensation waiting for me at the cottage.
A message had been left on the answerphone.

'Hi there, Harry. Samuel. That trip to North Shore Hotel for a
round of golf, well, I'm up for it the Monday after Huntingdon
races. I've spoken to Mike. All OK with him. Thought we could
all go to the coast in my car – save petrol.' He chuckled. 'Unless
I hear from you that you can't make it, I'll pick you up at around
six thirty, Monday morning. We can grab a bacon bun and coffee
in the hotel before we tee off. Look forward to seeing you.'

I reached for the desk diary and made a note. As I did so, a
thought occurred to me that assuming I didn't have a bad fall on
Sunday, I'd still be alive and kicking on Monday.

I turned the page over to the following day – Tuesday, fourth of
October – and made another note: *Southwell racecourse – meet Jake
Smith!*

There was a clatter from the cat flap in the kitchen and moments
later an enormous ginger tom edged himself round the partially
open office door and glared balefully at me. He let out a bellow
loud enough to be heard by my nearest neighbour – half a mile
away – before launching himself up on to my shoulder and rubbing
his head hard against my chin.

'OK, your dinner, right?' I hoiked myself up and went to the
kitchen, undid a tin of smelly cat food, to Leo's great delight, and
made myself some coffee. Taking my drink through to the lounge,
I sprawled on the settee and thought about Annabel's theories.

Taking it from the closest relation first, that made Jake's father front runner. To find out where he lived would also give me an advantage next Tuesday. It seemed likely Jake was also living there since his release from prison. But I knew nothing about Jake Smith, hadn't even known he existed until I'd received that note at the races.

Carl Smith had worked in racing stables in the village of Dayton, near Newark, but he would most likely have lived in lads' quarters near the stables. The trainer, Fred Sampson, would have Carl's home address on file, but with the data protection restrictions, he wouldn't be able to tell me.

So who could I ask?

Carl certainly wasn't the only stable lad working for Sampson. Maybe his mates would know. The only way to find out was to ask them. And that meant tracking them down at their favourite watering hole – usually the nearest pub to the stables.

I drained my cooling coffee and grabbed my car keys.

Twenty minutes later, I was ordering a pint of beer in the Purple Dragon at Dayton. Three lads, one of whom I recognized, were seated at a nearby table.

'Mind if I join you?'

There were assenting grunts and I slid my glass on to a spare beer mat.

'Not on your own patch, Harry?'

Being champion jockey had its uses at times. No way could I disguise who I was. But it also had its drawbacks. I had to keep this light, spontaneous. It was the best chance I had of getting the information I needed. If they thought the address was important, it was possible they wouldn't let it slip.

'No, on my way home. Fancied a beer.' The lie rolled off my tongue and tasted sour.

I lowered the level in my glass halfway and waited until their glasses were empty.

'Have one on me.' I handed a note to Tony, the lad I recognized. The gesture went down well and they began relaxing, chatting easily. I gave it ten minutes and then dropped a question into the conversation.

'Which one of you replaced Carl, then?'

Two fingers pointed to the third lad.

'I got the start.'

'Live locally, do you?'

'Nah, come from Strelley.'

I nodded sagely. 'Too far to travel in.'

'Yeah, well, Carl lived in. I took his room.'

'Right.' I nodded again. 'Where did he come from, then?'

Tony answered. 'Up Wellington Street, Newark. Lived with Fred, his dad.'

I didn't push it any further. 'Any runners on Sunday?'

'Dayton Princess is running in the one o'clock.'

The same race as one of my rides for Lord Edgware, as I informed them. And the conversation steered itself smoothly and safely away from the subject of Carl.

I stood them all a further round, cried off having another myself – 'Sorry, have to drive back' – and stepped outside into the chill night air.

Once home, I dug out the telephone directory and looked up F. Smith of Wellington Street, Newark. The telephone number Jake had written down had been a landline, not a mobile. Turned out the house was number twenty-nine.

I checked my watch. Just short of eleven o'clock. Too late to go swanning off to Newark tonight, but I intended to run over and take a look at the Smith homestead tomorrow. I might just get lucky and spot Jake Smith going in or out. Actually put a face to a name. Did they still insist on short haircuts in prison? Anyway, for an offence of GBH, it wouldn't have been a short sentence. He couldn't disguise prison pallor. A dead giveaway. I should be able to pick him out.

He'd been keeping check on me. Now it was my turn.

'M'Lord.' I touched the bright green peak of my silks where they sat covering my crash cap. The equivalent, I suppose, of a latter-day tugging of the forelock. Racing was steeped in tradition. And I wouldn't have it otherwise. It was somehow a comfort and conveyed a sense of security. A total illusion, of course. Racing was right up there amongst the most dangerous of sports. Which was why it held the fascination it did.

Lord Edgware smiled in acknowledgement and nodded, still deep in conversation with Mike. We were all assembled in the parade ring at Huntingdon races, ready for the off in the first race on the card. The bell rang for mounting and Mike gave me a leg-up on to Joyous Morning, an iron-grey filly belonging to Lord Edgware.

'I wish you all good luck. I know you'll do your utmost. That's why I asked Mr Grantley to put you up.'

'Thank you, Your Lordship.' I executed another deferential touch to the cap. 'Certainly do my best.'

Mr Grantley, trying to hide a grin, slapped the filly on her neck. 'No instructions. Just build her confidence and get back safely.'

Darren, the lad who looked after Joyous Morning, clicked encouragement and led the way from the parade ring out on to the course.

We cantered steadily down to the start and circled around with the other seven runners. I remembered Tony from Fred Sampson's stable saying Dayton Princess was running. She wasn't a no-hoper, but not far from it. The rest of them were mediocre, except for Bright Dawn, a superb bay from a stable down in Lambourn – a long trip which told its own story. She was starting favourite at five-to-four-on, was a strong front runner and would take all the beating. I had to get Joyous Morning tracking her right from the off to stand any chance.

The starter shouted to the jockeys to get into line and the tape flew up. Predictably, Bright Dawn set a blistering pace and the field strung out behind her. I settled Joyous Morning on the outside in third place and ran three-quarters of the race uneventfully holding that position.

However, three fences from home, the horse in front misjudged the take-off, scrambled over, but pecked so badly on landing the jockey was shot off and their chances of winning hit the ground with them.

That left just Bright Dawn out in front, who was going like a train, meeting all the fences brilliantly. She continued to do so and nothing was going to get past her. At the post, she was twelve lengths in front and fully deserved her win. I brought in Joyous Morning in second place, pleased with the filly's performance and knowing she had enjoyed her race and would do all the better next time.

Lord Edgware was a fair-minded man and happily congratulated us in the second slot in the winners' enclosure.

'You handled her beautifully. Just look at her! On her toes, hardly blowing at all – looks like she could go round again.' He beamed at me and I accepted his praise gratefully. He was one of a breed of owners who had racehorses in training and went racing strictly for the pleasure of it. Winning was a bonus.

With some other owners, it was a 'win or be damned' attitude, with the focus on how much the prize money was likely to be. This type nearly always blamed the jockey, had long memories and made their displeasure clear by never putting you up again.

But a jockey is self-employed and needs the riding fee as basic bread and butter. Any winners were a triumph and put jam on top, but that particular sort of jam couldn't be relied on.

I unbuckled the girth and, with the saddle over my arm, went to weigh in. As I walked across the grass, I spotted Tony, grinning from ear to ear, putting the cooler over Dayton Princess who had actually come in third. I was pleased for him. He'd likely get a cash backhander from the owner with a bit of luck. With the poor wages paid to the stable lads, a little bit extra made a lot of difference.

The second of Lord Edgware's horses came nowhere but, fortunately, it didn't dent his intrinsic good humour. He seemed very pleased to have had one come second.

My last ride of the day was on one of Samuel's horses. Lucifer – a misnomer because he had the sweetest nature – was a massive seventeen-hands gelding with powerful quarters, stayed for ever and never gave up trying. He was a very genuine horse and a joy to ride.

We won by five lengths.

Samuel was higher than high, couldn't contain his delight.

'Just wait till Chloe hears about it,' he chortled. 'She thinks you walk on water as it is.'

'Just doing my job.'

'Oh, no.' He waggled a forefinger at me. 'This calls for a bit of a celebration.'

'Really—' I began, but he steamrollered me.

'Chloe would never forgive me if I didn't show our appreciation.'

'No need, Samuel,' Mike backed me up.

'What? His first full win at Huntingdon! No.' He looked from one to another of us and then started to grin wickedly and added, 'And I know *just* the right celebration.'

'What are you hatching?' Mike narrowed his eyes.

Samuel laughed out loud. 'I'll tell you guys tomorrow, when we've slaughtered eighteen holes at North Shore Golf Club. Now, don't forget, I'm picking you up at six thirty in the morning.'

NINE

I slapped the alarm off at six o'clock Monday morning. Trotted down to the kitchen, fed Leo and carried a cup of tea back upstairs. Took a swift shower and drank the tea whilst I was getting dressed.

I heaved my golf bag with full set of clubs out to the front gate and was all ready and waiting by six twenty-five.

As promised, Samuel arrived on the dot of six thirty. Mike was already sitting in the passenger seat. Samuel lowered his window.

'Boot's undone. Stow your golf things with ours.'

I did so and climbed into the back seat of the car. 'Morning, Mike.'

'Hiya, Harry. Seems like we've got a good morning for it.'

It was a windless, dry day, just right for a round of golf. I felt my interest quicken. North Shore Hotel, with its superb golf course situated right beside the beach and North Sea, was unrivalled. Not only was the golf course a beauty to play on, but the hotel was convivial, with the friendliest of staff and great food.

Samuel was an excellent driver and drove fast. Within an hour and a half, we were turning off the Roman Bank road which led us straight up the incline to the hotel car park beside the beach. We crunched in over the gravel and parked as close as we could to the angled line of buggies parked near the Pro's shop.

'OK, lads.' Samuel rubbed his hands together. 'First stop, reception, then straight into the dining room. I've already arranged to meet Victor in there.'

We walked up the steps and went in through the back door. The dining room was off to our left. Samuel put his head round the door.

'Victor, hello.' He lifted a hand. 'Just on our way to sign in. Be with you in a couple of minutes.'

We walked on down the hall to the reception desk which was manned twenty-four hours a day. It was flanked on the right-hand side by an enormous glass-fronted cabinet that reached from floor to ceiling and housed an impressive array of silver golf trophies.

Gavin was on duty behind the desk. His broad grin lit up the whole entrance hall. I'd never ever seen him without his genuine, thousand-watt smile. I hoped the management paid him a generous salary. His good nature was so much a part of the whole North Shore experience. He welcomed everyone in like an old and much-valued friend.

'So nice to see you again, gentlemen.'

'Great to be here, Gavin.' Samuel waved a hand towards us. 'You know my friends – Mr Mike Grantley, the racehorse trainer, and Harry Radcliffe, champion jockey, of course.' Gavin inclined his head and smiled. 'We'll all be playing in a party with Mr Victor Maudsley.'

'Oh, yes, sir, Mr Maudsley arrived a few minutes ago and he's in the dining room at the moment.'

Samuel nodded. 'I've just spoken to him. We'll go through and join him if that's all right.'

'Perfectly all right, gentlemen. Do enjoy your breakfast.' Gavin's smile notched up ever more wattage. 'We had a lot of onshore wind yesterday, but today's a great golfing day. It's lovely and calm.'

We went through to the dining room and were served with huge, delicious bacon-filled baps.

'Good to see you, Victor,' I said. 'How're things?' I hadn't seen him for several months and I didn't really need to ask. He looked a different man, relaxed and palpably at peace with himself. So very different from when we had met earlier in the year.

'I'm fine, never better. Good of you all to invite me for a round.'

'Now, now,' Samuel said around a mouthful of bacon, 'we appreciate your company – and your expertise. Help us to raise our game.'

I laughed. 'With my handicap, I need all the help I can get.'

'I'm not exactly achieving eagles either,' put in Mike.

'You don't need to – pleasure's the real name of the game.' Victor turned to Samuel. 'Wouldn't you agree?'

'Oh, yes, I definitely would. Whatever's going off out there,' Samuel said and waved an expressive hand towards the wide windows overlooking the sea and the outside world. 'As soon as you get here, life gets better immediately.'

We sat chatting and downing hot coffee until our teeing-off time approached, then went back down the steps to the car park to collect our golf bags from the car and to see the delectable Nikki in the Pro's shop for our score cards.

The course was eighteen holes. Samuel actually managed to pull off the tricky seventeenth tee shot. He'd played a blinder and sent the ball soaring over a grouping of trees, avoiding the dog-leg and landing on the seventeenth green. Unsurprisingly, Victor and Samuel were clear leaders, with Mike and me trailing a long way behind. We trooped back later, tired yet exhilarated, our lungs rejuvenated by five hours of breathing in the healthy ozones. We'd all enjoyed ourselves immensely and the thought of tackling one of the hotel's dinners was no hardship at all. And with Samuel driving us all home, it freed Mike and me to enjoy our drinks without risk of overdoing it.

But even as the happy thought occurred to me, another one counteracted it. Today had been a pull back from the graft of normal life, but tomorrow I was going to meet Jake Smith at Southwell races. Even before I'd downed my first pint, that thought was sobering. However, I shrugged it away. That was tomorrow's problem.

Right now, I followed the others into the bar and joined in the banter with the ever-effervescent Dan, the barman. He, like Gavin, was an indispensable part of the North Shore experience. And today he was in sparkling form, flirting with the ladies, cracking jokes and making sure all the men had swiftly pulled pints. I sighed with satisfaction. It was good to be here, good to meet up with mates again. I was determined to enjoy the rest of the day.

Tomorrow could definitely wait.

I arrived mid-afternoon at Southwell racecourse and went straight into the bar for a drink and a recce. Carrying my beer across to a table, I was accosted by Nathaniel Willoughby, the horse racing artist.

'Harry, good to see you. But what brings you? It's a flat meeting.'

'Hello, Nathaniel,' I said, cautiously. The last time I'd met him had been at Leicester races, and during that conversation I'd discovered a vital piece of incriminating evidence. Nathaniel hadn't realized as he chattered on that the information he was telling me held dire results for a friend of his. A very good friend. Now, I was unsure of his reactions. However, I needn't have concerned myself, as his following words proved.

'Great blow, you know, about the conviction.' He jumped right in as though he were reading my mind. 'I'd never have suspected – well, with some people, you take them as they present themselves. It's a massive shock to realize they are capable of such violence.' He shook his head sadly and consoled himself with a large gulp of gin.

'I'm sorry it had to be me who blew the whistle, Nathaniel.'

'Oh, crikey no, my dear chap,' he said and flapped a hand. 'I understand exactly. You were trying to safeguard your sister. Admirable, really. Besides,' he downed another mouthful before adding, 'if it hadn't all come out, I'd still be involved with . . . the family.' He hesitated over the last two words. I didn't say a thing. No point in embarrassing the man. Like all the rest of us, he'd had the wool pulled cleverly.

Nathaniel was an artist of great skill and, despite my apprehension regarding the upcoming meeting with Jake Smith, an idea entered my mind that certainly wouldn't have done had I not bumped into him.

'Nathaniel, could I commission you to paint a portrait for me?'

His face lit up. 'Work! Oh, yes, I do love being propositioned when it's not expected.' He rubbed his hands with relish. 'So, who is it?'

I smiled. 'Actually, they're not here on the earth yet.'

His face sagged. 'Wha . . . at?

'It's a portrait of a baby. Is that possible?'

'Ha, I see. Well . . . yes . . . well . . .' He passed a hand over his chin thoughtfully. 'I've never been asked to do one.' Then his shaken confidence returned in force. 'But I'm sure I could.'

I was sure, too. I knew his work. It was good; in fact, it was excellent. 'I'm sure you could.'

'So, when is the ETA?'

'Not sure, sometime in the next four, five months.'

'Hmmm . . .' He nodded. 'Might be best to leave it until the baby is, say, three months old – that way the features will be a little more formed. And the little one will be able to sit up.'

'Yes, I'm sure you're right.'

There wasn't much I could give Annabel to celebrate the birth of her first baby. Like the saying goes, what can you give someone who has everything? With Sir Jeffrey's deep, deep pockets, she didn't go short in any direction. But a personal, one-off painting of her baby? Well, that was something else.

'I'll pencil it in my work diary then and give you a bell to finalize the date.'

'Lovely.' I fished in my wallet and took out one of my cards. He nodded and pocketed it.

'Buy you another?' He drained his glass eagerly.

'Unfortunately, one's enough for me.' I stood up. 'Need a clear head.'

'You always were a cautious devil.' He clapped a hand on my shoulder. 'I'm off for a refill. See you, Harry.'

I went out into the bright sunshine. Cautious? I thought about my upcoming meeting. Nathaniel couldn't be more wrong.

I walked over to the parade ring and stood at the end of the line of prospective punters, making sure I was as conspicuous as possible.

The eight runners for the four o'clock were parading round, awaiting the arrival of the jockeys from the weighing room. One of the lady trainers – *the* leading lady – was standing in the centre talking to an owner. Barbara Maguire was acknowledged to be the expert in getting her horses fit to race on sand.

The punters loved Barbara. When they looked at her horses they saw pound signs on four legs.

Barbara looked nothing like a racehorse trainer. She was tiny, a doubtful five feet, with luxurious, flowing, chestnut locks. Her figure was similar to her namesake Barbara Windsor's. Rumour had it her head stable lad was employed half his time as a minder to see off the many interested males who got too close.

Her husband, Sean, had started their stables in the nineties. Progress had been slow and no doubt tough going with sparse winners. However, after his swift and unexpected death eight years ago, Barbara had focused all her energy on seeing off all the hopeful opposition – both on and off the racecourse. She'd been leading trainer on the All Weather for the last three years whilst remaining an enigma and a challenge to any man trying his luck.

But she had remained faithful to Sean's memory. It was probably his memory that drove her to make such a success of the stables. She was undeniably one of racing's characters – I'd known her for years and I admired her tremendously.

Turning to look at the jockeys, who were all streaming out now ready for mounting up in the parade ring, Barbara caught sight of me and flashed her famous smile. I raised a hand a few inches above the top rail that bounded the parade ring.

I could always rely on copy about Barbara's stable for the racing column I wrote for one of the papers. I always wrote in a positive, complimentary way, and she had thanked me previously for what she saw as the help I was giving her. In fact, anything I wrote was always the straight-down-the-middle truth and she didn't need to feel beholden in any way. But any parties she threw usually found me receiving an invitation. They were always damn good parties, too.

I found it reassuring to know there were friendly faces around I could call on if the tight spot facing me became too constricting.

I'd spent an abortive three hours doing a recce in Wellington Street in Newark. I'd drawn a total blank. I'd seen nothing and nobody entering or leaving number twenty-nine. I had absolutely no idea what Jake Smith looked like. He, along with a good percentage of the general population, knew my face well. Now all my senses were on top-level alert. To feel so vulnerable wasn't pleasant.

The bell rang and jockeys were thrown up into tiny saddles and led away up the horses' walkway and out on to the course. I ambled along beside the winners' enclosure and weighing room, taking my time.

'Far enough, *Mr Radcliffe*.'

Although the voice was hardly above a whisper, the menace in the tone was clear.

I froze. Felt my jacket move slightly at the back and something cold slide up inside against my ribs. Felt the sudden pain as the point of a knife pierced my skin. I drew in breath sharply. Tension bunched my muscles.

'Don't move – just talk.'

'No.'

'You what?' The point of the knife pressed harder. I felt a hot trickle running down inside my shirt. Blood.

'Take the knife away – now.'

'I'm the one giving orders.'

'And I'm not taking them.'

He was the one now taking in a sharp breath. A silent, quivering tension stretched between us.

I was banking on him wanting me in one piece to supply the information he needed. If Jake slid the knife between my ribs now, he'd never get any answers. But if I was wrong and he was mad – or bad – enough, he could finish the job right where we stood. I'd taken a massive gamble. The next second or two would decide if I'd won – or lost.

'Start walking. Head for the car park.'

I felt the knife slide away, felt the sudden weakness of relief. Obediently, I began walking. He was at the side of me now, matching me pace for pace.

'Don't try anything. Don't look at anybody.'

I started to turn my head to get a look at his face.

'Walk!'

I wasn't pushing my luck. At least the knife was gone – for the moment. But with despair, I heard the tannoy conveying the happy news for Barbara that her horse, Silvercloud, had just won the last race. All I had to do was wait. Help would be here within moments when she arrived in the winners' enclosure.

I walked on.

TEN

We walked to the car park. I followed his prompts and we fetched up beside a battered green Rover. He unlocked and motioned me into the passenger seat. For a brief moment, I considered refusing. Once I was inside, that was it. No telling where he was intending to take me. Right now, it was just us – one to one. But it was possible he would drive me to where two or three of his mates were waiting. Life could get more tricky. I hesitated.

'In.'

He was obviously a man not given to long sentences. Did I even have a choice? I climbed in. So did he.

'Belt up . . .'

I fixed my seat belt. His concern for my welfare was at odds with putting a knife to my ribs.

'Coppers on the gate.'

I nodded. Just out of prison, he was in no hurry to attract attention for a minor breech. He nosed the car out of line and bumped over the grass towards the exit.

'Where are you taking me?'

'Not far.'

I cast a sideways glance across the massed cars; my own Mazda – my escape route – was in there somewhere. It might as well have been the other side of the moon.

He drove for about a mile along Racecourse Lane towards Southwell. Then, to my surprise, he pulled in on to the grass verge beside a farm gateway.

He cut the engine and silence settled around us. Staring morosely across the fields, he said, 'How *did* you do it?'

I cast around. What was he referring to?

'Next clue.'

'Eh?' He swung round in his seat, eyebrows drawn tightly together across the bridge of his nose. Oddly, his eyebrows were heavy, black, whilst his head was shaved, totally devoid of hair.

'Do what?'

'Find out who did it.'

'I didn't kill Carl. I'm sorry he's dead.'

He flipped a hand sideways impatiently. 'I know *that*. But it was you, not the police, sussed it out – yes?'

I was forced to agree that, yes, I'd worked out the sordid mess.

'Carl's killer's being taken care of. So,' he sighed heavily, adding, 'that's him done.'

'You mean he's in prison?'

He stared at me aggressively. 'Did I say that? No, I don't mean *taken care of* . . . I mean *sorted* . . . I might be out of the slammer, but a lot of my mates are still inside.' He gave a gruff, snorting laugh. 'Mates that owe me, plus they were Carl's mates an' all.'

I felt a coldness hit my stomach.

'Understand?'

'Yes.'

We sat in silence. I had no idea what he wanted from me. If he didn't blame me, he wasn't after revenge. So what? His hands tightened on the steering wheel.

'My sister's dead.'

I heard the naked grief in his words. Recognized it immediately. They say it takes one to know one. By God, how true that is.

'I'm really sorry.'

He nodded, still clenching his hands. 'Thanks.' He flicked a quick glance at me. 'Likewise.'

'Hmm . . .'

We sat in silence again. All my apprehension had gone. Any violence that might have taken place now seemed unlikely. If I waited long enough, he was going to get around to telling me what he wanted.

'She was murdered.'

His first words shook me. But what he said next shook me even more.

'I want you to find her killer.'

'Whoa!' I held up the palm of my hand. 'I'm a jump jockey, OK? I'm not in the detective business.'

'Oh, no? You were the one who sussed out the last. You admitted it.'

'Well, yes, but—'

'So, you've done it once, you can do it again.' There was an edge to his voice now. 'I'm not *asking* if you want to – I'm telling you.'

'Now, look here—'

'Because if you don't, I'm going to come close to Chloe. Understand?'

The coldness was back in my stomach. 'Nothing to do with her.'

'Whatever it takes.' He shrugged. 'An' I reckon you're the right bloke for the job.'

'So, you're putting me over a barrel, eh?'

'You've been there before – and got results.'

'Let me ask *you* something. Did you, or someone you instructed, leave a set of false teeth on my doorstep?'

'What the hell you on about?' The eyebrows beetled their way tightly together.

His answer was good enough for me. Whatever else, the man

was certainly no actor. Annabel had been right. It hadn't been Jake. So who, then?

I stared out of the windscreen. A wood pigeon flapped its way lazily across the field. Freedom. I'd hoped for some myself once my life was under my control and I was, literally, back in the saddle. What a hope. I became aware Jake was scowling at me.

'Well?'

'The day I got your note, someone left a pair of false teeth on my doorstep.'

His eyebrows raised themselves to his hairline, or what would have been his hairline if he'd had any.

'They were replicas of Carl's.'

'Fucking hell!'

'Exactly.'

'Wasn't me.' He shook his head vigorously.

'Any ideas?'

'Nope.'

'Nor me.' I watched the wood pigeon head for the horizon and disappear out of sight. Lucky sod. 'Look, why not employ a professional detective agency?'

'I want you.'

'Is it the money?'

I was still unable to shake off the guilt about Carl's death. Irrational, ill-founded, but still guilt. Helping Jake to find his sister's killer, hand them over to the police, might go a long way to assuaging it.

'Nice try, Harry boy.' He shook his head. 'Won't wash. They'd play it by the book.'

'And I wouldn't?'

'You're a jockey, a jump jockey. You'd just get a result.'

He was right. A professional firm would do the work in the authentic manner, hide-bound by all the regulations and rules. Jake was watching me closely. He smiled.

'You see?'

'Yes.' I reluctantly inclined my head. 'Yes, I do.'

Wednesday morning, five thirty a.m., I stripped off the one item of clothing I was wearing – my boxer shorts – and, totally naked, stood sideways on in front of the bathroom mirror. Last night's hastily applied plaster had certainly stuck well. I hooked my thumbnail over the top edge and piggled the corner loose. Then, gripping the plaster tightly, I ripped it off. I could see the deep scratch had begun to heal cleanly.

Turning the shower on hot, I stepped in and let the water flow over me. The wound stung as the hot needles played against it, but I was simply relieved the injury was no worse. The whole meeting with Jake seemed surreal. I had gone to Southwell expecting the worst. At the point the knife punctured my skin and drew blood, my expectation of coming out of the confrontation unscathed had plummeted.

To find myself, half an hour later, sitting at the side of Jake talking about a relative's death and finding common ground was almost beyond credibility. But it had happened. From fear and dislike, my feelings for the man had swung round until I felt a certain fragile sympathy for him. Not a liking, but an understanding of his feelings of grief, loss, the need for retribution. All those things. They mirrored my own from a few short weeks ago.

However, the very fact that I couldn't shake off the guilt about Carl's death, despite it not being my hand that finished him, told me all I needed to know about getting revenge. It did nothing to help cope with the pain of losing someone close. Indeed, it seemed to increase the sense of futility of pursuing revenge as a lasting satisfaction and instead only increased the hollow emptiness.

But despite the empathy, I knew Jake was quite prepared to use whatever form of persuasion or violence necessary to achieve his own aim – tracking down his sister's killer. That he had decided I was the man he would use was my tough luck. If I didn't dance to his demands, innocent people might get crushed as he bulldozed his own way forward. However much I felt repulsed by the thought of handing over my own reins into his hands, he knew – I knew – I was going to do it.

I towelled off. Wiped the steam from the mirror. There was a streak of red along my ribs. I rooted in the first-aid box in the bathroom cabinet, found a plaster and secured it over the wound. I had no way of knowing if the knife had been clean or contaminated, but at least my tetanus jab was up to date.

Half an hour later, I drove into Mike's stable yard. He'd heard my car engine and a mug of tea was steaming on the kitchen table when I walked in.

'Still with us, then, Harry?' His flippancy didn't fool me. Genuine relief shone in his eyes. It felt good to know there was someone who did actually give a damn whether I lived or died.

I lifted the mug and took a gulp. 'Cheers. And before you ask, I am still all in one piece – well, practically one piece.'

'Eh?'

'The initial skirmish drew blood, but not much.'

'Are you going to give me the full SP about yesterday's meeting or not?'

I grinned and took pity on him. 'Sure.' I filled him in on the whole bizarre situation.

'Could only happen to you, Harry. An ex-con has his sister murdered and employs you to find her killer. Good God, man, how're you going to get out of it?' For once, his smiling countenance was clouded over with concern.

'Simple answer, Mike: I can't.'

'But surely you're not serious?'

'What choice have I got? You said it yourself, I can't let Chloe be put at risk. And you're right.'

'Tell the police. It's the only way.'

'And what will they do? Presumably, they've conducted an investigation into Jake's sister's death.'

'And presumably they've drawn a blank. So if, with all *their* resources, the police can't come up with the answer and the killer's name, what the hell chance do you stand? Be sensible, Harry. Look at this head-on. You've no chance.'

'You're wrong, Mike. *That's* what will give me a chance. A chance to get off Jake's hook. If I pay lip service to his demands and find out sweet FA, he'll have to back down. I will have tried and failed. End of story.'

'Knowing you,' he said and shook his head sadly, 'you probably will find something out. And if you do, what are the chances the killer won't come looking for you to close your mouth – and your eyes. That's what happened to Carl, don't forget.'

I looked at him steadily. 'Mike, I will *never* forget what happened to Carl. If I could rerun that particular tape, I would never have asked him to meet me. But since you can't undo the past, I'm stuck with it.'

'Yes, I'm sorry. That was crass of me. But for God's sake, don't go feet first into this snake pit. You might never get out alive.'

'I'm not thrilled at the thought, but reading the small print, I'm stuck with it.'

He sighed heavily, shoulders drooping in dismal resignation. 'All I can do is offer my help.'

'I accept your offer, should I—'

'I know, I know . . .' he lifted a hand, adding, 'should you find your back up against the stable door.'

I gave him a rueful smile. 'Something like that, yes.'

He shrugged again, drained his tea and stood the empty mug in the sink. 'Come on, let's get some work done.'

I followed him outside across the stable yard, glad to put the whole messy business out of my mind and concentrate on riding out first lot.

By late morning, and having ridden out second and third lots as well, a car drove up that we both recognized. Not hard to do. We had ridden in it to Skegness and back on Monday.

The doors opened and Samuel and Chloe got out, both wearing wide, happy smiles. At the sight of Chloe, all the grim thoughts I'd successfully pushed out of my mind for the previous four hours rushed back. She was a beautiful woman, a sweet person. I groaned inside. I couldn't risk that beauty being spoiled or that sweet person taking some horrendous physical beating – or worse, because I was quite sure Jake was capable of extreme action if he didn't get what he wanted. Whatever it took, I thought – and was instantly reminded that Jake himself had used the very same words to pin me to the cork-board.

'Hello, lovely to see you. How's my darling White Lace?'

I knew Mike would have kept Chloe informed of the vet's findings, but I wasn't sure if she knew about Annabel giving the mare healing.

'Great to see you both, too. White Lace is doing very well. Come and see for yourselves.'

'Marvellous day last Sunday, Harry,' Samuel said. 'Enjoyed it no end.'

'Oh, yes. And I enjoyed Monday's golf as well.'

Mike came striding up, having seen the car arrive. 'Me too, Samuel. Hello, Chloe, you're looking well. Racehorse ownership suits you.'

She laughed at him. 'You don't have to give me your 'owner's spiel' to keep me on your books. Just try keeping me out.'

'I wouldn't dare,' he laughed.

We all walked over to the mare's stable and she obligingly stuck her head out over the half-door.

'She looks very calm now – don't you, my darling?'

'Yes,' Samuel agreed with his daughter. 'Looks a picture. The shoulder's healed very well, too. Surprisingly well, because it was nasty.'

'Got to admit it,' Mike said, 'Annabel's healing has had a most positive effect on her. Settled the nervousness and speeded the flesh knitting up.'

'Annabel's healing?' Chloe queried.

'Spiritual healing,' I clarified.

'Wow! She's a qualified healer, then?'

'Yes.'

'But that's marvellous. I mean, look at my mare. She's so improved.'

'I'm certainly impressed. And I shall use her again,' Mike said. 'Like Annabel told us, animals respond very well, much better on the whole than people, because they have no mental blocks that throw up obstacles. They just accept the healing and allow it to do just that.'

'She's a very useful lady to have around, I can see that,' Samuel said, nodding, and put out a hand to stroke the mare. 'White Lace has really benefited. Would you pass on my thanks to Annabel, please, Mike?'

'Certainly will.'

'And now,' Samuel said, a wicked twinkle in his eye, 'talking of white lace . . . You boys didn't remind me of what I said on Sunday at Huntingdon races, did you?'

'Remind us.'

'I said after we'd slaughtered eighteen holes at North Shore, I'd tell you what I have in mind for a celebration.'

'And we thought we'd got away with it,' Mike joked.

'Uh-huh, oh, no. I want you both to agree. It will give Chloe and me a lot of pleasure if you do.'

'Agree to what, Samuel?' I asked. 'And what's it got to do with White Lace?'

'Nothing,' he chuckled. 'Well, not the mare; it will be the bride who'll be wearing white on Saturday. There's a wedding taking place at North Shore Hotel and you chaps are invited. It's an all-day job, stay overnight and play a round before leaving on Sunday if you wish.'

'Well, it's not really my scene, Samuel—' Mike began.

'Nor mine,' I backed him.

'Look, I know it's short notice, but two of the original guests have had to cry off. One of them has been whipped into hospital to have his appendix removed. The room has already been paid for and will now be empty.'

'But who's the bride? Will she even want us there? After all, it's her day.'

'She's a friend of mine,' Chloe answered. 'And you're friends of mine, too, so she's happy with the arrangement. Oh, do say you'll both come and join in the fun, please.' She caught hold of my arm and squeezed it. 'Pleeeease.'

Mike, ever the sucker for a pretty girl, turned to me. 'You've no racing on that day. We could make it. What do you say, Harry? Shall we?'

Before I could answer, Samuel, seeing Mike as good as won over, steamrollered me.

'Of course you're coming. You've had a lousy year, got yourself in a rut. You're due a bit of excitement.'

I raised an eyebrow at Mike who grinned and looked away. Right now, I had all the excitement I needed. But they were all waiting expectantly on my reply. It would be churlish to refuse. And, anyway, Jake Smith had told me to expect a visit from him in the next day or two. He wouldn't be able to find me if I went to the east coast.

'Thanks, Samuel. Yes, I'd love to.'

ELEVEN

The water level rose to within a few inches of the top of the bath and I twiddled the hot tap and stopped the steaming water gushing out. Tentatively, I dipped a toe in. It was bloody hot. And it needed to be. Taking the towel from around my waist, I draped it over the radiator.

Screwing my head round, I had a look at my naked right thigh. An ugly hoof shape of purpling flesh marked the spot where Lobalong, living up to his name with aplomb, had planted his near fore racing plate.

Earlier in the day, Samuel and Chloe had stayed to sample roast beef and mustard sandwiches for lunch at Mike's before we had said our goodbyes. They drove off in Samuel's car, leaving me to head the Mazda down to the racecourse at Towcester. I had just the one ride there in the last race on Thomasina, an eight-to-one shot.

I'd not ridden her before, but right now I was willing to take any rides offered me as I sought to build up my standing after being out for months. After a good start, joint first and a second, I needed to follow up. Owners needed confidence in a jockey before they instructed their trainers.

But like a lot of other professionals – golfers, writers, etc. – jockeys were only as good as their last success. A track record helped, of course, but you still had to repeatedly produce results. In a way, it was catch twenty-two. Achieving winners restored owners' confidence, but rides were needed in order to get winners. And, as yet, I was in no position to pick and choose the horses I rode. I was just damn grateful to get any rides – full stop.

Right now, Joe Public was unsure of my fitness to ride. Looking down at my right leg, I could share their uncertainty.

Thomasina had carried me safely over all the fences at Towcester – no mean feat, it was an extremely taxing course – until we approached the third last. Instead of sailing over, she had stumbled into it, ploughed her way through and dropped me on the far side. Lobalong, right behind us, had tried to twist away on landing and almost made it. Except for kicking my leg on his way past.

It had been a jaw-clenching limp all the way back up the course. The walking would have helped the injured leg from stiffening up, but I was relieved when I reached the entrance of the horses' walkway.

Thomasina, thank God, apart from some superficial scratches, was uninjured. One of the stable lads had managed to catch the mare and was waiting for me. I removed the saddle and struggled into the weighing room.

I was even more relieved to be told that my femur was uninjured. However, there would be no racing for me for the next three days. The leg needed hot baths and resting. Falls were an everyday possibility and an acceptance of this grim fact was firmly hardwired into every jump jockey.

Driving back, with my leg throbbing and on fire, the journey had taken close to three hours, with roadworks and the inevitable daily accident on the A46. The ongoing improvements to the road layout were supposed to ease the traffic flow, make it safer. As far as I was concerned, its claim to fame so far was to increase the price of shares for the cone manufacturing companies, confuse all the drivers and increase the accident statistics.

With great relief, I swung in through the gate and parked by the back door to the cottage. There was no better place to be than home when illness or injury struck. However, the cottage was empty. Leo was absent. No doubt out on a scouting trip for willing queens. I immediately downed a generous whisky, locked up and, after switching off all the downstairs lights, crawled upstairs to the bathroom. I was about to give the leg injury some much needed TLC.

Wincing, I lifted the leg to get into the bath. At that same moment, the light bulb blew. The spare light bulbs were downstairs under the kitchen sink. It would mean negotiating the stairs – down and up. I swore strongly. Not this side of Christmas! In the airing cupboard in a corner of the bathroom, there was a box of tea-lights, candles that Annabel used to light whenever she'd taken a bath when we lived together.

I groped about in the semi-gloom inside the cupboard and found them, together with a sturdy box of Cook's matches. Lighting several and placing them around the edge of the bath, I had to admit that, without the main light on, they did add a definite air of tranquillity. I climbed into the bath and slid down, letting the hot water cover my thighs completely. I'd probably come out wrinkled and bright red, but right now the feeling was bliss.

I closed my eyes and let go of the day.

For the next hour or so, I dozed, reheated the water, dozed some more. I don't recall thinking much about anything. Drifting in and out of consciousness whilst the supporting, healing water did its job, I was suddenly jolted into sharp awareness. Someone was banging loudly on the cottage door. A clutch of apprehension gripped my guts.

Outside it was pitch-black, the cottage isolated, and my leg injury rendered me unable to move faster than a hobble. I was not expecting anyone, nobody at all. No one except, possibly, the one person I really didn't want to meet – Jake Smith.

Struggling out of the bath, I grabbed for the towel, secured it around my waist and hobbled down the landing and into the bedroom overlooking the back door. I angled myself behind the curtains and risked a glance out of the window.

Out in the lane, parked beyond the garden gate, was a large car. As I watched, the moon drifted from behind clouds and illuminated the vehicle: an old green Rover. I recognized it because I'd had an enforced ride in it – down Racecourse Lane. It belonged to Jake Smith. Although, from this angle, I couldn't see who was banging on the back door, it was odds-on that it was Jake.

I had two options. One, I could struggle downstairs, switch on the electric lights and open the door. Face him undressed, wet, extremely vulnerable. Two, I could remain where I was, completely hidden behind the thick curtain, and wait and watch until he got fed up with nobody surfacing. The fact that none of the downstairs lights were on helped my case that I was not at home.

I stood and listened to the hammering on the door. Jake couldn't be sure I was inside, unless he'd trailed me back from the races. That didn't hold water because I'd fixed a drink and then spent more than an hour in the bathroom. He wouldn't have bothered waiting if he'd been tailing me. No, he couldn't be sure.

I stayed put behind the curtain.

Now it was my decision where and when we met.

The next day, I treated the injury with respect and went to ground at the cottage, took hot, healing baths and rested the leg.

However, on Friday, I'd reached the 'sod it' stage and drove off over to Mike's stables at six o'clock. It wasn't easy – nor was it pain-free – but I managed to ride out two lots.

After the second ride, Fleur, who had been in the string as well, tugged off her crash cap.

'Don't you think you should be resting that leg?'

'I did. Yesterday.'

'Hmmm. You expect it to be better in one day?'

'No,' I said truthfully, 'but I needed to get back in the saddle again.'

'I see,' she said, poker-faced.

'And it's not what you're thinking.'

'Really? And what would that be?'

I grinned. 'Unlike my leg, my nerve is quite undamaged.'

For a moment or two, she eyed me up and down, and then her lips quirked up slightly at the corners. 'I believe you.'

'Doesn't make any difference if you do or not; it's the truth.'

'It may well be,' Mike said, coming up behind us, 'but you've ridden two lots. Now, get yourself back home and give it a chance. Don't forget, the wedding's at North Shore Hotel tomorrow. No resting there. Think of the toasts. It will be all arm lifting.' He grinned.

I saw his point. 'OK.' I shrugged resignedly. 'I'm off. I'll go and join Leo. He's got his head down. Been out on the tiles for the past two nights giving the queens a thrill.'

'Lucky Leo,' Fleur murmured and shot me a sideways glance under her lashes. Mike, never a man to miss a trick, smirked knowingly.

'Your turn soon, Harry. Off you go; give that leg a chance. I'll see you in the morning.'

I drove away, obsessively checking my mirrors for cars, but I didn't need caution: no one was tailing me.

Yesterday, alone at the cottage behind locked and bolted doors and windows, I'd spent most of the time asleep – when I wasn't taking hot baths. Nothing had disturbed the peace. No snail mail or emails arrived, the phone never rang and, above all, nobody came to the door. Of Jake Smith, there was no sign. All I needed to do now was keep my head down for the rest of today. If he came round tomorrow, he wouldn't find me. I'd be over on the east coast attending the wedding.

I turned in at the gate of Harlequin Cottage, parked up and stumbled awkwardly over the gravel to the kitchen door. My leg was hurting like hell.

In the kitchen, Leo, curled up in his basket, opened one emerald eye, sighed heavily and closed it again. The 'do not disturb' sign was very clearly in place.

'That's females for you, fella.'

I brewed a mug of strong tea, struggled upstairs to the bathroom and ran yet another hot bath. Sitting, soaking, sweating, I supped the hot tea and thought about where my next rides were coming from. But the heat was both soothing and soporific. Finishing the tea, I lay back and closed my eyes. I never saw the door open; just heard the voice.

'If I didn't know better, Harry boy, I'd think you were avoiding me.'

My eyes snapped open. Jake Smith was leaning against the airing cupboard door, lazily chewing gum. His eyes were cold, expressionless. He glanced down into the bath.

'Saw your accident. Watched the race in the bookies. Called round later to make sure it wasn't going to put you out of action.'

I said nothing. My mind ranged round the cottage boundaries. How the hell had he got in?

'Expect you wonder how I'm standing here.' He was reading my mind now. 'You left a transom open in the conservatory.' He gave a mirthless snort. 'You should be more careful, Harry, boy, you might get a visitor you don't want.'

I levered myself up and reached for the towel.

'Ooooh . . .' He sucked in breath sharply and shook his head. 'Now *that* looks painful . . .'

'You're not wrong.' I wrapped the towel round my waist and towelled off my shoulders and chest with another. 'So, that's what you're here for, is it? To see how badly I'd copped it?'

'Yeah.' He chewed on a wad of gum, shifting it around his mouth. 'So?'

'You're walking . . . an' you've ridden out two lots this morning.'

I dropped the towels on to the linen basket. 'You've been tailing me?'

He shrugged. Pushing a hand into his pocket, he drew out an envelope. 'This is a photo of my sister, Jo-Jo. I'll leave it with you, but you'd better not lose it. I really wouldn't like that. I want it back.'

I struggled into underpants and jeans and took the photograph from him. She was a looker: long black hair, tall, slender but with a beautiful pair of breasts. Dressed in a scarlet evening dress with incredibly high heels, she was every male's must-have.

He watched me keenly, noted my reaction. His mouth twisted up on one side and he chewed harder on the gum.

'Yeah, stopped traffic, she did.'

I could believe it. With her life cut short, beauty like that was a loss to the world.

'How did she die?'

'How was she *murdered*, you mean?' He thrust his face aggressively close to mine.

'OK, take it easy. So far, I don't know anything at all, right?'

'Sure.' His shoulders sagged. 'She was in a car smash.'

'Her own car?'

'No. She was with this bloke. He was loaded, o'course. I mean, she was high class, not one of your street-corner girls.'

'You're saying she was a prostitute?'

'She had this flat, y'see. He paid for it all.'

'Right.'

'He's dead as well.'

'And what was his name?'

'Frame, Louis Frame. The car was a Jag. It was totalled.' As he spoke, Jake took out a single sheet of paper from the envelope. 'Here, all the dates an' details an' people are listed. They were coming back from the races when it happened.'

'What did they run into?'

'Horsebox.'

My immediate thought was to hope the horses had escaped injury but, prudently, I didn't say anything. He was so screwed up about losing his sister there was no room for concern for anybody else, human or equine.

'What was the police verdict on the accident?'

'Useless arseholes, said it was careless driving. Raining y'see. Couldn't stop in time 'cos they were really motoring.'

I nodded. 'Who was driving?'

'Frame was. Jo-Jo said he always drove fast. For an old bloke, he was full of energy.' His mouth twisted.

'You didn't like the set-up?'

'Would you? If it had been your sister?'

'No.'

In the following silence, it was there again between us, that tenuous link.

I didn't have a sister but I thought about my half-sister, my horrifically disabled half-sister. Given the choice between Silvie's disability or her being a prostitute, I'd opt for the latter – by God, I would.

'What makes you think it was murder, not an accident?'

'I reckon Jo-Jo was in the wrong place, wrong time. It was Frame that was the target, not her.'

'Why should he be a target?'

'He was in two dodgy situations that I know about. Like, he was involved in a crash about a year back. Took out the driver of the other car. His relatives might be wanting some comeback. Two, a mate of mine was sent down on Frame's evidence in court a while back. His wife, Alice, was spitting tacks in court, swearing she'd get him. She was a big mate of Jo-Jo's.'

'Well, *she* wouldn't set out to kill Jo-Jo.'

He glowered at me. 'Like I say, wrong place, wrong time.'

'Do you know if there was something wrong with the car?'

'Yeah. The fuzz gave it out there was a brake fluid leak but still classed it as careless driving – got too close, y'see, couldn't stop in time. Frame had driven it up to Doncaster races, so it was OK then. But the crash happened on their way back home.'

'So, it could have been tampered with at the races?'

'Yeah, looks like it.'

'Whose horsebox did they run into?'

'Robson's. Used it to take up a seller and was coming back empty.'

I sighed out a deep breath of relief. No horses injured, then.

'You think Robson was involved?'

He shook his shaved head. 'No. Apparently, the driver was gutted by the deaths.'

'Right.'

I took the sheet of paper and photograph from him and replaced them in the envelope.

Jake stopped chewing. He took the gum from his mouth and pitched it into the waste bin underneath the wash basin. 'You'll sort it, then?'

'Do my best to get a result.'

He thrust his face two inches from my own.

'You'd fucking better, if you want to keep breathing. Somebody's going to pay the price for Jo-Jo's death, and if you don't find who's responsible . . . it will be you!'

TWELVE

On Saturday, kick-off for the wedding was twelve thirty, so plenty of time to ride out at Mike's before we had to leave. My right leg had now decided to concede and, whilst not fully healed, the pain level was such I could override it.

After seeing off three lots on the gallops and one of Mike's tasty breakfasts, showered, suited and booted, we motored east in his car.

Traffic was light until we arrived at Skegness, but turning left at The Ship on to Roman Bank, it was nose-to-tail for a couple of slow miles before we swung off round the willow tree corner on to North Shore Road.

Now, not a car in sight; instead, a wide spread of glorious green golf course culminating in the hotel at the top of the rise – an oasis of calm with a unique atmosphere guaranteed to increase the pleasure of being alive.

In front of the hotel, a red carpet royally invited us up the steps and in through the main entrance, where we were greeted by Mark, the manager, and shown into the St Andrew's Suite. Nearly all the guests had arrived and everybody was now anticipating the bride's entrance.

I spotted several racing acquaintances. Samuel, already halfway down a glass of Pimms, spotted us and beamed his way over. He noted my acknowledgement of two or three of the guests.

'Friends of the bride's late father. Louis was a great one for going to race meetings.'

'Louis?' I queried, my heart shifting a bit.

'Louis Frame. Used to be my business partner – had fingers in other business pies as well, mind. Great shame he died suddenly. A big shock to Lucinda.' My heart was now below foundation level. Yes, this was the same man we were talking about – us and Jake Smith.

'Lucinda, the bride?' I queried.

'Yes, damn good job she's got Brandon.'

'He's the husband-to-be, I take it?' Mike said.

'That's right. He's been Lucinda's boyfriend for the last six months. I think it's so reassuring for her, y'know, that Louis knew him and approved. Like, now Louis is gone, he's handed Lucinda's care on to Brandon.'

I listened to the conversation and thought about the cause of Louis' passing. Was it simply a shocking accident? Or could it really have been murder?

Jake wasn't interested in the loss of the man, only in his sister dying. If it proved to be murder, then it was just possible Jo-Jo had been the intended victim, but I doubted it.

What I needed to discover was a motive – against either of them. Given that, it would clearly point to the identity of both victim and murderer. And it seemed that coming here might provide me with the opportunity. Could it be fate was getting involved, pushing me down the right path? Possibly, but I was a pragmatist – I dealt with facts every day. In my own choice of career, bloody hard facts.

I surreptitiously ran a hand down the outside of my right thigh. It was still giving me some stick.

Dan came bustling up with a tray of Pimms.

'Hello, Mr Grantley, Mr Radcliffe. Do help yourselves to a drink. The bride will be here very shortly now. Just heard it on the early warning system.' He was in full fizzing form, brightening up the already happy crowd. People responded to Dan. He had a knack of getting on with, and getting the best out of, people.

'Cheers, Dan.' Mike reached for a glass and took an appreciative swallow. 'Lovely stuff.'

I took a more moderate sip. 'What time are you on till tonight?'

Dan chortled. 'Last man standing.' He was in his element and his high spirits were infectious. He disappeared through the crowd, who by now were really getting in the mood as good-natured laughter flooded the dazzling room. It was decked out with an impressive balloon arch in shades of lilac and pink, and the colour scheme was continued with displays of flowers everywhere.

From being lukewarm about turning up today, weddings not being my thing, I was actually beginning to enjoy myself. It looked like being a fun day, and since the disco was scheduled to go on until two a.m., a fun night to follow.

Music sounded through hidden speakers. Robbie Williams' chocolate-smooth voice singing 'Angels' filled the St Andrew's Suite and spilled out down the hall, through reception and reached out to greet the bride as she arrived. Upholding tradition beautifully, she was just a tad late. Accompanied by two bridesmaids, one of whom was Chloe, Lucinda clung to the arm of a tall, thin, middle-aged man and picked her way carefully along the red carpet into the St Andrew's Suite.

They say every bride looks beautiful and she did, but at the side of Chloe . . . there was no contest. Although radiant, Lucinda's glow owed a great deal to an expert application of cosmetics and an exquisitely fitted white gown.

Chloe, her long brunette curls dancing on her shoulders, wearing a full-length dress of deep pink satin, was stunning. I shot a glance at Samuel standing beside me. His expression was one of awe and overwhelming pride as he gazed at his daughter.

Chloe and the second bridesmaid bent to ease the bride's train through the doorway to the St Andrew's Suite.

The other bridesmaid, I learned later, was Juliette, Lucinda's cousin, the daughter of Edward, the thin middle-aged man. She was a fresh-faced, pretty girl who had the most unusual hair I'd ever seen. Totally natural – impossible for any salon to replicate – it contained a dozen different shades of blonde, and the overall effect was of shimmering creamy gold. I gaped. I guess a lot of the other men did, too. It was unbelievably beautiful hair.

I could have begun to feel sorry for the bride, flanked as she was by two gorgeous, eye-catching girls, but both bridesmaids, to their credit, gave full centre stage to Lucinda.

With eyes shining with love and firmly fixed on the bridegroom waiting at the far end of the room, Lucinda walked forward as the song 'Angels' reached a sublime climax.

The music moved me more than I'd have thought possible. I'd chosen it to be played at the celebration service for Silvie, my half-sister. It brought so many precious memories back. This particular song had been Silvie's favourite, giving her joy every time she heard it. Picturing her dear face, I found myself swallowing hard several times.

The song ended and, as she reached her husband-to-be, Lucinda's marriage ceremony began.

Later, after pronounced man and wife, Brandon, looking hand-some and very sharp in a smart suit, drew Lucinda into his arms and delighted the guests by giving her a long, long kiss.

Mike, standing beside me, gave an almost inaudible sigh. I shot a quick look at him. His face was sombre and pinched. *Monica*, I thought with a flash of insight; he's remembering Monica and their wedding day. I didn't look away in time and his eyes met mine.

'They're both in a better place,' he murmured, meaning Silvie as well as Monica.

'We can hope.'

'Come on,' he said and punched my arm lightly, 'let's drown our sorrows. And then I'll introduce you to Edward.'

'He's Louis' elder brother, right?'

'Yeah.'

'Is he likely to know anything about the accident?'

He shrugged. 'You can ask.'

The bridal party was shepherded outside for photographs and we followed the guests for drinks and canapes in the garden.

Sited on the east side of the hotel, the garden ran almost parallel to the beach. For the time of the year, the day was a beauty – sun shining, warm and a view right out, far, far out, over the glittering sea. We ate delicious nibbles, enjoyed the peace and listened to the soft boom of the sea. Lucinda would certainly remember her wedding day taking place in such a special place. Her happiness was obvious, but I'd no doubt it also covered a lot of sadness at the loss of her father.

Would my looking into Louis' death help? Or would it make things worse for her? I had no way of telling, but surely she'd want to know the truth. I could see now my actions were likely to affect quite a few people I'd not considered. If it was humanly possible to duck out, I would, but I had absolutely no option.

Where to start, I'd no idea, but if it wasn't an accident that had seen Louis off, then someone knew the truth. I just had to ask the right questions, try to get a loose end to unravel and hope it would lead me to the solution – and the murderer.

For now, I was going to assume it had been murder. I was also going to assume the intended victim had been Louis – not Jo-Jo.

But to eliminate Jo-Jo entirely, I needed to find out a great deal about her. Jake had supplied all the information he had, which wasn't much, but at least gave me a starting point.

If I followed up any information I discovered from any of the people involved with Louis and Jo-Jo, sooner or later a pattern would emerge.

As I'd found out a few months before, one piece of information inevitably led to another, and when all the pieces were put together, intuition took over at some subliminal level and a gut reaction pointed to the truth – even if, as in that case, the truth seemed incredible.

Right now, it looked to me as though all this amateur sleuthing was going to be very time-consuming. My challenge for champion jockey, already way behind schedule, looked increasingly like a no-hoper. Important though the championship was to me, I had to weigh it against Chloe's life. Chloe, looking stunning in her long pink satin bridesmaid's dress. Only one answer – ironically, the same one Jake had used: *whatever it took*. Whatever the cost to me personally didn't matter. What did matter was that Chloe retained her beautiful face and, indeed, her life.

We all stood around in the garden enjoying our food, the drink and the warmth of the sun on our faces. I'd allow myself an hour's grace to pull back and enjoy the present before I started off on the trail of the murderer. He must have harboured a great hatred towards Louis to have coldly killed him. Had that hatred been satisfied by Louis' death? And what of the motive behind it? Had his death achieved the expected result? Or, if not, did it carry over to his daughter?

The distasteful thought occurred to me that it was quite possible he was here amongst us right now. After all, this was Lucinda's big day – and she was Louis' daughter.

In spite of the sun, my skin felt suddenly cold.

THIRTEEN

Mike and I had been allocated the east turret room. Our overnight bags had been carried up for us. I turned the key at number 115 and went in.

The bay windows all overlooked the beach, sea and golf course in every direction, and the views were superb. The one direction it didn't cover was west – inland. I took off my jacket, laid it on one of the twin beds and went over to let in some of the ozones.

Bay window was a very good description. From every one of them was a view right out to sea, plus from the north-facing window an uninterrupted view down the tenth fairway, edged by sandy beach, and away to the adjacent community of Winthorpe. It was breathtaking.

As last-minute fill-in guests on a cancellation, we had really landed a great room. The only one to surpass this would be the bridal suite, number 105, which was sited right at the farthest north-eastern corner of the hotel and shared this same view but with a much wider aspect over most of the golf course to the west. Mike had pointed both rooms out to me from the car park below. All the other rooms had windows facing straight out east to the sea. How fortunate, if there had to be a cancellation, that room 115 had become vacant. I appreciated our luck. This was a perfect place for a holiday or a honeymoon.

And what a howling shame I had to bring down the vibes by trying to find out who had killed Louis Frame.

Reluctantly turning away from the windows, I unzipped my overnight bag. From inside, I drew out the envelope Jake Smith had given me. I tipped the contents on to the bed. Jo-Jo's photograph slithered across the bedspread and lay there.

Her face looked up at me, beautiful, a knowing smile on her lips that spoke of her power to seduce with her looks and body. But staring down at her, I could see the tell-tale worldliness in her eyes, the hard edge of disillusionment behind her come-to-bed smile that said you can't tell me anything about this wicked world of men that I haven't already found out for myself. It was an *experienced* face.

On that first sighting, when I was clad only in a towel in my bathroom and Jake had held it in front of me, all I'd seen was a glamorous woman. Now, studying the photograph minutely at close range, in addition to her glamour it was obvious her blatant sexuality came from experience. She had ended her life as Louis Frame's lover, but before that there was obviously a string – a whole stable full – of other men. And I could see the experience had tainted her beauty.

I wondered why she'd become a prostitute. With those looks, she could have been a model, commanded high earnings. Was she – had she been – over a barrel, too? She smiled out from the photograph. Her eyes drew me in and I found myself feeling sorry for her. I'd started out thinking I'd try to discover who the killer was strictly for Louis' sake, never mind the prostitute. Now, seeing Jo-Jo for the first time as a person with every right to live, I saw the need to bring her killer to justice, too.

Moving the photograph to one side, I unfolded the single sheet of paper. The writing was sparse and direct – like the note I'd received at the races – and listed several names, one or two with addresses, all with telephone numbers or emails. Further down the page he'd set out the logistics of Louis' journey to Doncaster races that day. And as a final paragraph had listed the names of the people who had a possible grudge or motive – the same ones he had told me about when he'd handed over the envelope. Included in that paragraph was the name of the man against whom Louis had given evidence – who was currently serving time – plus the name of the prison. I hoped to hell I wouldn't need that information. Prison visiting was not something I felt drawn to in any way.

I scanned down the list of names. Edward Frame wasn't on the list. Nevertheless, I'd decided, apart from Lucinda, he'd been the closest person to Louis and was my obvious starting point. Louis had been his younger brother. He'd doubtless been present at the funeral and he was here now, in the hotel. He was bound to know the subtext to his brother's life, always assuming they'd got on. And I had to assume they had. Today, Edward had acted as stand-in for his brother – Louis' daughter was getting married and needed giving away. Not only that, but the way Lucinda had clung to her uncle's arm spoke of a close family link.

I put the paper and the photograph back into the envelope and carefully stowed it away in the inside pocket of my jacket. Putting on the jacket, I picked up the key and closed the door of 115 behind me. Going down the back staircase, I bumped into Mike who had just come up from the billiard-room toilet on the lower floor. Dinner was scheduled for five o'clock in the dining room and it was now a little after four.

'Let's grab a seat outside somewhere, Mike. I've something to show you.'

'Why not take a coffee out on to the balcony?'

Dan having provided the drinks, we went up the west staircase and out on to the fortuitously deserted balcony. The view took in the whole of the golf course, right out to Roman Bank.

I took the envelope from my inside pocket and passed it to him. The photograph was uppermost, and just as Jake had watched my own reaction, I watched Mike's. I suppose it reflected my own.

'Phew, some looker!'

I nodded.

'Who is she?'

'Was.'

'Eh?'

I tapped the photo. 'That's Jo-Jo, Jake Smith's sister. She's the one who died along with Louis.'

'Bloody shame. What a waste . . .'

'She was a prostitute, Mike, but she was also a human being. And I'm going to find her killer. The sheet of paper still in the envelope is a list of possibles Jake Smith has drawn up.'

He took one last look at the photo, shook his head and drew out the sheet of paper. Reading quickly down the list of names, he looked up.

'No mention here, Harry, of Edward Frame.'

'Exactly what I thought. But he's the one I'm going to ask a few leading questions.'

'Hmmm . . .'

'It doesn't mention Samuel either, but he told us Louis Frame was his business partner.'

'Good God! Samuel's above suspicion. I mean, Chloe's his daughter. He wouldn't put her in jeopardy.'

'Right now, Mike, he doesn't know she *is* in jeopardy.'

He grudgingly acknowledged the fact. 'But I can't believe he would have anything to do with murder. It's preposterous.'

'I don't want to believe that either, but right now anybody, everybody, is a suspect, whether we want it that way or not. Until I can prove exactly who did kill those two people, it's a lousy situation. Don't forget, I've been here before, Mike, and look how *that* turned out. Would you have believed who the murderer was then?'

He shook his head violently. 'Not in a bloody million. Still can't believe it, to be honest.'

'Exactly.'

'You've got a right job on your hands, Harry. I honestly can't see how you're going to get at the truth this time.'

'That's two of us, then. But if I don't, where does that leave Chloe?'

'With her head on the block.'

We stared at each other in silence.

He eventually replaced the two items inside the envelope and handed it over to me.

'I think you'd better watch your own back, too, Harry.'

I hadn't told him of Jake's threat against me, wasn't going to. My problem.

Mike glanced at his watch. 'It's nearly five o'clock. We'd better get downstairs.'

I slid the envelope out of sight inside my jacket and stood up.

'Let's shelve it for the next hour and enjoy the chef's skills.'

And he was certainly skilled. We worked our way through three courses with great enjoyment. Or, rather, Mike did. Mindful, as always, of my riding weight, I helped myself to a couple of mouthfuls from a couple of courses and indulged myself a little more on the main – Guinea fowl with a tomato and ragout sauce. The volume of noise in the dining room was a good indication of the quality of the food. From a light buzz as everyone took their seats and began the meal, it took a long time to rise to any perceptible level.

But as the meal drew to a close, Richard Lutens, the best man, stood up, raised a glass and tapped it with a spoon, requesting silence.

'Ladies and gentlemen . . .'

His speech was everything it should be: the right length so as not to bore, full of humour, flattering to the bride – ribald, bordering on slightly risqué, comments directed at the groom – before outrageously and wittily flirting with the bridesmaids. He also included Edward, before consummately glossing over the absence of Lucinda's parents and the bald fact that none of the other guests were members of her family. It was a cold, harsh fact that she had no other family.

And throughout, Lucinda, cheeks deeply flushed, smiled prettily and blossomed from all the attention.

There was spontaneous clapping and cheering when, smiling widely with relief his speech had gone down a storm, Richard resumed his seat, took a handkerchief and passed it quickly across his forehead.

Everybody raised charged glasses of champagne and toasted enthusiastically. Already, the amount of liquor consumed would have filled a bath – and it was still only six o'clock. With another eight hours to go, I could ever more appreciate Dan's comment that he would be the last man standing. He might well be. But drink loosened inhibitions and normal discretion ceased to operate. The more the evening went on, the more the odds were shortening in my favour. This certainly seemed the right place to start asking questions.

The important part of the wedding now over, the rest of the evening, from eight o'clock until two o'clock, would be given over to a disco with buffet. And as the guests replaced their glasses on the tables and began to drift out, free to mingle, whilst staff cleared the dining room, I caught Mike's eye.

'I'll start with Edward,' I said in a low voice. 'Can you casually introduce me?'

'Sure.'

We wandered out into the main hall and watched the rest of the guests as they streamed from the dining room and arranged themselves in happy, talkative little groups.

Edward Frame, chatting to Brandon, patted him on the shoulder and walked off down the back steps to the car park. We meandered over to the window and watched him take out a cigarette and light up.

'OK,' Mike said. 'I think I need to collect something from my car, don't you?'

'Oh, yes.'

We in turn trailed off down the back steps and crunched over the gravel to the massed lines of cars. Making it look good, a few yards away Mike pressed his remote control and unlocked his car. Sliding in behind the wheel, he pretended to fish in the glove compartment. Moments later, he climbed out, relocked the car, and we strolled back, fetching up near Frame.

'Lovely ceremony, Edward,' Mike said.

Frame swung round to see who it was. 'Ah . . .' He struggled to remember.

'Mike Grantley. We met at one of Samuel's dinner parties.'

'Ha, yes, yes.' He beamed. 'Always a relief when a wedding goes off so well. Prone to cock-ups, I believe.'

I couldn't meet Mike's eyes, but Edward didn't see the funny side of his remark.

'Can I introduce a friend of mine? Edward, this is Harry Radcliffe, my retained jockey. Harry – Edward Frame, Louis' elder brother.'

'Pleased to meet you.' I shook his hand firmly. 'Good of you to step in and give Lucinda away.'

'Nice to meet you, too, Harry. Least I could do for my late brother. Lucinda has no other family, you see.' We nodded solemnly in unison. We already knew.

'Lucinda's mother died a long time ago . . . cancer.'

I dropped in the baited hook. 'Louis never remarried?'

'No, no . . .' Edward took a long, deep draw on his cigarette. 'Said he'd had the best wife a man could have, stupid to think he could ever replace her.'

I felt a prickle of anger at the hypocrisy of the dead man. Jo-Jo wasn't good enough to marry, but he'd had his full share of bedding her.

'Surely,' I said, 'Louis was a comparatively young man; didn't he have any female companionship?'

Mike threw me a wry look and I suddenly realized this scenario I was putting forward could fit him, too. I'd have to watch what I said. I didn't want to hurt Mike's feelings or antagonize him.

'Well . . . y'know . . .' Edward smirked.

'Yes?' I prompted innocently, thanking heaven that he clearly had a fair amount of alcohol on board and it was clouding his discretion.

'To be honest, it was me who put Louis on to it.' He took another long pull at the cigarette and I hoped it would last out long enough for us to discover something useful.

'I don't have a lady of my own, either . . .' Mike said.

I gaped at him. There I was, trying not to step on his toes, and he was jumping straight in himself.

'Ha, I see . . .' Edward's smirk spread wider. 'Well, since you could say we're all men of the world' – he winked – 'you could try Daddy Dating.'

Mike blinked. 'Say again?'

'A website, my dear chap. I put Louis on to it. It specializes in finding the . . . "right" young ladies for older gentlemen.' He dropped the stub of his cigarette and ground it out on the path. 'You'd be surprised just how many, er . . . ladies, are looking for a . . .'

'Father figure?' Mike proffered.

'You're so right.' Edward clapped Mike on the shoulder.

'Louis found a lady, then, from Daddy Dating?'

He turned and stared at me as though I was naïve.

'Yes, of course. Jo-Jo was ideal for him. Oh, she wasn't *my*, er . . .' He struggled.

'Your lady friend?' I helped him out; the word 'tart' was inappropriate but he was clearly considering it.

'That's right.' He smiled with relief. 'Alice told Jo-Jo.'

'Alice?' Mike murmured.

'My, er . . . lady friend.'

'Also from Daddy Dating?' I asked.

He nodded.

'Jo-Jo died in the car crash, too, didn't she? I seem to remember reading it in the paper.'

He sighed. 'Terrible tragedy. She was a lovely person, really cared about Louis.'

'At least they died together . . .' Mike kept the thread of conversation going.

Edward dropped his voice and leaned in closer to us. 'And not just the two of them.' We were treated to a blast of alcohol fumes.

'No?' We egged him on.

'Oh, no. 'Course, with her being only a little late it didn't get in the papers.'

'Pregnant?' I queried, practically whispering down his ear, inviting confidences. He swayed ever closer towards me and tapped a finger down the side of his nose.

'But don't let on. Wouldn't want it to get out now, 'specially not today. Don't want to upset Lucinda.'

'Oh, no, no, 'course not,' we chorused, shaking our heads.

'As the grave, Edward,' Mike said, raised a finger and moved it side to side, 'as the grave.'

In view of the circumstances, his choice of a reassuring phrase wasn't in the best of taste, but it satisfied Edward who then excused himself to go and join the other guests.

We watched him walk back into the hotel.

'Yet another motive, Mike?'

'Could well be. But how come it wasn't made public, reported in the press? You know what reporters are like – titillation of any sort will add to their readership numbers.'

'Mike, she was sitting in the passenger seat, at the front. Louis was driving like the proverbial bat and their car ploughed head-on into a ten-ton horsebox. Death was instantaneous. The firemen had to cut them out.'

I had a sudden mental picture of Jo-Jo's beautiful face, as it had been in life. The following picture that my vivid imagination was about to show me, I censored.

The door opened behind us, and Lucinda and Brandon, hand in hand, Lucinda still clad in her gorgeous white gown, came down the steps to speak to us.

FOURTEEN

'We'd like to thank you both for coming.' Brandon opened the conversation with words he'd obviously been repeating all afternoon and by now must have been totally sick of saying.

'Thanks are due from us,' I said. 'It's a beautiful place, and a pleasure to be here for your wedding ceremony. We wish you a long and very happy life together.'

'Indeed we do,' Mike added.

'How kind.' Lucinda smiled. 'I don't want today to end, it's been so perfect. I suppose by now I should have changed, but you only wear a wedding dress for one day and I'm making the most of every minute. I shall keep my dress on until bedtime.' And then she blushed. She struck me as an innocent little girl. She was the total antithesis of Jo-Jo. Brandon put an arm round her waist and gave her a quick possessive hug.

'You do whatever you want, my love.' He looked at her proudly. 'It's *your* day.'

'You're spending your honeymoon here?' Mike enquired.

'Only tonight. Tomorrow evening we fly to Barbados.'

'Very nice, too.'

'And then we'll fly home to start our life together.' Lucinda looked lovingly up at her husband.

'And what's your line of work?' I asked Brandon.

'I'm in partnership with Richard. We supply horse feed. You may have noticed our delivery truck – B and R Lutens?'

'I can't say I have.' I shook my head. 'I'm more into filling horses' saddles than filling their stomachs.'

'Well, maybe one day we'll be able to supply Mr Grantley.' Brandon gave Mike a wide, confident smile.

Mike smiled back. 'Actually, I'm very satisfied with my own supplier, thanks, but I'll keep your firm in mind for the future.'

'Great; that's what I like to hear.' He started to pat his pockets, ended up laughing. 'What am I like? It's my wedding day and I'm in all my finery.' He gave Lucinda a hug. 'I'll slip one of my business cards under your door later. What room are you in?'

'One-one-five.'

'Now, no more business. How are you both enjoying the day?'

'A lovely wedding,' Mike murmured.

'I think everybody's enjoying the day,' I said.

'And there's more to come. We have a disco starting at eight o'clock.' Lucinda smiled. 'Not sure how I'm going to dance around in my dress,' she smoothed her hands down the white satin, 'but it's staying on. Right till the last possible minute before bedtime when I take it off.' Then she glanced up at Brandon, charmingly turned bright red and giggled. He laughed at her discomfort and gave her another squeeze.

'You're in room one-o-five?' I queried.

'Yes, it's the one with the lovely views over the golf course as well as the beach. It's even got a fire escape in case of emergency.'

'Not too likely these days,' Mike put in, 'not now they've introduced the no-smoking ban.'

'Daddy smokes . . .' Lucinda's smile died. 'Used to smoke.' Her face crumpled. 'I forgot,' she gulped. 'For a moment, I forgot . . . Oh, Brandon.' She pressed her face into his chest.

'OK, darling, it's OK. Everyone understands.' He shot us a quick glance. 'If you'll excuse us, I'll take Lucinda for a little walk – go across the car park and look at the sea, probably.' We nodded.

'Look after her, Brandon,' Mike urged. 'She's in a fragile state.'

We watched them walk away.

'Would have been better if they'd waited a bit before getting married – y'know, give Lucinda time to grieve.'

'Maybe it's better this way. She won't have time to dwell on losing him.'

Sombrely, we turned and went into the hotel.

'Just catch the bastard, Harry.'

'The thing is, Mike, does Lucinda think the crash was simply an accident? Or does she have any idea it could be murder? I mean, as yet we don't have any proof it *was* murder.'

'You'll have to keep on digging. Jake Smith thinks it was murder. And what about that pair of false teeth on your doorstep? They didn't get there by themselves.'

'No. At the moment, they're locked in my desk drawer at the cottage.'

'And you say Jake denies all knowledge of them?'

'Yep.'

'So, who *did* put them on the doorstep?'

'Someone who wishes me ill, that's for sure.'

We went on up the back stairs to our room. Whilst there was a pull-back in activity before the disco began, we might as well pace ourselves. It looked like being a long night.

I shrugged off my jacket and switched the kettle on.

'I'm for a cup of tea. Want one?'

'Don't ask damn fool questions.'

'I take it that's two teas, then.'

We sat in the bay window and looked out at the darkening landscape with the sea stretching mysteriously away into the distance.

'I'm going to start right at the beginning, Mike. Find out who the driver of the horsebox was. Yes, I know Jake said he was gutted by the accident, but he may have noticed something, somebody. Say I give him a call . . . what d'you reckon? Worth a try?'

'Sure. Anything's worth a try.' Mike levered himself out of the chair. Kicked off his shoes, stretched out on one of the beds and closed his eyes.

'Very relaxing, this place.'

I smiled ruefully and silently promised myself that when this little caper was over I'd come here for a few days' break and really appreciate it.

I flung myself down on my own bed and reached for the telephone.

Eventually, having been given an outside line and the trainer's number, I found myself talking to Robson. I didn't know him personally, only as a racing man. I told him who I was and asked him about the driver of the horsebox involved in the crash. This was one of the occasions I was grateful for being famous. It did seem to open doors.

He was a blunt, no-nonsense Yorkshireman and didn't bother asking why I wanted the information.

'Bad business, that, Harry. Two killed. Didn't stand a hope in hell. I told John it wasn't his fault. He took it hard. But it's like coming off a horse, is driving – you have a smash, you've to get behind the wheel straight away, otherwise you're done for.'

'And he's driving again?'

'Oh, yes. No good going soft. Next day, set off from Redcar down to Cheltenham. If box driving is your livelihood, you've no choice.'

'And can you tell me his name? I know there's data protection but . . .'

He made a noise like a dog swallowing a wasp.

'O'course I can tell you. His name's John. John Dunston. OK?'

With the greatest difficulty, I assured him that was OK and very slowly and carefully replaced the phone.

'So?' Mike had opened one eye and was watching me.

'You're not going to believe this.'

'All right, I don't believe it. But tell me anyway.'

'Frank Dunston's the bloke who finished Carl in the toilets at Leicester races, right?'

'Right.'

'The box driver's name is John Dunston, his father.'

'Bloody hell!' Mike blew out a silent whistle.

'Yeah, as you say, bloody hell.'

'I think we've just gone from accident to murder. What do you think?'

'What I think is, not only were Louis and Jo-Jo murdered, but we've also discovered the identity of the person who left the false teeth.'

'And I'm sure you're dead right.'

We stayed in our room, chewing over the staggering information, until the sound of music filtered upwards and declared that the night was wearing on and the disco had begun.

'Better show our faces, Harry.'

'I've lost the appetite.' I shook my head. 'Thought I'd put all that mess in the summer behind me, now it's come back to life. I ask you, of all the people it could have been driving that horsebox and it happens to be John Dunston.'

'It didn't just happen, Harry. It was a carefully planned-out killing. And Dunston's not the brains at the back of it. You can be sure he's had a handout – a big handout – to do the dirty business.'

'Must have put on a convincing performance of being gutted. Even Jake bought it.'

'Come on.' Mike slapped my shoulder and headed to the door. 'At least we know one more crucial piece of jigsaw. Let's go and find a few more.'

I followed him down to the St Andrew's Suite which was now a gyrating swell of bodies. Standing out in the midst, dancing away in the white dress, was Lucinda. Maybe Mike was right. Bury the grief as soon as and get back in there. We found a spot to hitch ourselves and took a drink off Dan as he sped past.

'Not on your own, Dan?'

He grinned and gestured to the other side of the room.

'No, Tom's doing the honours as well.' His grin grew wider. 'That's if he can keep his mind on the job. His wife went into labour last night and they've shunted her off to the hospital this morning.'

'So why isn't he with her?' I asked.

'He took her in, but they told him it's likely to be a long job, so go home and ring later.'

'Keep calm and carry on,' Mike murmured.

'Something like it. But I dunno about the keeping calm bit. He's a complete bag of nerves.'

We all looked across to where a thin, harassed-looking young man was circulating with a loaded tray.

'Working is better for him than biting his nails down, waiting about at home.'

'You'll note from that, Dan, that Harry is one of the world's grafters. That's why he gets on so well with you.'

'Takes one to know one,' chortled Dan, and disappeared to refill his empty drinks tray.

'Where *have* you two been hiding?' Chloe clutched my sleeve and gave it a little tug. 'Naughty boys.'

'Taking a pull,' I said.

'Hello, both,' Samuel said. 'Supping tea and having a bit of peace and quiet, I bet.'

'You bet right,' Mike laughed.

'Ha, ha, nice if you can manage it. I doubt anybody will be getting much sleep tonight.'

'I heard that.' A buxom woman with chestnut hair, laughing her head off, deliberately bumped against my arm.

'Barbara, didn't know you were here.'

'You know me, Harry. Love a good party.'

I grinned back. 'Tell me about it.' Barbara's parties usually didn't end until it was time for morning stables. I nodded a greeting to the man she was dancing with.

'Must find the gents. Can you point me in the right direction?' he said.

Mike took pity on him. 'Have to go myself. I'll show you. It's down the lower-level stairs and to your right.' He nodded to Barbara. 'Good to see you. You all right?'

'Oh, yes, Mike. Fine, fine. Got several new owners quite recently.' In the present economic situation, it was extremely good going and showed confidence in her stables.

'Well done.'

'Seven new horses. Had to increase my feed order from B and R. They were pleased.'

'Toilet?' Barbara's companion said in an aggrieved voice.

'Sorry,' Mike said hastily. They slipped away through the crowd as the harassed wine waiter worked his way past with yet another tray of drinks.

'Chloe? Barbara?'

'Oh, yes, please, Harry.'

I took two glasses from his tray. 'Everything going well with your wife, Tom?' I enquired. He looked surprised.

'Er . . . er . . . yes, well, she was doing OK, the hospital said when I rang up about an hour ago.' Then he added defensively, 'I was on my break.'

'I'm sure,' I nodded reassuringly. 'All the best to you both.'

'Your wife's having a baby?' Barbara asked.

'Yes.'

'What are you hoping for?' Chloe said.

'Wife wants a boy. Me, I'm not fussed. Just want to finish my shift and get over to the hospital to see her.'

'Surely,' I said, 'they'd be able to get a stand-in if you want to go.'

'Oh, no! No.' He looked agitated. 'I wouldn't even ask. Now she's going to be a mum, she's given up her job, so she's relying on me to support us all.'

'But why?' Barbara crinkled her forehead.

'Do you *know* the cost of child care?' His voice rose. 'I'm sorry. Didn't mean to . . .' He looked round nervously to make sure nobody was taking notice. 'It wouldn't pay us to do it. She was only on basic wage rate, y'see . . . not worth it.'

'So much better for the baby if she stays at home to look after it.'

He shot Chloe a grateful look. 'We think so, too. But o'course that means it's up to me to keep working. Daren't risk losing my job. Got a mortgage, y'see.'

We all saw and commiserated with him about the state of today's world. An awful lot of people had their backs pushed hard up against the wall. Another guest a few yards away raised an empty glass and waved it in our direction.

'Must get on.' He lifted the tray and eeled his way through the crush.

'Let's hope his wife holds on until he gets there. Would be a shame if he misses the birth.'

'Ooh, yes,' Barbara agreed with Chloe. Then she turned to me. 'Got one of my parties booked for the end of next week. You up for it? And you, too, Chloe, if you fancy it.'

'I fancy it.'

'Me, too,' I said.

'Great, always room for a couple more.'

They sipped drinks and we watched as the dancers parted like the Red Sea as the band struck up 'Brown Sugar'. It was a while since I'd heard it, but it was definitely a party song. Into the wedge of clear space on the dance floor, Lucinda and Brandon really got into the spirit of the music. They danced very well, despite Lucinda's dress, and finally, panting and laughing, collapsed into chairs at the side. There was cheering and clapping as the guests roared their approval before going back to have another go themselves, this time to 'Rolling in the Deep'.

Mike forged his way back to us as Barbara was whisked off into the heavy beat dance by her partner.

'Going very well, isn't it?'

'Certainly is, but now we've established Louis' death wasn't an accident, I could do with having another word with Edward.'

'He's tucked in over there by the windows, chatting to that trainer from Leicester, Clive Unwin. We'll break it up. I'll take Clive, you go for Edward.'

It was a major operation crossing the room, but we eventually fetched up next to Edward. Mike cleanly cut out Clive with talk about an upcoming race and I was left wondering how the devil I could broach awkward questions in the present venue. But the awkwardness was swept away by Edward himself.

'Such a shame Louis can't see her dancing.' He nodded in Lucinda's direction. 'Having some fun and being happy.' He shook his head. 'A tragedy.'

'Yes.'

'If I'd known what was in store, I'd have gone to the races at Donny myself, driven us back.' He paused, 'Jo-Jo as well.'

Big of him, I thought. But it answered the first of my questions for me. Edward hadn't been to the races that day.

'Edward, can I ask you if you know of any threat against Louis? Had he any enemies?'

There was no subtle way of asking it except head-on. He peered at me, taken aback by the question.

'Eh?'

'Do you think it could have been a deliberate smash? Not simply an accident?'

'No, 'course not. I know there're some idiots about that cause an accident on purpose, claim on the insurance, but no, no, it was just a terrible tragedy. Nobody to blame.' He took a handkerchief from his trouser pocket and gave a good blow.

'So,' I persisted, 'Louis didn't have anybody gunning for him?'

More than half-drunk by now, Edward peered at me closely. 'He was a tough man in business. There could have been competitors who wished him off their backs. Maybe not *pleased* he died like he did, but . . . not too sorry he's out of the way, I suppose.'

'No more personal disagreements?'

'Funny thing, but I think Alice, my, er . . . lady friend . . . wasn't too keen on him.'

'Oh?'

'Yes, said something once about doing a man down. Wouldn't say what or who, though, when I asked her what she was on about.'

'Couldn't have meant it. I mean, she put Jo-Jo on to DaddyDating. That's where Louis met her.'

'S'right,' he slurred, 'must've got it wrong.'

'I expect so,' I said. 'What was Alice's surname?'

'No idea, my dear chap,' he said, a laugh rumbling in his throat at the absurdity of my question.

'Could it have been Goode?'

'Can't answer you that' – his laughter bubbled up – 'except she was – *bloody good.*'

I nodded and looked across at Mike who was still valiantly holding court with the other trainer.

'Better mingle, Edward,' I said.

'Oh, yes, definitely.' Adroitly, he reached for another drink from the passing waiter. 'Enjoy the evening.'

FIFTEEN

The buffet was an excellent spread. It was deliciously tempting, but Clive, the trainer from Leicester, had offered me a ride on Tuesday the eleventh at Huntingdon races. Mike filled his boots. He deserved to: he'd set me up with Clive.

At eleven o'clock, the waiters and waitresses swiftly cleared the tables and left for the night. The dancing continued now in earnest. The band, fortified by both their break and the food, struck up with gusto. And the guests were only too ready to party.

I found myself grabbed by Chloe for a hot number. I danced like a camel with three legs, but she could have been a professional.

And whilst laughingly, skilfully, avoiding my size nines, she threw herself into 'Staying Alive' with ferocious energy.

Mike, meanwhile, was being twirled around the floor by Juliette. She, too, her hair flying freely in a golden cloud around her shoulders, was giving it her all. Mike looked younger, happier. It was about time he started dating, found himself a suitable woman, one who made him happy.

I found myself filled with light-hearted pleasure at being here. Devoting myself to Silvie and to race riding for so long, I'd lost the ability to switch off and simply enjoy myself. Being here, where the atmosphere was one of total carefree enjoyment, brought it home. I'd been lacking something in my life without realizing the lack. I was suddenly very glad to be here.

Chloe claimed the next three dances, but by that time my right leg was giving me aggravation. To call a halt to the dancing was unthinkable since the disco wasn't due to finish until two a.m. Some paracetamol would keep me going and there was a packet in my room that I'd brought with me just in case.

Leading Chloe to the edge of the dance floor when the music ended, I fetched her a drink.

'I'm just going up to my room for a moment. Won't be long.'

'Brandon and Lucinda have gone up,' Chloe said and gave a knowing smile, 'but I don't think it's for the same reason.'

'No, I don't. But I'll be back soon.'

'I expect they'll be a bit longer, probably half an hour or so.'

'You're a naughty girl.'

'Hmmm . . .' she said, her eyes sparkling, 'I could be . . . with the right man.'

I excused myself.

From the St Andrew's Suite it was quicker to use the main staircase opposite the reception desk. I followed the stairs as they turned left at the top, left again and then right down a short landing. At the end of which was door 105, the bridal suite. From the noises coming from inside, it was obvious Chloe's assumption had been correct. I grinned and tiptoed past.

Reaching my own room, I snapped on the lights. It was dark outside, although the moon was up and it was a full one. Going into the bathroom, I opened the packet of paracetamol tablets, filled a tooth mug with water and swallowed three.

On the point of leaving the room, I'd actually stepped out on to the landing when I remembered my mobile phone had been left charging since dinner. I was about to go back to collect it when I heard a cry. The cry was muffled and followed directly afterwards by the sound of a door slamming. I hesitated. The landing was deserted. It was unlikely anybody else would have heard anything. Although the cry had been indistinct, there was distress in it – and it had come from room 105. But I could hardly go barging in to see if there was anything wrong.

Instead, I went back into my own room. Going over to the north window, I looked out. The upper part was open and all I could hear was the boom of the sea as the waves broke on the shore. There was no other sound. A cloud had obscured the moon, leaving only starlight, but from this vantage point I could see the window of 105 at the end of the hotel. The lights were on inside, but that was all I could make out. No movement, no sound. I gave it two or three minutes. Apart from the noise of the waves, it really was as silent as the grave.

Calling it quits, I reached up to pull the curtains ready for night.

And the cloud slid away from the face of the moon. Instantly, everything was bathed in brilliant moonlight. With puddles of darkness and shadows in shades of grey and silver, it was magnificent. The sea itself appeared to be gilded with silver. I halted, taken aback by the sheer beauty of the landscape.

Away down the dark ribbon of beach, a flash of pure white drew my eyes. For a second, I couldn't imagine what it was. It resembled a white shadow. But it was moving, quite fast, and as I watched in fascination, I could make out the shape of a person. Realization came to me. It was Lucinda. Lucinda still wearing her white bridal gown. She was running along the shore, by herself.

Apprehension ran down my spine. Something was very wrong here. And at that same moment, I saw a second shadowy figure. A figure very difficult to discern, dressed all in black.

Whoever it was had been totally invisible until then, hidden by the sea defence escarpment. Built to withstand the full fury of the North Sea, the escarpment was substantial. Between the edge of the beach and the low shrubs that marked the boundary of the golf course ran the line of enormous sea defence rocks.

As Lucinda drew level, the man in black suddenly emerged from behind one of the rocks. Totally oblivious to danger, Lucinda never saw him as she ran along the sand. Watching in impotent horror, I saw him lunge at her, knocking her to the ground. But almost instantly she was up on her feet again, battering at the man with both hands. It was hellish to watch, knowing there could only be one winner and there was nothing I could do – I was too far away to help her. I could only watch helplessly as the man pinioned her arms and dragged her up over the rocks and down the other side, out of sight.

He was heading away from the beach towards the golf course. The low boundary of shrubs edging the course would prove no barrier to him. I strained to see which direction he would take. But sod's law was operating. Another cloud came across and the moonlight blacked out. Any advantage gained by staying in the room to keep the man in sight was obliterated.

I snatched my mobile phone from the electric socket where it had been charging and ran for the stairs. Outside, the buggies were all lined up – securely locked in place. And I needed wheels to overtake the bastard before he injured Lucinda. She was such an innocent, sweet girl. I blanked off what he might have in mind for her.

Outside the Pro's shop was the greenkeeper's buggy. I sprinted across, flung myself into the driver's seat. The key was in! I knocked it into forward, wrenched the wheel and sent it surging and slithering up the slope by the side of the hotel, along the yellow stone track and out on to the course.

Within yards, the track had petered out and the buggy was travelling down the grass on the tenth fairway. I switched on the overhead spotlight and found the Klaxon horn – the noise was tremendous. I hoped to heaven people in the hotel would hear it above the sound of the music. I needed back-up desperately but had no time to waste asking for help. Remembering the mobile in my pocket, I drove with one hand and fished for the phone. It was no use: I couldn't operate the mobile and steer.

Driving at top speed, I sent the buggy hurtling and bucking down to the bottom of the long fairway that ran parallel to the beach. But there was no sign of either the man or Lucinda. Her white dress would have been a dead giveaway, impossible to miss.

I swung the wheel hard left, inland now, away from the beach, and careered up a steep bank. Teetering at the top, I sent it plunging down the other side. The beam of the spotlight on top of the vehicle dipped and spun madly as the ground fell away and the tyres dropped solidly into steep hollows, bouncing me around against the sides of the buggy.

The landmark of the lighted hotel had completely disappeared from sight. I was driving into darkness. I lost all sense of direction. All I needed was to run straight down the side of a sand-filled bunker and that would be that. Although the night air was chill, I dragged a forearm across my face. I was dripping with sweat, from both nerves and exertion.

The blackness pressed in on me from all sides. It was surreal and spooky to be out on the golf course in the middle of the night. I found myself crashing through some very rough ground covered in straggling low undergrowth and bushes. The buggy ran aground, came to a bone-shaking halt, the tyres spinning wildly and ineffectively.

Swearing and sweating, I knocked the one lever into reverse and gave it some hammer. The tyres spun backwards, found purchase and slammed me hard against the seat as the vehicle suddenly shot backwards down a bank.

Totally disorientated, I drove round in a wide circle searching for a landmark I could recognize. It was all so very different from walking the course in daylight. But the circling paid off. I felt the difference in the tyre grip and then I was back on one of the yellow tracks. Cutting the speed so I didn't overshoot if it ran out suddenly, I followed the track round two tight bends.

Up ahead, I could just make out a line of post-and-wire fencing dissecting the course. I was approaching the public footpath called Granny's Opening. The narrow path ran from the main road at Roman Bank, west of the golf course, right through to the beach on the east side. I wasn't lost now; I knew exactly where I was.

I stopped, cut the engine and the Klaxon, and listened. Except for the sough of the wind in the trees lower down the course near the seventeenth tee, and the boom of the sea breaking on the beach to my right, the night was silent.

The cloud cover shifted again and the moonlight provided much needed illumination. I took out my mobile and tapped in Mike's number.

'I need your help, mate.' I gave him directions where to find me.

'What the *hell* are you doing out there?'

'Trying to save Lucinda from a crazy bastard. Can't explain, no time. Just get me some back-up out here – quick. Get Dan to unlock the buggies and drive – it'll be quicker than on foot.'

Mike didn't waste time on futile questions.

'I'm with you, Harry. Hold on.'

The phone went dead and I pushed it back into my pocket.

Leaving the buggy parked up, I walked a short way to the left along Granny's Opening, shouting out Lucinda's name. My voice echoed weirdly – but no one answered. The course was eighteen holes, seventy-one par playing distance, well over six thousand yards. It was unlikely I'd find her on my own. More manpower was needed. I retraced my steps and started off along the right-hand side of the pathway. I called her name every few yards, but the night mockingly tossed my voice back to me.

A lot of shrubs and tangled undergrowth grew at the side of the path, but shortly I found myself facing a high, very steep bank on the top of which I could just make out a flag flying.

An onshore wind was blowing, whipping against my face and bringing with it a strong, salty smell that I could practically taste. If the light had been better, I knew it would show the flag was red because this was the fourteenth green and I was standing in the hollow called Devil's Hope.

Maybe, if I were to climb up to the top of the bank, I could see further towards the beach. I moved forward a few paces and almost tripped. I'd been focusing on the highest point, looking up at the flag for direction. Now, glancing down into the hollow to see what had snagged my foot, I saw something lying on the ground half obscured by the undergrowth.

Something white.

I went closer and moved back some of the foliage. Fear for that innocent young girl sent my pulse racing into overdrive. I looked down at the little heap of white and felt I'd been punched very hard in the guts.

It was Lucinda – I'd found her. But how I wished to God I hadn't.

Lucinda's precious white gown was no longer pristine. A ragged tear ran from ankle to groin and an ugly stain on the bodice had spread all down the left-hand side. Although it wasn't light enough to make out the colour of the stain, I didn't need light. I could smell what it was – blood.

A great, suffocating sorrow swept over me. I drew in a sharp, rasping breath and dropped to my knees, calling out her name.

There was no response.

I pressed my fingers beneath the line of her jaw, desperately feeling for a pulse. Her skin felt soft, warm and yielding against my fingers. But it was already too late. There was no pulse.

Lucinda was dead.

SIXTEEN

Twelve hours ago, Lucinda had entered the hotel full of life, happiness, pride in her new husband, her wedding ceremony, her beautiful white gown. She had entered the hotel to the song 'Angels'.

Now she had gone to join them.

Gone was her life and her happiness, her marriage; her pristine gown defaced, ruined.

And I was the only person to have seen her killer.

I knelt beside her limp body and longed to gather the girl into my arms to cradle her, comfort her – and I couldn't. This was murder. A foul wickedness perpetrated against an innocent girl.

I rose slowly to my feet and made a silent pledge to Lucinda, as she lay on the cold ground, that I would track down the bastard who had snatched away her life, her future. My feelings were running so high with anger against him, all I wanted to do was jump into the buggy and drive off at full speed around the golf course and hunt him down.

But I didn't. Lucinda couldn't be left – she needed me to stay with her, stand guard. I reached for my mobile.

'Mike, it's me. Bad news, the worst. I've found Lucinda . . .'

'She's dead?'

'Yes.'

'How?'

'Looks like she was stabbed.'

'The bastard.' Mike ground out the words.

'Bottom of the pond.'

'Want me to phone the police?'

'Yeah. I'm staying here with her. Actual location is Devil's Hope near the fourteenth green – you know, at the base of the bank?'

'Got it.'

I stood in the cold, lonely blackness and wondered where the killer was right now. Could he have already got off the golf course? Be on his way, leaving Skegness behind? Had there been time to get away? Or was he still very close? My nerves prickled at the thought. He wouldn't think twice about killing again to save himself.

If I'd seen him through the hotel window, it was feasible he could have seen me standing there. More than feasible. I'd been looking out into the dark, moonlit landscape, whereas he'd have had a clear view of me at an illuminated window. And I was the only person to witness the attack. OK, I couldn't identify him – but he didn't know that. The east turret room was an outstanding distinctive feature. If he managed to suss out who was staying in it, I'd be in the frame. But so would Mike. The realization of that brought me up sharp. An extremely enjoyable weekend had now turned into a ghastly nightmare. And I couldn't begin to guess what repercussions might follow.

A bush rustled behind me and I spun round, pulse jumping. But it was only the wind gusting in from the sea. I felt vulnerable down in this hollow of dark shadows, so aptly named Devil's Hope, and would have preferred to climb up the steep bank, get on to the flat, smooth top of the fourteenth green. From that vantage point, I'd be able to see anybody coming at me.

But this was a murder scene, not to be contaminated by careless wandering. I'd already blundered about searching for Lucinda. If there had been clues to be found, it would be a miracle if they'd survived my big feet. Best if I didn't obliterate any possible further clues. I would be doing Lucinda no service if I hindered the police in their search for her killer.

So I stayed where I was, wary and apprehensive.

In the distance, a low hum slowly grew louder. I took a deep, steadying breath – the posse was on the way. It didn't matter to Lucinda, but it mattered a great deal to me. I could hand over the responsibility to the police, let them take over, use their new technical knowledge of DNA. It was bringing criminals to justice who would, years ago, have got away with crimes.

But even if they caught him, secured a conviction, it still wouldn't matter to Lucinda. Because it wouldn't give her back her life.

A rush of sound filled my ears, bringing me back to the moment. It sounded like the entire fleet of buggies had just drawn up by the side of Granny's Opening.

'Harry, you here?' Mike's voice bellowed through the blackness.

'Yes.'

Several strong torch beams swung in my direction.

'Turn right, walk a few yards up and turn right again at the base of the slope. Be careful. It's a crime scene.'

A minute or two later, stepping extremely carefully, a man joined me.

'I'm Dr Paulson. One of the wedding guests. Just need to establish she is dead.'

'Right.'

It only took seconds. He breathed out gustily as he stood up. 'I'm afraid so. But, then, you knew Lucinda was dead, of course.'

'Yes. I felt for a pulse. There wasn't one.'

'A tragedy.' His voice had a catch to it. 'I was the doctor who attended at Lucinda's birth, known the family for years.'

'I'm very sorry.'

'A police matter now. They've been informed; shouldn't think they'll be long.'

'You want me to stay with her until they arrive?'

'If you would. I'm going back to the buggies, break the bad news to Brandon. I'll try to restrain him from barging in. As you say, this is a crime scene.'

'The killer's on the loose on the golf course somewhere, unless he's managed to get away by now.'

'Do you know who he is? Did you see him?'

'I saw him from my hotel window. Couldn't identity him, but I saw him knock Lucinda down and drag her away over the rocks on to the golf course.'

He sighed heavily, shook his head and went back to join the others.

It seemed an eternity, waiting for the police to arrive, but it was only a few minutes. I heard the wail of sirens as the cars hurtled along Roman Bank and came up North Shore Road. I learned later that the greenkeeper had taken his buggy back to the hotel and was waiting to transport them across the golf course.

'Thank you, sir,' said the inspector, appearing at my elbow. 'We'll take over from here. You'll be required to make a statement later.'

And I was dismissed.

The air of outrage and shock still permeated the atmosphere on Sunday morning. Guests stood around in groups, talking in lowered voices. It was doubtful if any of them, Mike and me included, had slept much at all. Sombre-faced staff had served breakfast to those guests who could actually stomach food. Mostly, it seemed, coffee and toast sufficed.

The police were present and preparing to take statements. I found myself called first. The interviews were to be conducted in what Mike and I called the leather room because it was furnished with sumptuous, dimpled leather, chesterfield settees, but was actually the North Shore lounge. I was waved to take a seat in one of the chesterfields.

'Your name, sir?'

I knew he was already aware of my personal details. They'd been verified the night before. I humoured him.

'Harry Radcliffe.'

'And your home address, email address and telephone numbers?'

I filled in all the gaps for their official records.

'I understand you were the person who found the body.'

I winced. The words 'the body' put the whole nightmare into perspective. Lucinda was no longer a person, but simply a dead body. I nodded. 'Yes. I found her.'

They asked for the whole scenario, from when I first saw her as she entered the hotel for the ceremony, to seeing her fleeing figure going away down the beach, and finally stumbling, literally, across her lifeless body at Devil's Hope. They asked endless questions about my hearing the muffled cry and the time I subsequently spent in my room watching from the north window. I began to wonder if they were seriously considering me as number-one suspect. Their next question did nothing to allay my apprehension.

'Think very carefully, sir. At the point you discovered the body, did you climb up the bank at all?'

'The fourteenth green, you mean?'

'Yes, sir.'

I thought back to my perambulations in the dark, first aboard the buggy and then on foot. At no time had I been on the top of the green.

'No.'

'You're absolutely sure about that?'

'Yes, I'm sure.'

'What shoes were you wearing at the time you were searching the golf course?'

'Shoes?' I repeated stupidly, frowning at him.

'Just answer the question if you will, please, sir.' The inspector's face was impassive.

'The shoes I'm wearing right now. I only brought the one pair.'

'And what size would they be?'

'Size nine.'

'Perhaps you would be so good as to remove the left one, sir.'

I did so. Another officer stepped up and handed the shoe to the inspector. He turned it over and scrutinized the sole.

They were perfectly normal shoes, black slip-ons with a leather sole and heel. I'd had them repaired fairly recently and at the outer edge of the heel I'd instructed the cobbler to put a metal tip to prevent them wearing down too quickly.

'Thank you, sir. You may put your shoe on again now.'

I ventured a question. 'I take it you've discovered a footprint. My shoe doesn't fit, does it?'

'Yes . . . and no.' He permitted a tight, little smile to cross his face. 'On the top of the bank by the side of the fourteenth green is a sand-filled bunker. A footprint was discovered there. We needed to eliminate your own shoe, sir.'

'Thank you, very much.'

He inclined his head a tiny fraction.

It was likely he'd noticed my anxiety about being a strong suspect and could have been trying to alleviate it. I appreciated the snippet of information that he hadn't been obliged to reveal. I took it as a positive sign that I wasn't seriously being considered as a cold-blooded killer.

Or it could also have been he'd done a good check-up before calling me in. If he had, he would also know I'd discovered a dead body before – at Leicester races. And he would also know I'd helped the police considerably and had actually apprehended the killer.

The questions went on, but eventually the inspector concluded.

'We shall need you to sign your statement down at the station, sir. After that, you will be free to go, but we may need to speak to you again, so—'

'I won't be going far from home, Inspector.'

He nodded. 'Very good.'

I was shown out and the next person shown in.

I walked down the hall to the restaurant and bar area. A strong coffee was definitely needed. Tom, the wine waiter from the previous evening, scurried past, more whey-faced than ever. I wondered if his wife had had her baby yet.

The hotel was very good. At one o'clock, a light lunch of cold salmon and salad was provided for any guests who felt up to eating. I sat with Mike, Samuel and Chloe. None of us had been able to face eating breakfast, but we at least attempted some lunch.

Chloe's eyes were swollen and red-rimmed from crying. Her pink satin bridesmaid's dress had been exchanged for a pair of black slacks and a silk shirt.

'Have some salmon, Chloe,' Samuel encouraged. 'You'll feel a little stronger with some food inside you.'

'I can't believe it,' she kept repeating. 'Can't believe it. I'm waiting for someone to tell me it's not true, that it was just a nightmare.'

'Her death is unbelievable,' Mike said gently. 'You need time to take it in.'

I reached for her hand across the table and gave it a comforting squeeze. 'You're still in shock, Chloe. Your nervous system's shot because it was so unexpected.'

Desultorily, she chased a piece of salmon around her plate. Then suddenly jabbed at it with her fork.

'They *have* to catch him, put him away for ever.'

'And they will, darling,' Samuel said. 'He won't get away.'

Mike and I exchanged quick glances. Despite an ongoing search of the golf course, no one had been found. The killer had melted away into the night and left no trace. Except perhaps for that one footprint in the sand. By now I expect they must have checked out everybody's shoes. But it was possible that the footprint had been made prior to Lucinda's wedding and wasn't relevant at all. Whatever else the police may have discovered during their search, they were keeping to themselves.

Brandon wasn't present in the dining room. I'd seen him briefly during the morning coming out of the leather room, looking like a sleepwalker. Face the colour of a sheet of A4, and legs about to give way. Apparently, he'd told Dr Paulson that the reason for Lucinda's rushing off, most likely down the fire escape and out on to the beach, was a text message she'd received. The message telling her Louis had been murdered had also said the murderer was actually in the hotel and coming for her. The mobile phone had been taken away as evidence. This had been confirmed by the police.

He'd also told Dr Paulson that, after making love, he had returned to the guests whilst Lucinda took a shower before joining him. The message was assumed to have been sent after Brandon had gone down into the St Andrew's Suite, which seemed to point to the murderer being one of the guests. The object of the message had been to panic Lucinda into running away from the hotel.

Which explained why the police had been so interested in asking me if I had seen anybody lurking on the landings. Regretfully, I'd had to say that, as far as I was aware, there hadn't been anyone hanging about. However, with more than one staircase and a network of interconnecting landings, it would have been only too easy for someone to conceal themselves.

Brandon wasn't the only one missing out on lunch. Edward and Juliette were also absent. I had no doubt Lucinda's death would have been devastating for them. First losing Louis and now Lucinda. It was the end of the family line.

Another thought entered my mind. If Jo-Jo had lived, the line would have continued. She had been pregnant. But she, too, was dead, and the baby as well. Whether the pregnancy had prompted the 'accident' with the horsebox could only be guessed at, but the body count was now four.

I pushed my plate away. There seemed little I could do right now. To go around questioning the other guests was not on. The police were in charge and would not take a generous view of my interference.

My best bet now was to start at the other end of the trail, question the people on Jake Smith's list. And I couldn't do that here.

Later that afternoon, given police permission to leave, we said goodbye to Samuel and Chloe and, with Mike driving, headed back to the stables in Leicestershire. The atmosphere in the car going back was a total reversal of our light-hearted banter travelling to the wedding. Conversation was minimal. We were both at saturation point with mulling over the tragedy.

Arriving at Mike's, I didn't linger; just picked up my car and took myself home. With great relief, I drove in through the open gate and parked up.

I'd got as far as putting my key into the lock of the kitchen door when, without warning, a heavy boot smacked savagely into the back of my kneecaps, knocking me flying and landing me face down, hard, on to the unyielding gravel.

Falls from horses were expected: you instinctively rolled into a ball to minimize damage. This came out of nowhere and, with the full force of all my weight behind it, my face took a good smashing.

Blood spurted everywhere.

SEVENTEEN

I couldn't see a thing. Blood had flooded my eye-sockets and everything was a red blur. I was sure there was only one man, but it felt like half a dozen. His boots repeatedly thudded into my ribs, bruising and battering.

I curled up, bringing my knees to my chest, judged the moment his boot was about to connect with my ribs again, then kicked out with both feet. An explosive howl of pain brought me a moment's satisfaction as the man staggered back, gagging.

Slewing around in the gravel on my back, I dashed the blood from my face. He was doubled up, clutching his guts. I repeated my double-barrel kick, trying to use it as a springboard to regain my feet. But the man recovered quickly, side-stepped and deflected the blow. Grabbing my legs, he bent them backwards, sending pain screaming through my kneecaps. I gasped for breath, but the damage already done to my ribcage negated the effort. I felt like a landed fish, out of its natural element, fighting for life. Next second, he was on me, kneeling on my chest, hammering his fists into my face.

As I began to lose consciousness, he abandoned the punches. He was weakening, the effort making his breath hiss in his lungs. Instead, grabbing both my ears, he worked my head up and down, bashing it against the gravel. If the driveway had been concrete, it would certainly have been goodbye, but now the gravel worked in my favour. It was already churned up into dips and hollows and with each impact it shifted and rolled, reducing the deadly force.

Suddenly, he released me, lurched upright, pressing his bloodied fists to his chest, breath sawing loudly. I lay motionless, drifting on the very edge of consciousness. Through slits, I watched him stagger drunkenly away. I seemed to hear a vehicle start up, but I couldn't swear to it.

The next time I swore was through pulped and swollen lips when I resurfaced on an overwhelming tide of pain to find myself still lying on the ground near the back door. I opened my eyes. It was pouring with rain. In fact, it was stair-rodding. Sharp needles drummed down on to my face, exacerbating the pain from my injuries. A shallow puddle of water was cradling my head. The water was a disturbing shade of pink.

I rolled over on to my side, pushed up on to my knees and nearly passed out again. Picking up a large piece of pea gravel, I put it in my mouth, bit on it then forced myself upright. It was fractionally less painful to stand than to kneel.

The key was, mercifully, still sticking out of the keyhole in the back door. I'd never have found it otherwise. Shuffling like an old man, I made it into the kitchen, clung to the edge of the sink and removed the pea gravel. Looking into the mirror, I didn't recognize myself, but if I looked as bad as this now, what the hell had I looked like before the rain had washed off the blood?

Without warning, I vomited, urgently, into the sink. It told me a lot. One of the things I'd got was concussion – one of the many. I drank a couple of glasses of cold water and did a body check.

My ribcage felt as if it had been trampled by an entire race card of horses. I tried a tell-tale cough; wished I hadn't. However, it was reassuring. No blood, scarlet and bubbling, came up. No perforated lungs. My ribs were agonizing, but if they were simply bruised, not cracked, I'd got away lightly.

Both arms, both legs, all worked. The right kneecap would be sore for a while but would heal. Tried to bend the left knee – now that was a different story. I didn't know how much damage had been inflicted. It was the kneecap that had copped it months ago at Huntingdon races following a fall. It had landed me in hospital for weeks on end, with a dire prognosis that it would never allow me to ride again. Undoubtedly fragile, how much hammer it could stand was debatable.

Locking and bolting the back door securely to repel any possible boarders, I dragged myself upstairs by dint of a backwards ascent of the staircase on my backside. With sweat heeling out of every pore, I stood in the bathroom, stripped all my bloody, saturated clothes off and stood under a very gentle, lukewarm shower. I wasn't going to attempt a hot bath; I doubted I would be able to climb out again. Amazingly, there was only one deep wound where the skin had split along the edge of one of my ribs – I stuck a plaster over it and slapped arnica over the rest of my body. Wrapping a towel round me, I fished in the bathroom cabinet and came up with some powerful painkillers. I knocked three back.

My bedroom was still as I'd left it yesterday morning. Was it only yesterday? Good God, it felt like a lifetime. The bedside clock read almost ten past five. I drew the curtains, shutting out the pounding rain, and gratefully crawled under the duvet. For the next twelve hours – or more – the world could take care of itself.

I awoke to a painful bladder demanding to be emptied on Monday afternoon at two o'clock. Nature had been doing sterling work and repairing my battered body whilst I slept on unawares. I no longer felt sick, didn't have a headache and, holding up one finger, that was all I could see – one finger. So my concussion was getting much better. If I didn't bash my head again over the next couple of days, that was one problem gone. The rest of me was sore and hellishly stiff, but I could at least draw breath now without biting on pea gravel. So probably no cracked ribs.

I stood starkers in the bathroom. I was not a pretty sight – nearly the whole of my chest was covered in purpling bruises. This time I risked taking a bath, running it hot and high.

It must have been after three when I clambered out. But I felt better, considerably better. The right kneecap now just a dull ache, but working. The left one? The jury was still out. I swallowed another three strong painkillers and hobbled down to the kitchen.

Leo was there. He was not amused. I must have closed my bedroom door last night – I knew I'd made sure of the window – otherwise, he would have been in there on dawn patrol demanding food. He was demanding food now.

'Please, Leo' – I lifted a hand – 'stop it, I'm feeling fragile.'

It cut no ice; the decibel level increased. I hastened to fill his dish.

Then I fixed a meal for myself: ham omelette with three eggs. It had been twenty-seven hours since I'd last eaten. I realized I was starving hungry. And that told me a great deal, too. I was mending fast. And I needed to. Today was Monday – tomorrow, Tuesday, I was riding for a different trainer, Clive Unwin. If I rode a winner, there'd be the chance of further rides.

I finished the food and poured a mug of strong tea. Then I sat and thought about the moment I'd arrived home yesterday. I'd not noticed a car parked up, but there must have been one. The man hadn't simply walked up to my cottage. The man. My overall impression had been of an older man. Strong enough to give me a right pasting but . . . before he could finish the job, if that's what he had intended, his strength had run out. It smacked of a lifetime of smoking because he'd been wheezing and struggling for breath at the end. A young man could have kept going.

But maybe the attacker thought he had finished the job. As far as I could recall, I'd been pretty much out of it, covered in blood . . . If the gravel hadn't absorbed the blows, I would have been a goner.

So the big question was who was he? And the second question: why had he attacked me? And attacked me with such violence. It wasn't simply a frightener; much more like personal revenge. Unless it was the golf course killer . . . but surely he couldn't have worked out my identity and got here before me. Say it had been him, and he thought he'd done the job on me, who next? Next was Mike.

I snatched up my mobile. He answered from down the stable yard.

'Hello, Harry, how you doing?'

'I've been better. And you?'

'Keeping busy. Best antidote for just about everything. Oh, and propping Samuel up.'

'Samuel's there, with you?' I asked stupidly, mind going full gallop at the possible reasons why he might be there.

'Harry, he's feeling it because of Chloe.'

'Yes, yes, of course.'

'Heard anything from North Shore – any developments?'

'No, nothing.'

'If the police had caught him, it would have been on the news.'

'That's true.'

I tried to avoid saying that news, whatever it was, had passed me by for the last twenty-four hours. No sense in telling Mike my state of health. But at the same time, I needed to warn him.

'I've been thinking, Mike, the killer's still free. It's possible he saw me watching from the turret room. He could have worked out you and I were billeted in there.'

'You're saying, watch my back?' Mike was ahead of me.

'Exactly.' I breathed with relief that the message had gone home without me letting on about my injuries.

'By God, I'd like him to try,' Mike growled.

I wondered what he'd say about my own sorry efforts to defend myself.

'Just take care, Mike. He's a dangerous bastard. Don't let him take you by surprise.'

There was a long silence.

'I hear you, Harry.'

'Yeah, well, I can't spare the time for hospital visiting right now. I'm riding for Clive Unwin tomorrow.'

'D'you know, I'd forgotten. Huntingdon, isn't it?'

'Yes.'

'At least you've broken your duck about riding that course.'

'That's not a problem. The problem's winning.'

'Pheeewww.' He blew air disparagingly through pursed lips. 'It's a walkover.'

'Such faith.' I had to laugh. 'Anyway, must go, let you get on with evening stables.'

I didn't really think Samuel was in the frame as a suspect. And now I'd warned Mike, there was nothing more I could do. Except try to work out from the meagre pieces of jigsaw puzzle already in my possession what my next move should be.

I mashed another mug of tea and spread out Jake Smith's list on the kitchen table. I'd already contacted Robson, the trainer. I drew a line through his name – one down.

Jake had put the names of people with a possible grudge or motive in the final paragraph. The first name was Goode, a misnomer if ever there was one: the man was in prison. Louis had given evidence in court that helped to get him banged up. I really didn't fancy prison visiting.

I went to the next. Alice Goode – his wife. Edward Frame had been associating with an Alice found on DaddyDating. She had put Jo-Jo on to the website and subsequently on to Louis. Was it possible it could be the same woman?

Only one way to find out. And I'd better do it whilst the pain-killers were still working. I'd be in trouble when they wore off. I tapped in the telephone number beside her name.

Half an hour or so later, I parked the Mazda at the kerb in Grenville Street, Newark. Thankfully, with the edge of pain dulled, I'd managed the clutch. However, I tried to disguise my hobble as I went up and knocked on the dirty, peeling paint on the front door. I'd seen the twitch of curtains and knew my approach had already been clocked. Any weakness was best disguised. There was no telling who the information might be passed on to.

The door was opened by a woman wearing a mini skirt. A very short miniskirt.

'Bloody hell fire!' she said.

'As a greeting, that's not very nice, is it?'

'Have you seen your face, mate?'

'I don't need to, I can feel it.'

'I'll bet.'

'You are Alice Goode?'

'Oh, sure. And you're Harry Radcliffe, ain't you?'

'Yes.'

'I can see he found you, then. Mind, I'm surprised you're still with us.'

My heart started pounding. What information did she have? If I

could persuade her to tell me, another piece of the jigsaw would
fall into place. And given enough pieces, I could guess the full
picture.

'Aren't you going to invite me in?'

EIGHTEEN

'Of course, I never turn a gentleman away.' A sly, sexy smile
spread over her face.

'I'm not a customer.'

''Course you're not.' Her lips curved wider.

I contemplated making a run for it. Wouldn't work. I could only
manage a hobble. She stepped back into the tiny hall.

'I don't bite. That is, not unless you want me to . . .' Her laughter
lingered behind her as she walked away into the lounge.

I took a deep breath, closed the door behind me and followed
her. She knew her trade. The swaying buttocks were enticing in the
tight, black mini and would have got any man going. Well, almost.
Not me. I was far more interested in finding out the identity of the
man who had attacked me. Sad, really.

She spread herself out on the settee and patted the cushion next
to her.

'Have a seat. Tell me what you're after.'

I ignored the settee, took a seat by the window: it was safer.

'I'm after information.'

'Well,' she said and shrugged one shoulder, 'we can start with that.'

'Are you married to the man who's doing time for fraud? Darren
Goode.'

She opened her eyes wide. 'I didn't see that one coming.'

I waited.

'I don't see what it's got to do with you, but yes, Darren's banged
up.'

'And you've been seeing a chap called Edward whom you met
on the DaddyDating website?'

'A regular little Sherlock, ain't you?' Her smile had faded now.
'Where's all this leading?'

'You haven't answered the question.'

'Yes.'

'Thank you. And you introduced a friend of yours to this same website. She clicked, if you'll excuse the pun, with her contact, didn't she?'

'You talking about Jo-Jo?'

I nodded.

She slid off the settee, went over to the mantelpiece and helped herself to a cigarette. Taking a deep lungful of smoke, she swung round to face me. 'You know a lot, don't you?'

'I'm over a barrel. I have to find answers or I'm for the chop.'

'By who?' Her eyes narrowed as she blew out a column of smoke. There didn't seem any reason to withhold his name.

'Jake Smith.'

'It wasn't Jake who worked you over.' It was said as a statement.

'No?'

'Oh, Christ, no.' She shook her head firmly. 'If it was, you'd have been measured for a box by now. He doesn't mess about.'

She knew what she was talking about. My heart dropped further than it had already regarding Jake and what he was capable of doing.

'No, he doesn't.' I agreed. 'I've found that out.'

'Jo-Jo was Jake's sister, did you know that?'

'Yes. It's the reason I'm over a barrel. Jake's sure it was murder. I'm the patsy who's got to find her killer, or join her on the other side.'

'I don't know who killed her – well, her and that sod she was seeing.'

'Louis Frame.'

'Yeah,' she blew a plume of smoke, 'him. He put the boot in for Darren, at his trial, y'know.' She stared at me intently.

'But he did embezzle the funds.'

She flapped a hand dismissively. 'His sentence was increased. He won't be out for a long time. Why do you think I went on DaddyDating, eh? A girl's got to live, ain't she?'

I thought the word 'girl' was stretching things a good deal. Alice was so much older than I'd thought.

'Why did you encourage Jo-Jo to pick Louis, if you hated the bloke?' At this point, I was taking a considered guess but I didn't think it was a coincidence.

'He was wealthy, very wealthy. Jo-Jo could take him for a packet. Serve the soddin' man right. Only, it didn't run quite like that.'

'How do you mean?'

'Dozy cow fell for him, didn't she?'

'I see.' And I did. The only way for an ongoing future with Louis would be for Jo-Jo to get herself pregnant. And she had. Alice scrubbed out her cigarette in the ashtray.

'So, that all you want to know?'

'One more thing. You were talking about someone working me over. You know who it was, don't you?'

She shrugged. 'Might do.'

I took out my wallet and counted out some notes on to the coffee table. Her eyes followed my every move.

'Will that improve your memory?'

'I might be wrong, o'course, but he was shooting his mouth off about doin' for you.'

'Alice, who was he?'

'Frank's dad, John Dunston.'

I stared at her. Of course. I'd forgotten about the teeth on the doorstep. I nodded slowly.

'Yes, I think you're right.'

Her hand slid across the table with the speed of a striking cobra and the notes disappeared.

I threw a heavy at her. 'Did you arrange for Louis' accident?'

She snorted. 'Don't talk bullshit. Jo-Jo was my best mate. You didn't know she was pregnant, did you?'

'Yes, I did.'

'Oh.' She sat down suddenly. 'I thought I was the only person who knew.'

'I'm very sorry she's dead, Alice, I really am. And I'm going to do my damnedest to find her killer.'

'Really?'

'Yes, really. I know some of the picture already, but there's somebody pulling the strings – he's the one I'm after.'

'If I can help you, I will.' Her eyes were brimming over with tears now.

'Thanks, I appreciate it.'

'I cared about Jo-Jo, you know. We looked out for each other.'

I nodded. 'It's tough.'

She stood up, came close. 'We could give each other a bit of comfort right now, if you like.'

I put my hands on her shoulders. 'No, Alice, we couldn't. Thanks for the offer but . . .'

'I understand – a posh bloke like you doesn't need a slapper like me. You can take your pick.'

'I wish.' I smiled at her. 'If I find the killer, I'll come and tell you, OK?'

'OK.'

She saw me to the door. 'Don't forget.'

'I won't. But I've got to find him first.'

I drove home well satisfied with what I'd discovered. But I was glad to get back. The painkillers had done their job but they were wearing off now.

How the hell I was going to ride at Huntingdon tomorrow, I couldn't imagine.

I didn't drive straight in when I got to the cottage. Instead, I parked a short way up the lane and walked back. I didn't intend being caught out again. Inching in, I pressed close to the hedge. At that point I realized Dunston must have done the same because I'd not been alerted by the scrunch of gravel prior to the attack. I did a recce of both front and back gardens and tried all the windows and doors. They were all secure. As far as I could see, no one had gained entry and I was certain there was no one lurking in the gardens. I returned to the car, drove it on to the gravel and parked.

Letting myself in, I hesitated, listening, but the cottage gave off the unmistakable air of an empty house. I heaved a big sigh. Although the rest of my body was healing fast, the left kneecap was complaining like hell. It wouldn't stand any further harsh treatment. I locked the door, mashed a mug of strong tea, took it through to the lounge and switched on the table lamp. It shed a soft, golden glow on the dark October evening.

Slumped on the settee with my leg propped up took a bit of the edge off the pain. Clearly, the way forward was to give the knee the rest it required. But there was tomorrow's race to be ridden. I didn't like admitting I'd been jumped and worked over, especially by a much older man, but if I wanted to ride, it had to be done. The X factor in my personal first-aid kit needed to be played.

I reached for my mobile and tapped in Annabel's number. It went to answerphone. Swearing under my breath, I left a brief message asking her to phone me as soon as she could. I drank the tea, contemplated taking some more painkillers – and didn't. They were best saved for tomorrow. Adjusting the cushions underneath my knee for maximum support, I settled back with another one behind my head.

The meeting with Alice had gone far better than I'd hoped. She could be crossed off Jake's list. She had nothing to do with the deaths of Louis or Jo-Jo. I'd thought it safer not to let on that I'd already found out it was John Dunston driving the horsebox. Perhaps she already knew, but I'd bet the cottage she didn't know he'd been instructed to cause the crash. I was keeping that to myself for the moment. I was after the man who gave the orders.

There was a noise in the kitchen and I sat bolt upright, tense, ready. The door opened a crack. My fists instinctively bunched. And then Leo shoved his whiskers through the gap. The relief was out of all proportion. Obviously, it had been the cat flap.

'You young devil! You had me going there.'

He mewed loudly and stalked over to the settee. I didn't need to pat the cushion. With one bound, he was on my knee and stretched out across my stomach. He made a very good impression of a hot water bottle.

I started thinking about the next name on Jake's list – Benson McCavity. He seemed the next most likely contender. I needed to set up a meeting.

It was warm in the cottage; the tea was soothing and the settee likewise. Leo had stopped purring now and gone to sleep. Peace settled around me and, still mulling over my approach, I, too, must have drifted off to sleep.

An hour or so later the strident tones of my mobile jerked me awake.

'Hello, Harry. How're things?'

'Annabel, er, yes, thanks for calling me back.'

'You OK? You sound half asleep.'

'Matter of fact, I was. Didn't mean to drop off but I guess I must have done.'

'You're not ill, are you?'

'No, not ill exactly.'

'But . . .?'

'But I'm in need of some spiritual healing. To be honest, I've been on the receiving end of a punch-up.' I heard her intake of breath.

'Oh, Harry, darling. How bad *are* you?'

'Don't panic, I'm not too bad, considering. What is giving me a rough time is my left knee.'

'I could send you some absent healing. That's the one that's dicey, isn't it?'

'Yes.'

'Would you like some healing?'

'I would, very much so. But I have to say it's for selfish reasons. I'm supposed to be riding tomorrow at Huntingdon.'

There was silence for a moment. Annabel was the most unselfish of people. However, the reason we weren't still together was not because our feelings had died, but because she couldn't stand seeing me suffer the injuries a jockey inevitably incurs as part of his working life. Asking her for help and healing so that I could go ahead and risk my neck yet again on a racecourse was below the belt on my part.

'Harry, if you're suffering, that's all the reason I need.'

'Bless you. Have I told you, you're one in a million?'

'Yes, darling,' she gurgled with laughter, 'you have, several times. I'll have to watch it doesn't go to my head. In the meantime, take it steady. Sounds like you should put your feet up and rest.'

'I was doing.'

'Good man. You relax and I'll do the necessary. 'Bye, Harry.'

She was gone and I was left staring at the phone, cursing myself for letting her go out of my life. Life, when she was with me, had been bliss. But it was no good living with regrets. They got you nowhere . . . Life was constantly moving on, bringing you new opportunities, new people. I needed to forget the past bliss and look forward to finding bliss with another woman.

A picture of Fleur came into my mind. I'd taken a rain check on having dinner with Mike, his sister and Fleur. High time I reminded Mike to set another date. I'd definitely go and give fate, or destiny, whatever, a chance to work some magic.

I followed Leo's example and Annabel's instructions and fell asleep.

Something, later, brought me up from the lower depths to just below the surface. It felt a bit like a soft punch in the stomach. I knew what it was. Leo had used my stomach as a springboard.

I'd been dreaming. Dreaming of food, something delicious. I could practically taste it, certainly smell it. I took a last lingering sniff and, reluctant to wake up, opened my eyes.

The first thing I saw was a steaming mug passing slowly back and forth underneath my nostrils. The chicken soup smelled even better than it had in my dream. I raised my gaze to the person who was holding the offering.

Annabel smiled down at me. I was instantly awake, filled with a burst of pleasure.

'You're not safe to be let out,' she said and placed the mug of soup in my hand.

NINETEEN

'I didn't hear you come in.'

'No, but Leo did. He was doing his guard-cat routine.' She scooped up the ginger Tom who stuck his head in her neck. Lucky sod! He was purring for England. In his position, I'd be purring, too.

'I didn't intend dragging you away from Jeffrey.'

'He's away, as usual. Spends half his life zipping up and down the M1.'

'Even so, you shouldn't have come over.'

'Drink your soup.' She nuzzled Leo. 'How's White Lace?'

'Doing fine.'

'Good. I like to get feedback.'

I grinned. 'It's nice getting fed.' The chicken soup was home-made, a million miles away from the tinned variety.

'When you've finished, I'll give that knee a bit of attention.'

As far as I was concerned, she could give the whole of me a going over. But, prudently, I didn't say so. Instead, I asked her how she was feeling.

'I've passed the first three months. Most women seem to have morning sickness during that period, but, honestly, I've never felt better.'

'You're blooming; being pregnant suits you.'

'I'm like a kid looking forward to Christmas,' she laughed and patted a tummy that hardly looked any different. 'I can't wait.'

'What names have you thought of?'

'None, yet. I think when I see him, I'll know.'

'Is it a boy?'

'Well, I say him but I refused the chance to know for sure. It's more fun not knowing.'

'Do you want a boy?'

'I just want a healthy baby.' She took the empty mug from me. 'Now, let's see about giving your knee some healing. You're racing tomorrow.'

She ended up giving me a full healing – every energy centre, every joint – and also spent time on my battered face. The healing was more effective than the painkillers. I could feel the heat pouring out from the palms of her hands and it relaxed me totally. All the discomfort melted away. I knew from previous experience the value of accepting a healing.

Annabel had once flown over from Malta to be at my hospital bedside when I'd had a bad racing fall. She'd not only had to obtain the permission of the ward manager but had also had to check if the bone had been set in the correct position before she gave me any treatment. The healing energy was powerful, could even start a broken bone fusing.

Afterwards, the relief was wonderful and we sat in companionable harmony and drank tea before Annabel declared it time to be going home. Back to Jeffrey. I could have kept her at the cottage for ever. But I saw her out. And now I wasn't even hobbling. I held her car door open.

'I owe you, Annabel. I really didn't expect you to drive over to do the healing. I'd have been damn grateful for some absent. The pain's gone completely.'

'I'm very glad, Harry.' She leaned forward, gave me a chaste kiss on the cheek. 'Good job I've still got my key. But next time I'll send you some absent healing. Do rest your leg, though, as much as you can. Don't take liberties. That kneecap's vulnerable.'

'Yes, I know. And the man who gave out the kicking knows as well. That's why he targeted that spot.'

'If you will go in for playing detectives . . .' She shook her head, reprovingly. 'Even race riding's not as dangerous.' I hadn't told her the whole story, just an abridged version.

'Don't worry, I'm watching my back.'

'I do hope so.' She turned the key. 'If you need me again, just ring.'

I watched the car turn into the lane and drive away. Need her again? I needed her all the time.

The next morning, hearing Annabel's words repeating in my ears, I forfeited riding out at Mike's stables. I stayed at home and worked on my weekly column for the newspaper. Not a job I enjoyed very much, although the editor told me I made a pretty good fist of it. At least it kept me sitting down in a chair as opposed to sitting down in a saddle.

But the time crept round towards lunchtime and I needed to be making tracks for Huntingdon. I took a yoghurt, fruit and a bottle of mineral water with me, together with the box of painkillers, just in case. If I managed to ride in the race before it flared up again, I still needed to be able to drive home.

I pointed the Mazda eastwards.

My one ride for Clive Unwin was scheduled for three thirty, but I needed to be there at least an hour or so beforehand.

However, there was something else I was planning to do before walking into the parade ring.

Arriving at Huntingdon, I went into the weighing room.

'Back, then?' said one of the jockeys, about to go and ride in the two o'clock. 'Too bad about your leg, but I got the ride on Unicorn last Friday.'

'Right.' I'd been offered the ride on the horse at Carlisle but had to decline because of the fall at Towcester. 'Saw you rode a winner.'

'Dead right,' he grinned and walked to the door. 'Piece of cake.'

I grinned back. Next week, the situation could well be reversed and I'd be taking over one of his rides. Race riding was a dangerous sport. The valet in charge of my gear bustled up.

'How'd your wedding go, then?'

Nothing was secret in the weighing room. I'd mentioned last week that I wouldn't be riding on Saturday.

'The wedding went off beautifully . . .'

'I hear a "but" . . .'

'Afraid so. Surprised you didn't read about it in the papers.'

'What?'

'The bride was murdered.'

'No! Get away!'

'I'm afraid it's true.'

'Bloody hell.' He gave me a look that summed up how we'd all been feeling on Saturday night.

As gossip fodder, I suppose it did take some beating.

'The poor lass.'

'Yes.'

He looked at me sideways. 'You on the case, then?'

'Now, why should I be?'

'No reason,' he said and did a stable-lad sniff, 'except it was you that cracked the Leicester races murder.'

I groaned inside. I was not going to live it down.

'Doesn't make me a candidate for sussing the next one, does it?'

'D'y'know,' he said, unfolding a pair of white racing breeches, 'I reckon it does.'

I left him to his bustling and took myself off. Whilst I was on the computer this morning, I'd done a bit of spadework. Robson, the trainer I'd rung from the turret room at North Shore, had several runners here this afternoon. It was very likely his box driver might just be John Dunston. I was about to find out for sure. I'd parked in the normal jockeys' car park, but now I made my way over to the box park.

Every available space, it seemed, had a horsebox parked up. I was looking for a maroon-and-grey one. From a safety angle, I was pleased to see there were plenty of people about. The trouble was, I couldn't ask any of them where Robson's driver had parked.

Walking in and out of the lines of vehicles, I tried to look as unobtrusive as possible. But legwork ate up time and I was riding in the three thirty. Time was pushing on when I came round the rear corner of a large six-horse box and found myself looking right at Robson's box – and John Dunston.

We both stopped short. I recognized him immediately as the man who had given me a good rib kicking. What he saw, I don't know. His face dropped a foot with surprise.

Quickly, I walked the few yards between us.

'Thought you'd finished me, didn't you? Well, sorry, I'm not a ghost.'

His fists bunched themselves and I could see the knuckles were skinned and grazed from where he'd hammered them into my face.

'I wouldn't advise you have another go.' I waved a casual hand towards the other people. 'Look at it this way, Dunston, I've got you off a murder rap.'

'You've sent my lad down,' he croaked.

'Get this: your Frank sent himself down.'

'If you hadn't worked out who it was, he'd still be free.'

'For God's sake, man . . . He's a criminal.'

'He's behind bars, an' it's all your fault.'

I let my arms drop to my sides. No point in trying to bring any sort of reasoning into the conversation. He was totally blinkered.

'Behind bars,' he repeated, shaking his head. 'It'll be for a long time . . . be too late.'

'What are you talking about?'

Dunston simply carried on shaking his head and said nothing.

The alarm tone on my mobile gave out a sharp reminder. I'd set it when I'd left the weighing room. Time I was heading back to change into my racing silks. I felt baffled. Tracking down Dunston had been meant to clarify things – maybe come to some sort of truce. It hadn't. And there was no time to try further.

'I have to go.'

I turned and jogged away between the big boxes. There was no way of knowing if seeing me had brought him up sharp and I could draw a line under the possibility of any further assaults.

I felt it was just as likely he'd have another go, really make sure of finishing me. But a race is a race; it doesn't wait. I increase my speed and headed back towards the weighing room.

Mike had set up this ride for me. I'd just accepted the offer from Clive Unwin and had no idea who the owner was. Walking over to the parade ring with the other jockeys, I saw the man standing with Unwin and couldn't believe my eyes. It was Paul Wentworth, the man who had been driving the Audi on the day White Lace bolted.

'Harry, I'd like to introduce Mr Wentworth—' Unwin began.

'We've met, haven't we?' Wentworth's eyes twinkled. 'I have to say, not under the best of circumstances.'

'Oh?' The trainer was frowning.

'Nothing to worry about, Mr Unwin.' I hastened to reassure. 'It was at an accident, when my horse bolted.' The last thing I wanted was to get on the wrong side of a new trainer before my first ride for him.

'I'm pleased you're riding for us, Harry. Pen and I have not long had the horse. It'll put the cherry on the top when I tell her.'

'Do my best; can't guarantee the end result.' I'd be very surprised if I won because Dishwasher was running. He was the outright favourite.

'Whatever, I'm enjoying myself immensely just being here as an owner.'

I could do with more of his sort as owners.

The announcement 'Jockeys, please mount' cut short any further conversation and Unwin flipped me up into the saddle.

There were seven others in the race and I came a respectable second, the race going, as expected, to the odds-on favourite. But Unwin and Wentworth were still pleased with the result.

Back in the winners' enclosure, Wentworth pumped my hand.

'You must ride for us again, Harry.'

'Thanks, I'd like to.'

I slung the saddle over my arm and went to weigh in.

I stripped off my racing silks amidst the usual crush and smell of sweating men and spotted the valet coming over. Having ridden the one ride, I was free to go now. He stopped beside me, arms full of clobber.

'I did wonder, y'know, about the state of your face. Greenhill told me you was done over.'

The grapevine was working with its usual efficiency. I heaved off my racing boots and reached for my own shoes.

'He reckons it was old Dunston.'

'Does he?'

'Yeah.'

'Could have been.' I shrugged.

'Ha . . .' He bent to pick up some gear. 'You've got to cut him some slack, y'know.'

I looked up at him in surprise. 'I have?'

'Hmmm . . . Well, Frank's banged up now – 'course we don't know yet how long for, but it'll be a good stretch, even if he gets remission.'

'So?'

'She'll likely be gone, time he gets out.'

'Who will be gone where?' I finished dressing and stood up.

'Dunston's missus, Lilly. Frank's mother. Confined to bed now. She's got terminal cancer.'

The words slammed into me like Dunston's fists. That explained why he'd attacked me with such frantic viciousness. I knew it wasn't a simple warning or working over. The attack had felt personal, held a desperate, frustrated fury. And now I could understand why.

If his wife was bedridden, there was no possibility of her seeing her son in prison, nor him getting out to visit her. And it was a terminal case. By the time Frank got out of prison, Lilly Dunston would be dead. Yes, in John Dunston's shoes, I'd probably have felt much the same hatred against the one man who had brought about Frank's incarceration.

'An' he's struggling, money-wise.'

I waited. There was no need to prompt him – he wanted me to know.

'Has to pay for carers to look after Lilly, sit with her. Can't drive boxes all over the country *and* look after her.'

'No.'

And a bit more of the jigsaw fell into place.

'So, is this common knowledge, then? I didn't know.'

'Reckon so. Well, you know how it is . . .'

Yes, I did know. Racing was a tight-knit community all of its own. Sooner or later, most things came out, knowledge was passed on. However, secrets that remained 'secrets' were the sort it was much safer not to admit knowing.

I had a long and thoughtful drive back home to Nottinghamshire.

TWENTY

Next morning, six o'clock, inside Mike's kitchen, supping hot, honey-laced coffee, I updated him on events.

'Somebody's pulling his strings, that's for sure.'

'So, who is it, Harry?'

'Don't know,' I said and shook my head slowly. 'But it's costing them pretty well. They've greased Dunston sufficiently well enough not only to take the risk of engineering the car crash, but also so he can afford to pay for round-the-clock care for his wife. That's not a cheap option, and it's ongoing until she dies.

'But it's not just the payment, Mike; they've traded on the man's grief. Double grief, actually. First for his son, and although we know he's a waste of space, Frank's still his son. And second, for his wife.

'OK, it's crazy to think I should have any sympathy for him because the man gave me a good working over. But right now, I feel bloody sorry for John Dunston.'

'Me, too. Talk about hitting a man when he's already down . . . This situation gives a whole new meaning to it.'

'And I thought I was over a barrel.'

'But you are, Harry. You can't escape. Jake Smith's doing emotional blackmail on you, too, don't forget. You can't just walk away, however much you want to. Jake Smith's got you by the balls. You know it, I know it. And it's not only Jake Smith; John Dunston's going to try again.'

I shrugged, spread my hands. 'I did try to defuse him . . . before I knew the bigger picture. Trouble is, Mike, the more I look into this whole mess, the more complicated it becomes. And the more people are getting hurt, emotionally as well as physically.'

'It's all down to motive, Harry. And where family safety is concerned, motive doesn't come much higher.'

The door opened and Fleur walked in. With unspoken agreement, we dropped the subject.

'Morning, Fleur.'

'Morning, Uncle Mike, Harry.' She poured herself a coffee. 'Got a second on Lytham, then, yesterday.'

'Yep.'

'Are you aiming for a crack at the title again?'

'Well, it's what you aim for. Getting it's another thing.'

'You could do with more rides.'

I chuckled. 'Dead right, I could. But they don't come that easily. You have to chase them.'

She took a swig of coffee and studied me. 'I did plenty of chasing for rides in Italy – flat, though.'

'Your Uncle's a dark horse himself. He never told me about your racing.'

She leaned across and ruffled Mike's hair. 'He thought you'd enough on, and you had.'

'So, what're your plans? Will you be going back to Italy? Or staying in England?' I found myself waiting expectantly for her answer. If she was staying, I'd definitely ask her out. The signals she was giving seemed to indicate she was interested in me. And I was pretty sure she would say yes. On the other hand, if she didn't intend to stay, why start something that would be going nowhere?

'Depends, doesn't it?'

'On what?'

'Much the same as you. I need work – rides. There's a job still, over in Italy. Well, not indefinitely, of course, but I could go back in a month or so and carry on where I left off.'

'But there's your mother . . .' Mike frowned.

'Yes, I know.' Fleur's brow furrowed charmingly.

'Mum's the reason I came to England. She's had a rough time, losing Dad. I wanted to help her settle in, you know, find somewhere to live.'

'Plenty of room here,' Mike murmured.

Fleur dropped a kiss on the top of his head. 'I know, and it's very sweet of you, but I think Mum wants to get her own place.'

Mike smiled and stood up. 'I'm sure she does. Anyway, work to do . . .'

I took my empty mug over to the sink and rinsed it out.

'By the way, Harry, you doing anything this evening?'

'No.'

'Feel like joining us for dinner?'

'Oh, yes, good idea.' Fleur nodded enthusiastically. 'Do come, Harry.'

'You were supposed to have a bite with the three of us last Friday.'

'Well, Annabel was on her own that night, so . . .'

'Yes, but you're free tonight, aren't you?'

'OK, then, Mike, thanks. Yes, I'll be here.'

'Great.' Fleur grinned and led the way out to the stables.

Third lot, back from the gallops, had just clattered their way into the stable yard when an Audi drew up. I recognized it. Far from covered in bright blood, the vehicle was a pristine white.

I dismounted, tossed the reins over the colt's head and led him across behind me as I went to greet the Wentworths.

'Harry. Not imposing, are we?' Paul Wentworth enquired.

'Not at all.' I shook his outstretched hand. 'Mike will be pleased you've taken up his offer to visit.'

'Actually, we popped round on Saturday afternoon, but you and Mike were attending a wedding, I believe.'

Pep stepped forward and ran a hand down the horse's neck. 'Did the bride look ravishing?' She smiled up at me.

'Er . . . I'm afraid it ended in tragedy.'

Her smile faded. 'Oh?'

'You may have read about it in the newspapers . . . Lucinda Frame?'

She stopped stroking the bay neck and her hand flew to her face. 'Murdered, the bride who was murdered, on her wedding day?'

I nodded. 'The same one.'

'Good God.' Paul shook his head in disbelief. 'And you and Mike . . . you were there, when it happened.'

'How utterly dreadful,' Pep said in a shaken voice.

'Did you see anything?' Paul asked.

'You mean, whoever did it?'

He nodded.

'No,' Mike's voice behind us said. 'No. Harry was unlucky enough to be the person who found the body.'

'Oh, you poor man!' Pep's eyes were wide with distress.

'Look, how about we all go in, have a coffee?'

'Damn good idea, Harry,' Mike said briskly. 'I'll take Pep indoors, get the kettle on. You stable up and join us. We can do the grand tour afterwards.' He threaded his arm through Pep's and gently drew her across to the house.

Paul watched them go. 'Something like this brings back unpleasant memories for her.'

'Oh?'

'She was attacked a few years ago. Plus a member of the family was killed suddenly in an accident last year.'

It was my turn to stare in disbelief at him.

'She's put it behind her really well. But just now and again . . . you know?'

We watched Mike and Pep disappear inside the house.

'Look, come into the stable whilst I see to the colt. Then we'll go over and get our drink.'

'Yes, OK.'

I led the big animal down the yard to his stable, attached a head collar and untacked him. Giving him a swift brush down, I rugged up and left him with a full haynet.

Walking back to the house, Paul said, 'They don't ask much of us, do they? And yet they give such a lot.'

'Have you had your horse very long?'

'No, Lytham's a recent investment – well, I'm not sure that's the right word. Probably "recent interest" would be correct. My cousin's experiencing some cash-flow problems with his business. Not his own fault – a main road's been rerouted and it's cut a lot of his trade. Far too proud to accept a loan, but when he suggested selling Lytham, I could see the sense from his point of view. It wasn't something he did lightly; he was very fond of the horse. Helene, his wife, called it Lytham after the place where they first met. I thought if Pep and I bought the horse, it would keep him in the family, plus help financially. And, as you know, Pep's devoted to all things horse . . .'

'So now you're racehorse owners.'

He grinned broadly, 'That's the size of it.'

'Once the racing bug bites, I'm afraid it's usually terminal.'

He gave a bellow of laughter.

'What made you decide to use Clive Unwin as a trainer?'

'What you're actually asking, Harry, is why didn't I use Mike?'

'I suppose I am.'

'Very simple. Unwin was already in charge of the horse's training. He was Benson's choice, really.'

'Benson . . . that's your cousin's name?'

'Yeah, Benson McCavity. Why?'

'I wondered if I knew him – you know, might have ridden for him.'

'Oh, I see. And have you?'

I shook my head. 'No.'

But as I said no, a voice inside my head was saying yes, yes, yes. I knew I'd never ridden for the man, never met him, but I was shortly going to. I had spoken to him on my mobile last night – and I was due to meet him at four o'clock this afternoon. It had to be the same man. There couldn't be two men with that unusual name. It would be too much of a coincidence.

Benson McCavity was the fourth name on Jake Smith's list.

At ten minutes to four, I pulled up in the forecourt of McCavity's place of work. He ran a garage and tyre-fitting company on an industrial estate on the southern outskirts of Grantham. The sign painted in orange over the door read *McCavity and Son*. It was a devil they'd rerouted the road. I could see the man would have a battle on now to maintain his level of business.

Walking into the big hangar-like interior of the garage, I saw a lanky guy in greasy orange overalls straighten up from underneath the bonnet of a Vauxhall.

'Help you?'

'We've an appointment at four o'clock. Bit early, I'm afraid.'

'Oh, right, you're Mr Radcliffe.' He frowned. 'Wait a bit, you're *Harry* Radcliffe, the jump jockey.'

'I admit it.'

He rubbed the worst of the grease from his hands with a rag and held out his right hand. 'Pleased to meet you.'

'Likewise.'

'So, what is it you want to talk to me about?'

'Might be better if we go into your office.'

'Yeah, sure.'

He retrieved a spanner from inside the Vauxhall, let the bonnet thump back into place and led the way through an internal door. Closing it behind us cut out a little of the fug of rubber tyres and oil fumes.

'Take a pew.'

He flipped a switch on an electric kettle housed amidst piles of invoices and work sheets.

'I think I should say straight away, this isn't about possible business.'

'Is it not?' He raised an eyebrow.

'Sorry, no.'

'Oh, well, life running true to form still.'

Brewing up two chunky Union Jack mugs still bearing the tea stains not only from yesterday, nor indeed the day before, but more likely three months before that, he pushed one towards me.

'You do know I don't own a racehorse any more? My cousin, Paul Wentworth, was good enough to buy Lytham off me. So, if it's not about racing, what is it about?'

'Tricky,' I said. And it was. How *do* you begin a conversation starting with *I understand your wife was killed in a car crash a while ago*? I realized I was hesitating too long, pondering how to ask the real question I needed an answer to. Like, *did you kill Louis Frame in retaliation for killing your wife?*

'Haven't got all day, mate.'

'I really don't know how to begin . . .'

'Start with one word. What's it about – me, my son, garage, elf and safety, not declaring my taxable income . . .' He took a long pull at the tea.

I jumped in. 'Your late wife.'

His hand jerked, tea shot over the rim of the mug like a brown tidal wave. More continued to drip over as his hand developed a shake.

'What . . . what about Helene?'

The man's grief was still visibly open, raw. It would be easy to empathize. I had to remind myself, yes, he'd lost his wife, but he could actually be Frame's killer.'

'In the car smash that killed your wife, the driver was Louis Frame. Did you know he's dead?'

'Yes, 'course I bloody know. If I'd had the balls, I'd have sunk a knife in and gutted him myself.'

'He was killed in a collision with a horsebox.'

'*I know*. Read it in the papers, didn't I? Killed instantaneously, it said. Too bloody good for the bastard. Should have suffered . . . like Helene did.' He raised tear-filled eyes to mine. 'Took her four days it did . . . to die. Hospital said she had multiple injuries, crushed organs.' His shoulders shook and he wiped the back of a greasy hand across his face. 'She was on morphine, because of the pain. I didn't want her to die. But the state she was in . . . God help me, part of me wanted it to be over, to end her suffering. There was no hope of her getting better, d'y'see? All that suffering, all for nothing. Would have been better if she'd gone straight away – like he did!'

'I'm truly very sorry. If it wasn't important, I wouldn't be here, asking you questions.'

Giving himself time whilst he fought for control of his emotions, he shakily tipped the mug and drained what remained of the tea.

'Why are you asking?'

'Because, like yourself, I'm in a situation I can't control. It's controlling me. Do you know a man called John Dunston?'

'Can't recall that name, no.'

'Can you tell me where you were on the afternoon Frame died?'

'Where the hell do you think I was? Here, of course. Grafting. Trying to make a living for me and Daniel.'

'Is that your son?'

'Yes. He's only seven, poor little bugger. Lost his mum. And if I'm not careful, we'll lose the business. Gone right downhill since they rerouted the main road. It's taken a lot, and I mean *a lot*, of passing trade away.'

'I can see it would.'

He flicked a quick glance at me. 'What you're really asking me is did I do the bastard in? Well, the answer's no. Sure, I'd like to have done. Can you understand that?'

'Oh, yes. I certainly can – been at that point myself.'

He nodded, took a ragged breath, 'Well, then . . . But I didn't.'

And although he certainly had the motive and all the anger and need for revenge, I didn't see him killing Frame. Not unless he was a brilliant actor.

I stood up and walked to the door. 'Thanks for your time. I'm sorry I've had to run you through the mill again.'

He shrugged his shoulders and stared out through the office window. 'I hope you can see your way out of things. Damned if I can.'

TWENTY-ONE

Back home in my office at Harlequin Cottage, I took out the list of names given me by Jake Smith. There was a line drawn through the first three. I reached for a pen and drew a line through Benson McCavity's name, too.

The options were going down. The elimination should be

making it easier to see where the trail led, but, in truth, I hadn't got a clue. I seemed to have simply shortened the odds. Without a definite lead to follow, though, it was not looking good. I could carry on down the rest of the names, and if I still had no idea when I came to the end, Jake Smith couldn't accuse me of not trying. But he was a man who expected results. I was going to have to dig harder.

Sliding the list back into the envelope with Jo-Jo's photograph, I put it in the drawer beside the pair of false teeth. They seemed to grin derisively at me. I closed the drawer.

My mobile burst into life. I'd had it turned off all afternoon. Any interruption would have been unwelcome during my visit to McCavity.

'Yes?'

'Harry, boy, what progress?' It was Jake Smith.

'Not a lot.' Before he had time to blow up, I continued, 'I'm working my way down your hit list – number four and counting.'

'Have you found anything out?'

'Well, I know who left the false teeth on my doorstep.'

'Who?'

'John Dunston.' There was a stretching silence. I could practically see the cogs turning. I waited.

'Yeah, it figures.' He sighed heavily. 'After Carl's funeral, me dad had the wake at our house. I bet he was there.'

'But you were in prison.'

'You any better ideas, Radcliffe?' he said belligerently.

'No.' I admitted, noting it wasn't *Harry boy* now.

'So, what next?'

'I plug on. All I can do.'

'I'm expecting results . . .'

'I know you are.'

'I've another name for you.'

'Oh, yes?'

'There was a man, fancied our Jo-Jo, really had the hots for her. She couldn't stand him. One day he came on strong, got violent, and she told him to fuck off. Bastard didn't take no for an answer. Hurt her . . .' He gave a snort of mirthless laughter. 'I sorted him. It was two weeks before he got out of hospital.'

'Had he anything against Frame?'

'It was before she was with him. Still, the bastard could have been jealous of Frame, after she met him. I mean, the bloke was loaded, and Jo-Jo was living in a flat he was paying for. You get my meaning?'

'Oh, yes. What's his name?'

'Aiden Dobbs.'

'The jockey?'

'Yeah. You know him?'

'I know him.' A ruthless, mercenary chancer, but a brilliant rider – who happened to be Barbara Maguire's retained jockey.

'Follow up on him, OK? Report back. Got it?'

Without waiting for a reply, he disconnected.

I opened the desk drawer again, took out the piece of paper and added Aiden Dobbs' name to the list.

Not that I was likely to forget it. I'd be meeting him on Saturday night. Saturday was the day Barbara was giving her party. It was odds-on Dobbs would be there. I didn't need to try to set up a meeting with him – I already had an invite to the party.

All I needed to do was show up.

But before that, I had to show up at Mike's tonight. It would make a change, having a meal cooked for me. On my own, I normally cobbled together anything that had the two factors I needed: high nutritional value and low calories. Eggs were usually on the menu. With Fleur being a flat race jockey, Maria was used to cooking for weight watching. It would be interesting to see what her choice of meal was for tonight.

Also interesting to speculate on was what Fleur's choice of outfit would be. I'd not seen her wearing anything other than work jodhpurs since the night she and Maria had turned up at the pub looking for Mike. Even then she'd been wearing slacks. I hoped she would wear a dress tonight. I found myself really looking forward to finding out what she looked like.

I went upstairs, had a meticulous shave and ran a hot, deep bath. It suddenly seemed important to smarten myself up. I'd not used aftershave in quite a while, but there was half a bottle in the bathroom cabinet. It was one I'd always used when Annabel lived with me. Maybe I'd slap some on tonight.

Stripping off, I climbed into the bath, slid right down until my chin was level with the water and closed my eyes. Right then, the landline phone rang. Too bad. Whoever it was could talk to the answer phone. I'd listen to the message later.

I dressed in a black shirt and cream slacks, smart enough yet still casual. Running a comb through my hair, I noted it was more than time I went to the barber's. Any longer and I'd start looking like a pirate.

Mike had said any time around seven thirty. Checking my watch, it was barely seven. I'd time to check the message that had come through.

I'd never been so popular.

'Hello, Harry.' It was Uncle George. 'Hope life's fine. Your Aunt Rachel's making a big thing about our wedding anniversary – next Thursday. Don't say I said so, but I suppose she's trying to make up for all the lost and forgotten ones we've had. Still, it is a biggish one – thirty years. Amazing how we've managed to achieve that, don't you think?'

I found myself nodding in total agreement. It certainly was amazing. It said a lot for the endurance of the human spirit – on both their parts – when placed under extreme emotional pressure. However, it proved it was never too late to build a relationship back up.

Aunt Rachel, believing Uncle George to have had an affair, had spent the last twenty-odd years in bitter resentment and it had been marital hell. Now, it was sorted between them, the coin had flipped and their marriage was full of bliss. George deserved every happy moment. Part of their reconciliation had sprung from George being taken into hospital in a hurry. He very nearly didn't come out again. Aunt Rachel had faced his imminent death and decided what mattered in her life – George mattered!

'So,' his message continued, 'what I'm saying is, Harry, your Aunt Rachel's arranging a big do and we want you to come. Bring Annabel. Rachel would love to see her. We still think of her as family. What do you say? It will be on Thursday, next week, at seven. Speak to you soon, I hope.'

I replaced the telephone. Then I sat with my head in my hands and thought about it for several minutes.

Rachel and George were family, George my late father's only brother. Rachel had never had babies – she couldn't, she was barren. At the news of Annabel's pregnancy, she had openly rejoiced. No matter that I wasn't the baby's father; just the fact that Annabel was going to be a mother was enough for Rachel. I'd dearly love to take Annabel. She'd grieved for the state of their marriage and would now be delighted. But I wasn't going to. A line needed drawing between us before I could go forward. Tonight, if I'd read Fleur's signals correctly, that line was going to be drawn.

I reached for the phone and dialled Uncle George's number. We hadn't spoken in ages – not since the celebration for Silvie, I guess.

'Uncle George, nice to hear from you.'

'Harry, glad you got my message.'

'Congratulations on the anniversary.'

'I know what you're thinking: *against the odds*, I'll bet.'

I chuckled. 'Wasn't going to add that, but yes.'

'And I'd have to agree with you, lad. But we hung in there and we want you at the party to share it.'

'Don't worry, Uncle George, I'll be there. I know what it means to you, and to Aunt Rachel.'

'And Annabel? Will you bring her? Rachel loves the girl.'

I hesitated. 'I think not.'

'Oh, Harry . . .'

I heard the disappointment in his voice.

'I'm sorry, but Aunt Rachel is reading too much into Annabel's condition. It's almost as though she's convinced I'm the father. Like, she's not acknowledging the baby is Sir Jeffrey's.'

'Oh, Harry,' he said again, 'I'm sure she doesn't.'

I smiled wryly to myself. The improvement in his marriage had ensured an even deeper degree of loyalty.

'Please, Harry, do bring Annabel.'

'I can't, I'm really sorry, but no. I can't. But give Aunt Rachel my congratulations and tell her I'll come to her party.'

'OK.' His tone held disapproving resignation. 'We'll see you there, then.' He disconnected.

I walked slowly upstairs and took out the bottle of aftershave from the bathroom cabinet – it was the only one I had. Tomorrow, I'd buy a different brand, one that smelled different, but for now . . . Let the evening begin. I unscrewed the top and slapped some on.

Fleur opened the door. 'Heard your car. Come on in, we're all in the lounge.'

'Harry,' Mike heaved himself up from the settee, 'glad you've made it.'

Maria walked across and kissed my cheek. 'Hope you like fish. I'm cooking Dover sole.'

'Can't wait.' I grinned.

Fleur pushed a glass into my hand. 'We've two other guests coming.'

'Oh?'

'I invited Pen and Paul Wentworth,' Mike explained. 'It seemed the right thing to do, seeing as they're owners now, albeit they're with Clive Unwin.'

Mike was not only a racehorse trainer but a shrewd businessman, too. It paid to remain cordial with potential clients.

'They've just the one horse, though. Are they anticipating buying any more?'

'Who knows?' Mike spread his hands. 'They got shunted into ownership because of family troubles.'

I gaped at him. 'How come you know that? I only found out this afternoon – from his cousin, Benson McCavity.'

'From Pen. She told me the whole sorry story.' Mike looked sheepish. 'Well, she was in a bit of a state when I brought her back indoors this morning. She needed a bit of consoling. And a shoulder so she could pour it all out.'

'Damsels in distress always find you, Mike.'

'They do seem to, don't they?'

'Always have,' Maria said. 'It's your "lived-in" face. It attracts them.'

'Steady on, Mum. Uncle Mike's what's known as ruggedly good-looking,' Fleur put in.

'So,' Maria laughed, 'how would you describe Harry?'

'Surprised you're asking.' Fleur gave me a sly, sexy smile. 'Harry, well . . . Harry's just drop dead. Wouldn't you agree?'

'Do you two mind? I *am* standing here.'

'Most certainly would agree,' Maria replied cheerfully. 'Pity I'm too old for him.'

'But I'm not.' Fleur gave an outrageous lewd wink.

'Come on, you two, cut it out. You're embarrassing the man. Away to the kitchen and rattle the pans, or something.' Giggling like schoolgirls, they took themselves off.

'Phew,' Mike said and wiped imaginary sweat from his forehead, 'thank goodness I'm related; at least I'm safe.'

'What about me?' I protested.

'Oh, you, well . . . I'd have to say you've pulled, mate. Better give in. Not worth struggling.'

A knock at the kitchen door and voices raised in greeting marked the arrival of the last two guests. Moments later Maria showed in Pen and Paul Wentworth.

'Lovely of you to invite us, Mike.' Pen reached up and kissed his cheek. 'I'm so glad we called this morning.'

'So glad we caught you in this time,' Paul said.

'Yes, sorry about that. As you know, Harry and I were attending this wedding at North Shore. A beautiful place . . . just dreadful that the murder occurred.'

'Please, Mike' – Pen clutched his arm – 'let's not talk about it.'

'No,' he agreed, 'no, let's not. Now, what would you like to drink?' They wandered over to the drinks cabinet and left Paul and me to chat.

'Do you do any consultancy or advisory work, Harry?'

'As in?'

'Buying racehorses.'

'Ah.'

'I'm looking to buy another. You know Pen and I bought Lytham . . . well, we'd like a horse with Mike. Lytham is with Unwin, which is fine. I get on well with him. I'm down his yard quite a lot. But Pen says she'd like a filly in training here with Mike.'

'I'd be happy to help you. The Newmarket sales will be held later this month. Probably pick up a yearling there.'

'Sounds good to me.'

'OK, everyone,' Maria said, coming in, 'dinner's ready. If you'd like to go through to the dining room . . .'

'Of course. I'm looking forward to your cooking.' Paul followed her through the door.

I turned to see if Mike was coming. He was standing very close to Pen, smiling down into her uplifted face. I noticed with staggered disbelief his fingers were caressing her hand where she held the wine glass. And the look on his face needed no interpreting.

After all these years on his own following Monica's death, it looked surprisingly like he was falling for a married woman.

TWENTY-TWO

I slipped away to the dining room without either of them noticing. I took my allotted place at the dining table with my thoughts whirling. Fleur was seated beside me, with Paul next to her. Maria, it seemed, was head chef and waitress.

She served me a grilled Dover sole that looked and smelled great. It was unfortunate I'd lost my appetite. She placed vegetable tureens on the table, one filled with garden peas and asparagus tips, and one with baby new potatoes tossed in butter and chives. There was a lemon butter sauce on offer, plus portions of freshly cut lemon arranged on a cut-glass serving dish. Obviously, it had taken time and skill. It would be extremely rude of me not to at least attempt to make an effort.

Paul was helping himself lavishly, exchanging light-hearted banter with Maria.

'Mike, Pen, what are you *doing*? Dinner's waiting,' called Maria.

My guts twisted as I thought of Mike and Pen in the other room starting something that potentially was going to hurt a lot of people.

'Come on, Harry,' Fleur said and nudged my elbow, 'tuck in.'

Obediently, I helped myself from the tureen containing the asparagus and squeezed lemon over my fish.

'You've not said if you like my dress.' Fleur pouted her lips.

I realized she was right. What with the embarrassment of the women's double act when I arrived, followed by the revelation of seeing Mike moving in on Pen, I'd not really noticed. Odd really, when I'd been interested earlier. It crossed my mind that if Annabel had been here, I would have noticed her dress immediately. I forced the thought away and, taking a forkful of the sole to give myself a few seconds' grace, took stock. She was wearing a floaty dress, pale green, with a neckline that, sitting next to her, I could see, when she bent towards me, not so much plunged as threw itself off a cliff. I swallowed the mouthful and cleared my throat.

'It's lovely.'

'You like it?'

'Yes, yes, I do.'

'That's OK, then.' She smiled happily. 'I seem to spend my life wearing smelly old jodhpurs. It's really nice to put a dress on.'

'And perfume . . .' I murmured, aware now of the seductive, sweet scent she was wearing.

Mike and Pen came in. To deflect attention from them, I congratulated Maria on her skill.

'This fish is first class. You're a pretty good cook, Maria.'

'Thanks,' she smiled. 'Actually, I enjoy cooking.'

'I've certainly eaten better since she's been here.' Mike showed Pen to her seat and sat down opposite me.

'Men need looking after,' Pen said.

'You do a good job looking after me. I'm very lucky,' Paul managed to say whilst busily chomping his way through a mound of baby potatoes.

I didn't look at them. I was having trouble getting the food down and it wasn't because of a fish bone. I deliberately focused my attention on Fleur.

'Good job you packed a dress. You're looking extremely feminine.'

For an upfront, flirty woman, who must have heard the compliment before, she seemed really pleased.

'I've packed two or three, actually.'

'We'll have to make sure they all have outings.'

'Hmmmm . . . that would be nice.'

'My Uncle George is having a party next Thursday. Well, I think it's really my Aunt Rachel's idea.'

'I'm sure it is,' put in Maria.

'What's the occasion, Harry?' Pen leaned across to help herself from the tureen.

'Thirtieth wedding anniversary.'

'Wow, that *is* an achievement.'

I found myself saying, acidly, 'It hasn't come easily. They've had to stick together through a hell of a lot of woe – on both sides.'

Pen blinked. 'That doesn't sound much like a marriage in harmony.'

'No.'

There was a tense little silence.

I saw Mike frowning. Looking directly at him, I raised one

eyebrow. Far from looking abashed, he gave a scowl. Well, whatever. My respect for him had taken a severe knock. I'd always thought of him as a straight player, a man you could trust.

Turning to Fleur, I said, 'Would you like to come to the party with me? Starts at seven.'

She gave me a beautiful smile. 'I'll wear dress number two, OK?'

'Very much OK. Especially if it's as lovely as number one. You'll have Uncle George's eyes out on stalks.

'You're sure your relations won't mind? I mean, they don't know me.'

I took a last mouthful of the delicious fish and replaced the knife and fork. 'They'll be delighted.'

And I could only hope. They would no doubt be harbouring a dream Annabel would turn up. How they'd react to my bringing another woman, I had no idea.

'If we've all finished . . . I'll bring in the pudding.' Maria collected the plates and disappeared to the kitchen.

'Harry's agreed to help us find another racehorse, Pen.'

'Oh, good.'

'He suggests we go to the horse sales at Newmarket.'

'As a market place, it will give you plenty of choice,' I said.

'I'm really interested in buying a filly, one that Mike can train for me, as a flat racer. You know, an interest in the summer months as opposed to Lytham jump racing in the wintertime?'

I nodded. 'Makes sense.' And – the unpleasant thought occurred to me – it would also give her a legitimate reason to come and see Mike.

'I could ride her for you, if I'm still here,' Fleur said.

'Yes,' Pen nodded, 'I'm sure you could.'

'Harry will be riding for us again, that's for sure,' Paul said.

'You couldn't do better.' Mike nodded.

Maria reappeared, bearing a tray. 'It's Milanese soufflé, nice and light. Guaranteed not to put pounds on.'

'Not too naughty, but still very nice.' Pen accepted her dish.

'Harry? You going to indulge?'

'Thanks, Maria, yes, why not? Your food is a privilege to eat.'

'Charmer,' she laughed, and handed out the rest of the dishes.

For a few minutes, conversation stopped as we sampled Maria's beautiful soufflé. It was not quite as low in calories as she'd made out, but what the hell. However, I discreetly removed the pistachio nut decoration. As far as I was concerned, tonight was a case of enjoying the good things as they happened, whilst trying not to think about what unpleasantness might be developing later. Whatever I personally thought of Mike's conduct, it wasn't going to alter anything.

I decided to direct my attentions to Fleur. By her acceptance of my invitation to Uncle George's party, it was clear she wanted my company. I was hoping there would be a chance to be alone with her after dinner. Where that would lead was an unknown, but all her signals were set to green.

It was a long time since I'd dated a woman. But it was nearly three years now since Annabel had chucked in the towel on our marriage. I would be all sorts of an idiot if I remained celibate any longer. Life was here, in the now, as it happened. And it wasn't fulfilled living if I remained on my own. There were no obstacles between Fleur and me. She was interested in me and she was a single woman. It was up to me to make the next move.

In the present situation, there was little chance of being alone tonight, but I figured there was a damn good chance if I volunteered to do the last round of the stables for the night. Mike would be only too pleased, I was sure. If Fleur offered to accompany me, we were home and hosed. If she didn't, well, I could invite her to – see what she said. It would be the only possible way for us to be together. As an intelligent woman, she would know that.

And then, if she agreed . . . I'd kick on.

'I'm afraid I need to change my clothes, Harry.' Fleur swished her hands down the floaty dress. 'Hardly the thing for stables.'

'Nor for the change in temperature out there.'

'Oh, I'm quite sure you can keep me warm.'

'Maybe,' I grinned, 'but I do think you should wear something not quite so thin and diaphanous.'

'You'd rather I wear Uncle Mike's long johns and top coat?' She wrinkled her nose at me then disappeared upstairs, leaving me in the kitchen. I'd not had to ask if she would accompany me. All it had taken was my offer to Mike to do the last check of the stables for the night. Almost before he'd agreed, Fleur had jumped in and said she would come with me. Mike had smirked and said what a

good idea. Under normal circumstances, we would probably have
exchanged a discreet wink between us, but tonight I wasn't playing.
Fleur was his niece and as such I understood his protectiveness, but
she was a grown woman. Very much her own woman from what
I'd seen. She needed nobody's approval for her actions.

Light footsteps came running downstairs. Fleur appeared in the
hall.

'OK, Harry, I'm ready. Let's go.'

We both took down coats from the pegs and I opened the door.
Immediately, the cold air hit us, dispelling the warmth from Mike's
central heating.

'Brrr . . . I see what you mean.' Fleur snuggled deeper into her
jacket. 'Good job I swapped my dress.'

'I preferred you in the dress, but I agree. The temperature drops
significantly at night now.'

I pulled the door closed behind us and she came in close to my
side, putting her hand into my pocket for warmth. I put an arm
around her shoulders and we went off down the yard.

It was a routine check we were doing, making sure all the horses
were rugged up and had adequate water. Checking none had got
cast. With more than forty horses, it took us quite a while, and as
we turned from the last stable, satisfied all was well, Fleur heaved
a deep sigh.

'Was that boredom, tiredness or contentment?'

She leaned in on me. 'Oh, definitely contentment, Harry. It's a
job I love, the last round of the day. There's such a feeling of placid
peacefulness about the horses. They're getting ready to sleep and
all is well.'

'And there was me thinking that the reason you volunteered to
come round with me was for the pleasure of my company. But it
was just to say nighty-night to the nags.'

She giggled and nuzzled her face into my neck.

'So,' I said, turning her round to face me, 'where do we go from
here?'

'Do I have a choice?'

'Absolutely, yes. A lady always has a choice.'

In the moonlight, I could see the glint of ice already forming on
the grass around the stable yard. We'd reached the tack room at the
end of the run of stables.

'If you're too cold, Fleur, we can go back into the house.'

'You know what you are, Harry?'

'No.'

'A gentleman. And a gentleman is a rare bird.' She reached up and wound her arms around my neck. 'I think,' she murmured in my ear, 'I think I'm very lucky to have met one.'

'And what would you like to do now you've met one?'

'Something mutually pleasurable . . . something rather like this. To begin with . . .'

She placed soft lips against mine. I kissed her back.

'There, you see, that was pleasant.'

'Oh, yes.' I tipped her chin upwards and took charge, kissing her gently, taking my time, running my fingers along her cheekbones and burying them in her long hair.

'You know something,' she whispered a little later, 'that was better than I imagined it would be.'

'I'm glad you're not disappointed.'

'Oh, I'm not. I've wanted you to kiss me from the first time I saw you in the pub.'

'Really? Let's go for a repeat performance, then.'

The second time was even better.

'Shall we go in now out of the cold, Harry?'

Disappointment ran through me. 'I thought you were finding this pleasant.'

'For what I had in mind, it might be warmer in the barn.' She ran a hand up under my jacket and slid a finger around inside my waistband. 'More comfortable as well.'

'What, with that pile of smelly muck sacks in the corner?'

'We'll be too busy to notice. I don't know about you but I can't wait.'

Her finger continued its journey round, but it had now dipped lower. If she expected to produce a growth result, I had to say she wasn't wrong. But whilst on the base level of a man desiring sex with a woman – and tonight was already heading for success – there was something about the way Fleur was producing and directing the play that was disturbingly off-putting. She was practically demanding I satisfy her by having sex. Her next words turned me off altogether.

'When I removed my dress, I also removed my thong. Thought I would make it easier for you. Save wasting time.'

I stared down at her. My male pride rebelled against the sexual dictates of a dominant woman. If there was to be seduction, I needed to be the one doing it. Up to now, I had considered her a lady. To turn down the offer wasn't chivalrous, and no doubt most men would simply take advantage of a sure thing.

But I wasn't most men. I became aware the growth result had diminished into negative return. What Fleur was offering – practically demanding – would, at best, simply satisfy a need. And I wasn't that desperate.

The last woman I'd made love to had been Annabel. *It had been an act of love, had been right . . .*

Suddenly, the present situation appeared what it was: shallow and extremely sordid.

I stood back from Fleur, removed her hand. 'I'm sorry. I'm going back to the house.'

'*What?*'

'I'm going back in. Sorry, Fleur, but—'

'It's Annabel, isn't it? You're still in love with her, aren't you?'

I could hardly say that I found her repellent because she was acting like a tramp.

I inclined my head. 'Yes.'

'You'll have to get over her one day.'

'Yes.'

'And I called you a gentleman.' She spat the words out. 'How wrong can you be?' Turning sharply, she marched away.

I watched her go. Gentleman or not, I had no regrets whatsoever. At least my self-respect was intact.

Fishing in my pocket, I drew out the keys to the large horsebox. I'd picked them up from their hook in the kitchen whilst waiting for her to change. I'd intended taking Fleur into the sleeping compartment inside the horsebox. A whole world away from rolling around near the smelly muck sacks.

I swung them from my finger a couple of times. They weren't needed, after all. I'd best go and put them back on their hook.

TWENTY-THREE

I was running late when I drove up Samuel's drive on Saturday evening.

Astonishingly, I'd had four rides earlier at Cheltenham race-course, which had resulted in two seconds and two firsts. It seemed my professional life was finally taking off. As I pulled up and stepped from the car, Chloe emerged from the house. She was dressed for a party in a red-hot scarlet dress, complete with red, strappy high heels.

'Lovely to see you, Harry.'

'Likewise.'

I held open the passenger door. She kissed my cheek, slid shapely legs in and sat in the passenger seat, laughing up at me.

'Do you think we'll stay the course?'

'At one of Barbara's parties?' I shook my head. 'It's doubtful.'

'I told Dad not to wait up.'

'Very wise.'

I engaged first gear and drove us over to Leicestershire.

As we pulled in through the wide-open gates that led up to Barbara's big house, the lights strung along the tree-lined drive twinkled in different colours.

'Wow, this is great – puts you in a party mood before you even get inside.'

I smiled at Chloe, pleased that she was being upbeat. I'd been to several parties here and was used to the trimmings. To be honest, I was relieved that she seemed to have got over the ghastly happenings that had followed the wedding. Lucinda had been her friend and losing her like that had been a terrific shock. Chloe was due an enjoyable evening.

'Barbara does her guests proud.'

'Seems to be an awful lot of them, too.'

Cars were parked in tidy rows in an adjacent paddock. I tacked on to the end of the last row and we walked over to the house.

Barbara herself answered my push on the bell.

'Harry, Chloe, so glad to see you.' Enthusiastically, she kissed cheeks and drew us inside. 'You did well this afternoon, Harry. I think two or three of my owners are about to ask for you to ride their horses.'

'Great. I'd be only too pleased.'

'How many horses do you train, Barbara?' Chloe enquired.

'I've fifty-three in at present – space for another five or six.'

'Sounds like a lot of work.'

'I've got some good lads. It's the secret to a successful yard. Keep your staff happy and you keep the horses happy as well.'

She led us through to the massive lounge.

'Come and have a drink. Now, what's your tipple?'

There was an impressively stocked bar in the corner and the wall opposite sported a roaring fire in the inglenook. It was all very welcoming and guaranteed to keep spirits high.

With a drink in our hands, Barbara introduced us to several of the other guests – mostly racing people and owners. Whilst we chatted, I scanned the room for Aiden Dobbs. I was gratified to spot him talking to one of the girl jockeys. I'd banked on him being here tonight.

He obviously had no problems with self-confidence. It poured out of every pore. It seemed to be working its magic on the girl. She was laughing and stroking his arm. I found myself hoping she'd go the distance at the end of the evening. From what Jake had said, Aiden was a man of high-octane sexual energy, who didn't like being thwarted in that department.

That thought led me to the distasteful non-event between Fleur and me. Tonight, in contrast, Chloe was genuinely warm towards me, had taken trouble with her appearance and was happy to let me take charge this evening. I knew she was no sexual predator as Fleur seemed to be. Chloe was a very attractive female and any man would be delighted to have her on his arm – or in his bed, come to that. Any man except myself, unfortunately.

With the situation surrounding her, it would be an absolute disaster for Chloe to go down that line. Her husband was sitting it out, awaiting a court case, whilst at the same time their divorce was going through the legal channels. It would most assuredly play into his hands if Chloe and I were to begin an affair.

I knew Samuel was well aware of how difficult it could get

should I make a move on Chloe. Both of us knew Chloe was not uninterested in me. The phrase he had used on my first afternoon back racing at Market Rasen had been both a statement of the fact and a veiled hint not to take advantage of her: *She already thinks you walk on water.*

Samuel was extremely protective of his daughter, and whilst acknowledging his debt to me for bringing the truth about her husband into the spotlight, he was making sure I understood where the line was drawn.

But his fears for her regarding myself were groundless. As far as I was concerned, Chloe needed all the combined help both of us could afford her, plus, in my own case, protection from Jake Smith.

Late last night, I'd logged on and checked whether Aiden Dobbs had been riding at York on the day of the accident. He had, achieving a first and third. The trainer he had ridden for was Robson. Undoubtedly, he knew John Dunston as a box driver, if not in any other way. But it was odds-on he was aware Frank Dunston was banged up. Which, taking it further, said he recognized me as a potential threat, should he be involved in anything shady, either on a racecourse or off it.

The difficulty now was how could I get into conversation with him – and how did I frame my questions without him reacting badly? Barbara had turned up the volume for the dance music, making conversation more difficult.

'Fancy a dance, Harry?' Chloe drained her glass and put it down.

I followed her example and emptied my beer.

'I warn you, I'm likely to crush your toes.' I looked down at her feet. 'Those little red things won't be any protection at all.'

She grinned. 'I'm going to risk it.'

Women seem to have more of an affinity with music than men, and are unable to resist dancing. Already, the girl with Aiden was, against his wishes, dragging him into the crush.

'Parties are great places for people to have a good time,' Chloe said, skipping nimbly out of the way of my size nines. 'It's ages since I threw a party. Have to have another one in two or three weeks.' As soon as she'd said it, her face crumpled. I steered her to the edge of the floor.

'What is it? What's the matter, Chloe?'

'Oh, Harry, that's where Lucinda met Brandon – at my party.'

She buried her face in my shirt, her shoulders shaking with emotion. 'We neither of us knew him, he wasn't invited – he gatecrashed, came with another friend.' She raised tearful eyes to mine. 'Lucinda said it was destiny. They clicked straight away. She was so in love with him . . .'

'Don't dwell on it, Chloe. At least they found happiness, even if it was for a short time.'

'Six months they knew each other, that's all.'

'She was happy, Chloe, remember that . . . well, until the last little bit.'

'Oh, she was. Brandon was so good for her. She blossomed when he was around. And her dad took to him straight away – that really made her up.'

'Some people never find true love. It's a precious commodity. The length of time doesn't come into it.'

'Yes.' She sniffed into a tissue and gathered herself. 'Sorry, it just sort of hit me . . .'

'You're doing great.' I squeezed her tight. 'Come on, let's go back and show them all how to do it.'

She nodded and allowed me to spin her back into the dance.

When that dance finished, we stayed on the floor and went for it, one tune after another. We were really letting it rip to an Elton John number, Chloe whirling around, when, taking a wild step backwards, she crashed into the couple dancing near us. The next moment, unable to save themselves, they hit the deck, legs waving in the air, the woman's dress rising up like an inverted umbrella over her face – black lace knickers exposed.

I grabbed for Chloe and managed to keep her upright.

'I'm so sorry,' Chloe gasped as she in turn helped the girl up, smoothing the dress back down over her hips.

'Not a problem. I'm fine, really, I'm fine.' The girl was laughing. 'That gave 'em all a thrill.'

I stuck out a hand and helped the man haul himself off the floor where he was laughing like a drain.

'Great view from down here.'

'Are you OK?' Chloe bent over him.

'If you've got to be brought down, might as well be decked by a beautiful woman. Makes a change from coming off a horse.'

It was Aiden Dobbs.

Recognition sparked in Chloe's face. 'I know you, don't I?'

'I think I would have remembered,' he sniggered.

'I don't mean in the biblical sense . . .' Her face had gone bright red. 'No, you came to one of my parties a few months ago.'

He stared at her. 'Chloe Simpson? Yes?'

'Yes, that's right.'

'I seem to remember gatecrashing your pad. Several others did the same. Word gets round if it's a good one.'

'That's when I catered for about thirty and ended up with more like fifty.'

'When's the next one, girl? You can put me down for it.'

He was openly ogling her now. Before his girlfriend noticed, I stepped in.

'Did you know a girl called Lucinda?'

'Eh?' He dragged his attention away from Chloe.

'She was at my party.'

'I only notice the good-looking ones, darlin'.'

'That's unkind.'

'Did you know her father?' I put in quickly.

'He was the bloke who bought it when he crashed into a horsebox, yeah?'

'Yes. And he had a woman with him.'

'That tart!' He spat the word at me.

'You obviously knew her.'

'So?'

'Weren't you keen on her at one time?'

'You move on, mate.'

'Everyone OK?' Barbara came up and put one arm around my shoulders and slid another around Aiden's waist.

'Sure, Barbara. Aren't we, doll?'

'Christ, yes! It's a million times better'n last Saturday night.'

'Why's that?' I asked innocently.

'Huh. Came off at the fifth fence at Chepstow, didn't I?'

'Afraid I missed the racing. Was away.'

'We spent the night havin' X-rays in A and E.' She giggled. 'All those beds and we couldn't use any of them.'

'Yeah,' Aiden grimaced. 'Bloody shame, that. We were there for hours.'

'Had an early breakfast at four o'clock next morning when we got home. Well,' she added, still giggling, 'I had a second one at eight.'

'Got to keep your strength up,' I said.

'Oh, listen to him.' She punched my arm playfully. 'It's Aiden who needs it kept up,' and she was off again in a paroxysm of laughter.

Grabbing her arm roughly, he said, 'Let's dance.'

'Regrettably short-fused,' Barbara murmured, smiling brightly at us. 'Do help yourselves to the goodies.' She waved vaguely in the direction of the bar and the laden tables. I took Chloe's elbow and steered her in the right direction.

Aiden's girlfriend, fluffy and giggly, had nevertheless done me a great favour. I'd been searching for a way to find out Aiden's where-abouts when Lucinda was murdered. As an unbreakable alibi, they didn't come much better than being banged up on a Saturday night in A&E. No way could he have committed the murder. And if he hadn't been involved in that, it was extremely unlikely he'd been party to the planning and execution, literally, of Jo-Jo and Louis.

I was quite sure that whoever was responsible for the first two – three if you counted the unborn baby – had been guilty of Lucinda's murder. Maybe not by his own hand, but certainly the brains, if you could call them that, behind it – the man pulling everybody else's strings.

We duly refilled our glasses and had great difficulty in choosing the least fattening of the food on offer. Well, I did. Chloe, with no such inhibitions, heaped her plate with delight.

Barbara, the ever-alert hostess, pointed to what she called the 'jockey bits'.

'Most are fat-free. I've a vested interest in keeping you boys' weight down, don't forget.'

She had imagination. The food was certainly low in calories. Little Gem lettuce leaves, used instead of a slice of bread, formed open sandwiches with choices of filling from tiny pieces of smoked salmon, cherry tomatoes, low-fat cheese spread, anchovies, chopped celery topped with minuscule chunks of lean ham . . . the list went on.

'But what about you?' Chloe asked. 'Are you not eating?'

'Dear girl, wish I could. One of my molars is playing hell. I'm off to the dentist first thing Monday morning. Haven't been to a dentist in years. I just hope he's good. Paul Wentworth recommended him. He was very satisfied with some work he had done.'

'Poor you.' Chloe pulled a face. 'Don't let it spoil your party.'

Barbara gave a belly laugh. 'Not a chance!' She drifted off to spread good cheer to the other guests.

TWENTY-FOUR

I dropped Chloe off safely at Samuel's house and received a less-than-chaste kiss. Then I drove down dark lanes that, at three a.m., were mercifully free from traffic. With no rides booked today, I intended going home to bed and having a rare and indulgent lie-in.

The quietness of the roads required little concentration and the meeting with Aiden Dobbs replayed through my mind. I wondered if the girlfriend was quite as fluffy as she made out or whether I had been set up. Aiden seemed to be unarguably in the clear, but something he'd said was niggling at me. Until I could recall what it was, work out the meaning, it would continue to bug me.

Jake Smith was expecting a report back about Dobbs, but although my gut instinct knew something wasn't right, all I could do was put forward the bald facts. He'd been in A&E, all right.

So that left any number of unknown business associates who might bear grudges – and one prison inmate.

Reaching the cottage, I swung in over the gravel and parked by the kitchen door. I was fairly sure there were no intruders tonight; I hadn't seen a car for miles. Leo, in his basket by the Rayburn, took a dim view of being woken up at four in the morning. He was attempting to make up the lost catnaps from the previous few nights spent queen hunting.

I secured the back door, waved him back to sleep and switched off all the lights. My own bed was waiting and very welcome.

What seemed seconds later, I was awakened by bright sunlight assaulting my eyeballs and the strident tones of, ironically, 'The Great Escape' assaulting my ears. Squinting and cursing, I checked the time, almost exactly noon – I couldn't believe it, noon? – and put a stop to Steve McQueen's blast.

'Yes?'

'Is that Harry Radcliffe?'

'Yes.'

'Sorry if I've disturbed your Sunday lunch . . .'

'You haven't.'

'Oh, oh, good . . .'

'Who is this?'

'We have met – well, just briefly, at the wedding.'

I scrubbed a hand through my hair, swung my legs out and sat on the side of the bed.

'You mean Lucinda Frame's wedding?'

'I'm Tom Jackson. I work at North Shore Hotel, as a waiter.'

'Right, I remember you now.' And I did. The whey-faced young man waiting anxiously for his first child to be born.

'I need to see you, speak to you.'

'About what?'

'That night.'

'Can't you tell me over the phone?'

'No way!' His voice had risen, shrill . . . barely in control.

'Hold it . . . just calm down. I take it this is important, right?'

'Oh, yes.' His voice dropped almost to a whisper. 'Oh my God, yes.'

'How about you drive over to see me?'

'I don't have a car, I can't drive. And I'm really stuck doing back-to-back shifts down here.'

'Can't you send me an email, a text?'

'I'm not putting *anything* in writing.'

'OK, look, we'll set a date. I can't come immediately. I've stuff to do, commitments at this end. Probably be the end of the week. That OK?'

'Have to be. It's just . . . now I've come to a decision, well, I need to hand over to you.'

'Shall we say Friday evening?'

'Yes.'

'I'll be at North Shore Hotel around eight. In the bar. See you then.'

I stood under the shower and ran it hot and long. Whatever it was Tom wanted to speak to me about, it was another piece of the jigsaw at least – maybe a *vital* piece that joined up the rest. But, then again, maybe it wasn't important – not to me. Obviously, to *him* it was a hot coal he wanted to drop into my hand.

But there were other things I had to do first, things I'd already set in motion that had to be completed and couldn't wait. Maybe they'd only serve to eliminate people, but I still needed to complete them.

His phone call had come out of nowhere, unexpected. I didn't know what had prompted him to ring. And I didn't know where it would lead, if anywhere. I wasn't banking on it being the Holy Grail. For now, he would have to wait.

In this game, I trusted one person only: myself.

Despite the frost, I was distinctly glad to be back in Mike's stable yard at six o'clock the following morning. I'd spent the whole of the previous afternoon turning my eyes square, peering at a computer screen. But by the time I'd logged off there was a treasure chest of information I'd discovered about Louis Frame's involvement in different business enterprises.

His brother, Edward, had commented that Louis had a 'finger in lots of pies'. He undoubtedly had, but the flavour was always the same. The man had catholic tastes but they all had a central, connecting theme: horses and horse racing. The various pies included suppliers of horse rugs and coolers, shavings and straw bales for bedding, hay, horse nuts, farrier equipment, saddlery and horseboxes.

Louis must have had a wide range of business contacts. It would certainly account for a good proportion of the guests at the wedding being drawn from horse racing circles.

What the information pointed out was that Louis Frame had been an extremely wealthy man. By spreading his wealth around, he'd insulated himself against being brought down should any of the companies descend into bankruptcy. I wondered about the possible knock-on effect to racing engendered by his sudden demise. But as I saw the wide scope of his business activities, my hopes of discovering his killer – never high – had dropped down the pan. It was like looking at the results of a stone chucked into a lake – ongoing circles, ever widening, that endlessly repeated themselves and pointed nowhere.

Still, this afternoon's sortie might turn up something interesting. At least where I was headed, it would be warm. Here at the stables, it was not only the weather that was decidedly frosty. I was getting a double dose from Fleur and Mike. I could understand well enough why Fleur had sent me to Coventry, but I wasn't sure why Mike had. It had to have been something she'd said to him about me. And somehow I didn't think it would be the truth. Couldn't be, because that would show her up in a very distasteful fashion.

I shrugged it off. When placed against having to speak to Jake Smith later today, it wasn't important.

Inside White Lace's stable it was considerably warmer. Horses were big animals and their sheer size gave off a lot of body heat. I picked up a Dandy brush and worked up a sweat grooming her coat and brushing with long sweeping strokes down the fall of her tail. She had fully recovered from the accident and was in fine shape. Turning her head, she blew gustily. It was like a hot air dryer being switched on.

It looked as though she had a pretty good chance of making the frame in the two races Mike had picked for her. I was pleased for Chloe that the mare was turning out so well. There was plenty of unpleasantness in store for Chloe regarding the result of the court case and her impending divorce. At least going racing and watching her horse come home with the winners would balance out some of the big negatives.

I tacked up White Lace and led her outside to join the rest of the lads on first lot. Fleur, I noticed, was keeping her distance and would be riding back marker. Her behaviour had been a sad eye-opener, and now that she was cold-shouldering me it was casting a shadow that wasn't lost on the stable lads. The last thing I wanted was to be the cause of disharmony in the yard.

'Harry, would you take the lead,' called Mike, 'and the rest of you fall in behind.'

We set off in a string into the bright early morning, the horses snorting white plumes of breath that hung in the cold air, iron shoes ringing on the frosty concrete and striking sparks.

I put everything on the back burner and concentrated on my riding.

Normally, at the end of morning stables, I would have stayed on at Mike's if I wasn't booked for a ride. But today, for the first time ever, I finished morning stables with relief and drove back home.

I was expecting a letter, but it was with conflicting emotions that I went to inspect the mail box. It would be a massive relief if the letter hadn't arrived. But at best that would simply be a rain-check job. I'd still have to face dealing with it tomorrow.

I pulled out two pieces of junk mail – and a franked letter. Taking them into the office, I chucked the junk into the wastepaper basket and opened the letter. The Visiting Order that would allow access to see and speak to Darren Goode, currently being detained at Her Majesty's pleasure in Nottingham Prison, slid out on to the desk.

I read it carefully, reached for my mobile and rang the prison. The visit – a rain-check job after all, because they required twenty-four hours' notice *after* receipt of the Order – was arranged for tomorrow. It had taken more than a week to get to this point, having set wheels turning immediately after seeing Alice. However much I might like to defer the visit, it was still irritating not to be able to press on.

I'd already begun to feel the same sense of increasing pace that I'd experienced with the murder at Leicester races. Nothing concrete, just a gut instinct that events were beginning to take over.

I drove down the A611 Hucknall Road in Nottingham and turned off down Perry Road. The prison was well signposted.

If I'd thought the procedure for a visit protracted, it was nothing compared with the security system in place when I actually arrived. Strictly routine – it was classed as a Category B prison – but by the time I'd filled forms, had an X-ray, a body search, a photograph and fingerprints taken, plus been sniffed for drugs by an enthusiastic spaniel, I felt like a criminal myself.

From the visitors' centre, we climbed the steep rise to the prison in groups of ten and were admitted into the blue-painted visiting room. Inside, it contained about thirty tables with attached chairs – all bolted securely to the floor – and made of clear Perspex. Practical, but bloody weird.

If ever I entertained ideas of breaking the law, all I needed to keep this side of the line was to remember coming here.

Across the table, Darren Goode glowered at me.

'So, what does the top jock want?'

'Hello, Mr Goode. Thanks for agreeing to see me.'

'You're the bod who sorted the Leicester races murder, right?'

'Yep. Guess I'll never live it down.'

'Word is, you're being fingered to sort out something else.'

He shot a sideways glance at the nearest prison officer as he patrolled past. There were prison officers stationed by each of the doors as well. I took the hint and couched my reply carefully.

'I've been to see Alice.' The effect on him was electric. He reared forward in his seat, eyes glaring hatred.

'You fucking keep away from my wife.'

I spread both hands, 'Calm it. We just talked, OK? She's on your side.' He eased back in his seat. 'Look, can you tell me anything about that car crash?'

'Like what?' he muttered.

'Alice wants to help if she can, but she doesn't know anything. Do you?'

'I know that bastard Frame opened his big mouth, dropped me in it.'

'But you were knocking off goods and falsifying the delivery notes for the horse supplies, weren't you?'

'Screw you,' he hissed.

'OK, Louis Frame found out and it increased your sentence, but you didn't organize his death, did you?'

'Don't expect any sob sympathy from me. Served the bastard right.'

'And Jo-Jo? She died too.'

He looked down at his bitten nails. 'Jake Smith's sister . . .' He shook his head. 'You don't go after anything of Jake's if you want to keep breathing.' He looked up sharply at me. 'Jake's got a bloody long reach; you should remember that.'

'Oh, I will.'

'Being banged up don't mean you can't contact mates on the outside. Works the other way an' all . . .'

'I'll remember.'

He leaned forward. 'Is Alice all right? She won't let on. Wonder if she's managing. I need to know.'

'Yeah, upset because of Jo-Jo's death, but otherwise OK.'

He nodded. I got the impression the only reason he'd agreed to see me was to find out. Well, OK, life's rules outside operated even under these circumstances – it was still a trade-off of information.

'Ah, she would be. Jo-Jo was her best mate, y'know.'

'So, it wasn't Jo-Jo who was the target?'

''Course it bloody wasn't. You thick or what?'

I didn't rise to the insult. He'd been speaking the truth. I'd never seriously considered Jo-Jo was anything other than an innocent victim, and now Darren had confirmed it.

'So, who do you reckon organized the murders?'

'If you think I'd tell you, even if I knew . . .' He snorted derisively.

'Do you know?'

'All I know is loose ends get finished off.'

I stared at him. 'Are you telling me there will be another murder?'

He shrugged. 'You're the detective. You work it out.'

TWENTY-FIVE

I reached home and poured a stiff whisky. God, what an experience. Not one I was going to repeat again if I could possibly avoid it.

Picking Leo up – he was in an affectionate mood, no doubt having caught up on lost sleep – I carried whisky and cat through to the conservatory. The late-afternoon sun, albeit a feeble offering compared with the high-season version, still provided a pool of warmth on the settee and I sat down with Leo on my knee. Sipping the restorative golden fluid and stroking the soft, sun-warmed fur, my nerve ends gradually ceased doing the zither dance.

How much information the prison visit had offered me was questionable. Certainly, it pinpointed Louis Frame as target. Jake Smith had been right about that. Jo-Jo, unfortunately, had been in the wrong place at the wrong time.

Darren Goode wasn't giving much away. I was certain he knew more than he'd let on, but just how much? The main disquieting thing was his oblique reference to another murder still to be carried out.

I took a gulp of whisky. I needed to press on, try to dig up some concrete evidence from somewhere before anyone else got injured.

It was a shame that having succeeded in calming my nerves, I was about to fire them up again.

Jake Smith answered my call on the second ring. 'You wanted an update on Aiden Dobbs—'

'Hold it. Not now . . . Meet me.'

'Where?'

'Make it down by the river. You can tell me when you see me, not over a phone.'

'Sorry. I don't think "down by the river" is the right place. I might end up getting chucked in.'

'You might.' He gave a low chuckle. 'Don't you trust me, Harry boy?'

'Afraid not.'

'Make it a pub, eh, neutral ground?'

'OK. The Royal Oak, here, at eight.'

He was still chuckling softly when I switched off my phone.

It was gone five o'clock. I pushed the cat gently from my lap and went in search of food. The fridge was three-quarters empty but there were eggs. Two scrambled on a slice of Hovis did the job nicely.

I took my supper tray back into the conservatory to eat. Not quite the condemned man's breakfast, but something along those lines. It didn't stop me enjoying the meal; I'd had nothing since breakfast. The trick to keeping weight down was to eat smaller portions and chew a whole lot more. After twenty minutes, the brain signalled full.

I'd got by using the method since my first winning ride way back when I was eighteen. In life, it paid to know who was on your side – your friend – and who was the enemy. Just where Jake Smith fitted in, I wasn't sure right now. It depended on the final outcome. It might have been safe meeting him by the river, but I wasn't about to take the chance. Inside a pub was a whole lot safer.

At ten to eight, I left the cottage and took the car down into the village to The Royal Oak. It was the pub where earlier in the year I'd met Uncle George. The meeting had led to a mind-blowing revelation. Tonight's meeting was unlikely to even come close in terms of emotional clout, but at least I could tell Jake his sister's death was not a premeditated murder. It was an accident. Not a lot of comfort – he'd still lost her – but it was some sort of closure. Especially if I wasn't able to come up with the answers to who Frame's murderer was.

What I needed was a solid lead I could chase up – and I didn't have one.

'Evening, Mr Radcliffe.' The barman raised a querying eyebrow.

'I'll have a fruit juice, thanks – grapefruit.' My supper needed a dose of vitamin C to help the absorption of iron. I needed all the strength I could get right now.

I took the drink over by the bay window beneath the old ceiling beams and looked out over the pavement. People were walking by, heading for the pub, to visit friends – doing normal things. Here I was, about to link up with an ex-con, a man who had done time for inflicting grievous bodily harm on a fellow human being. It was bizarre.

I suddenly felt very alone, isolated and strangely hollow inside. I had no wife beside me, no children. There was nobody I could call. I couldn't tell Chloe of the potential danger she was in, couldn't tell Annabel in her delicate condition, couldn't speak to Mike. He wasn't speaking to me, for whatever reason.

The one person I didn't want to speak to was coming through the doors right now – Jake Smith.

He stood, one pace inside, and swept the pub with an assessing gaze. I lifted my glass two inches from the table. With the merest nod, he ordered a drink and came across. As I watched him coming towards me, I realized with blinding clarity that I was back in the zone of not being able to trust anyone. It was an unpleasant, lonely place. I'd recognized it because I'd been here before.

Being suspicious of everybody had been essential whilst I was embroiled in what the rest of the world seemed to insist on calling the *Leicester races murder*.

Trusting only myself had been essential for my survival.

The situation I was now trapped in was following a similar path.

'Fill me in, then, Harry boy.' Jake Smith dropped heavily into the opposite seat at the table.

'You asked me to check out Aiden Dobbs. Well, on the Saturday night when Lucinda was murdered, he was in the hospital accident and emergency unit. Suspected fractured wrist.'

'On his say-so?'

'His and his fluffy girlfriend. She stayed with him, she says, until they were discharged in the early hours of Sunday morning.'

'Yeah, but that's only an alibi for Frame's daughter being offed.' I winced at his words.

'I agree. But in my book, these murders are all linked. Dobbs was actually riding at Doncaster the day of the crash.'

'So, he was around, then.'

I shrugged. 'So were an awful lot of other people.'

He stared moodily into his beer. 'An' that's all you've got to tell me?'

'Been visiting your hotel today.'

'Eh?'

'Nottingham Prison.'

'And?' He narrowed his eyes warningly.

'Spoke to Darren Goode. I think he knows more than he's letting on, but he did confirm one thing . . .'

'Which is?'

'Jo-Jo getting killed wasn't a premeditated murder. The target was definitely Frame. Her death was an accident caused by simply being in his car at the time he crashed.'

I reached for my glass and took a slow drink to avoid looking at Jake.

A silence, taut and practically vibrating, seemed to enclose our table.

When I finally emptied my glass and looked up, he was staring straight through me, eyes blank to the present.

I waited, unwilling to speak first.

'So . . . If she hadn't met him, she'd still be alive.'

I didn't answer. He had to pick his own way through the minefield of emotions that were obviously going through him.

The next morning, I gave Mike's stables a miss and stayed home to write up copy for my newspaper column and decide what my next move was.

For once, the writing proved the easier.

I made a strong coffee and ran through where my investigations had led. A chance remark at Barbara's party needed checking out. It could lead nowhere, but if my gut feeling was to be trusted, it could prove an alternative way of looking at the whole situation.

I reached for the telephone directory and checked out a name and address. I was lucky: the number was listed. I dialled and listened to the ring tones trilling out.

'Harry Radcliffe here. If you're not tied up this afternoon, could I drive over and have a word?'

Unfortunately not was the answer, but if I didn't mind driving over to Clive Unwin's yard, we could definitely have words there.

I didn't mind.

I left it until much later, because it was a racing stable, avoiding the traditionally slack time prior to afternoon stables.

I drove to Leicestershire and arrived at just after four o'clock. For the last ten miles, I'd been following a truck that sported the name *B & R Lutens*. It was no surprise when the vehicle turned in at the entrance to Unwin's stables. With no other stables close by, it was an odds-on bet. No peeling paint here, no wisps of hay lying around, everything pristine, and a big three-sided run of stables.

Brandon himself emerged from the cab. I swung the car in behind. He hesitated, then recognized me.

'Hello, Mr Radcliffe.'

'How're things?'

He screwed up his lips. 'Oh, you know . . . best to keep working.'

'Yes.'

He was shorter, stockier than I remembered. His face had lost the stark whiteness I'd noticed the last time I'd seen him coming out of the leather room after being interviewed by the police.

He fished in his pocket and drew out a business card.

'Never gave Mr Grantley this. Could you pass it on?'

'Sure.'

'You working here? Doing a write-up for your paper?'

'No, no, just talking teeth with Paul Wentworth.' Seeing the puzzled look, I laughed. 'As in dental work.'

'Oh . . . oh, right. The thing is, do you think you could mention my firm somewhere in your next column? Bit of a cheek, I'll give you, but, well . . . we could do with the publicity. A lot of people read your stuff, you know. You're very popular.'

'Thanks. Good to know. I'd rather be riding in a race, but it does bring in some coffers.'

'Exactly.'

'If I get the chance, I'll see what I can do.'

'Thanks, appreciate it.'

'Can't promise, of course.'

'No, no, I quite understand.'

Footsteps approached and we looked up as Unwin and Wentworth joined us.

I nodded to them. 'Good to see you.'

'And you, Harry,' Unwin said. 'Was going to give you a ring. One of my owners requested you ride his horse.'

'Thank you very much. Be pleased to.'

'Good, good.' Unwin rubbed his hands together. 'I'll let them know you're on.' He turned his attention to Brandon. 'Delivering the full order?' Receiving a nod, he continued, 'Unload it in the feed room, please. You'll find Pete, the head lad, in there.'

I remembered Louis Frame had had a business interest in the firm – one of his many. I wondered how much it had affected Lutens to lose the financial backing of so influential and wealthy a silent partner. But in view of his personal loss, I supposed its effect had been diluted. It would be later when the impact would be felt, although it already looked like he was trying to drum up more business.

I turned to Paul Wentworth. 'How are you doing?'

'Fine, just fine. I've come to have a look at Lytham.'

'Shall we . . .?'

We walked across the yard to Lytham's stable. I'd found the horse to be very genuine when I'd ridden him at Huntingdon.

'We'll set a date to go to the yearling sales at Newmarket,' Paul said. 'I'll leave it to your discretion. Just ring and let me know. I'll make myself available.'

'Will do.'

Hearing voices outside his stable, Lytham stuck his head over the open half-door and whickered in recognition.

'He knows me; I'm here an awful lot. You're a great lad, aren't you?' Paul rubbed the soft nose and palmed the horse a polo mint. Lytham crunched with pleasure. 'So, what did you want to see me about?'

I leaned in and patted the strong muscled neck.

'Just something I heard at Barbara's party the other night.'

'Barbara Maguire?'

'Yes. Apparently, you passed on the name of a decent dentist because she's having trouble with her teeth.'

'Well, I'd been to a good bloke a few months ago, a local chap. I gave her his name.'

'Which dentist was it?'

'The firm's name is White, Hubbard and Brownley. I saw Mr White.'

'Let's hope he's helped Barbara. She was going to see him last Monday.'

'Why did you want to know that?' He cocked his head to one side.

'Oh, it's not classified,' I laughed.

But even as I said it, I realized it might not be a good idea to give away information. The killer was not in my sights yet. I needed to maintain the self-preservation principle of not trusting anyone.

'How's Pen, by the way?' Not that I wanted to know, but I needed a distraction from the way the conversation was going.

'Going around like a dreamy teenager.'

'Oh?'

'It's called love. Seems as though when it strikes in mature years, it has an even more knock-over effect.' He chuckled. 'Still, I'm so pleased to see her happy.'

I looked at him in bewilderment. This was his wife he was talking about. It didn't add up.

'You'll have to explain.'

'Should have thought you'd noticed. After all, Mike's your best mate, isn't he?'

'Yes, but . . .'

'Regular couple of lovebirds, they are.'

I gaped at him. 'But I thought you and Pen were husband and wife.'

'Good God, no.' He cracked up. 'No, no, Harry. You've really got the wrong end of the stick. It'll have Pen in stitches when I tell her. She's my sister. We just live in the same house, that's all. It's convenient – well, it has been up until now.'

Relief wasn't the right word: an enormous weight rolled off.

'I'm a complete fool, Paul. You'll have to excuse me.'

No wonder I'd been getting funny, disapproving looks from Mike at the dinner table the other night. And it certainly explained his frosty manner. I'd assumed, wrongly, it was because of Fleur.

I needed to see him and straighten things out. How could I have been such an idiot?

TWENTY-SIX

'I owe you an apology, Mike.'

He grunted and pushed a mug of strong coffee towards me across the kitchen table. Six o'clock on a cold morning wasn't the best time, but this needed to be done immediately.

'You can bawl me out as much as you like. I've been an idiot.'

'As regards?'

'You.'

He scowled. 'What are you on about?'

'I got hold of entirely the wrong idea. I thought you and Pen were, well, getting close.'

Mike spluttered over his coffee. 'Not your business.'

'I agree. Except I *thought* Pen was married to Paul. Seems they are brother and sister.'

Mike stared at me for a moment and then exploded into great gales of laughter. 'Harry, you *are* a bloody idiot. Reaching across the table, he slapped me on the shoulder, still chuckling. 'Do you really think I'd make a play for a married woman? Come on, Harry, you should know me better than that.'

'Couldn't believe it, to be truthful. But I can recognize the symptoms.'

'Never thought it would get me again, old Cupid's arrow. But there you go. Just when you think you've got a handle on your life, that's when it strikes you. Can't deny it, mate, I think she's bloody marvellous.'

We stared at each other, then suddenly we were smiling and shaking our heads.

'Stupid buggers, aren't we?' he said. 'Heading into deep water – and possibly deep pain into the bargain – and we're still paddling as fast as we can go.'

'Sense doesn't come into it.' I agreed.

'It never did.'

'Still, it's taken a long time, Mike.'

'Since I lost Monica?'

I nodded.

'Never thought I'd find a woman to measure up to her. It's odd really – not a matter of measuring up at all. Pen's her own person, totally different. Did you know she's a widow? That's the reason she's living with Paul at the moment. She's had a rough ride this last year. Anyway, my feelings for her are different somehow, can't explain it. Monica's still my wife – you know, inside my head – but Pen is . . .' He floundered.

'Pen is your route to a new life. One that doesn't need to detract in any way from Monica.'

'Yes.' He seized on the concept. 'Yes, you're right, Harry. There's room for both of them, plenty of room. Pen's not crowding Monica out, not at all.'

'Pleased for you, Mike.'

'I know it's taken me a bloody long time. Don't make that mistake. It's high time you found somebody. I'd hoped Fleur might do the trick. But seems not, eh?'

'No, sorry, Mike. Doesn't work like that. Oh, I did think it might myself, but no' – I shook my head firmly – 'it's not going to happen.'

There was absolutely no need to go into sordid details. Fleur was family, his niece. He didn't need to hear anything damaging to her character.

I finished my coffee and rinsed out the mug. 'Better get some work done.'

Out in the yard, Fleur might still be giving me the frosty treatment, and I could understand that, but it was great things were OK again between Mike and me. And, thank goodness, I was riding at Ludlow this afternoon.

I had two rides, in the last two races on the card. Because the rides followed each other, it meant two stable lads were needed, plus the box driver, so I'd opted to drive down in my own car.

To say it was a cold day, there was a gratifying crowd of intrepid racegoers. With the roaring cheers that went up as I flashed past to win the second race, after already winning the preceding one, I think most of them had placed bets on me.

It was great to bring home two successive winners, giving me not only a decent bonus of prize money but also a priceless confidence boost. It was only the second time in months that I'd brought off a double.

Stripping off the silks in the changing room after weighing in, I was feeling pretty good. Until one of the other jockeys, on his way out, spoke to me.

'Have you heard about Dunston's wife, Harry?'

'No, what about her?'

'We all know about the aggro between you and Dunston, but go easy on him, mate. Lilly fell downstairs last night. They took her to hospital, but she was dead by the time they got there.'

His words shook me. There would be no chance of seeing her son, Frank, now. The effect on Dunston must be devastating.

'I'm really sorry. More than I can say.'

He nodded, picking up his saddle and jacket. 'Thought it best if you knew about it.'

'Yes, yes, thanks.'

'Well, seeing as how it was you who found out about Frank Dunston and got him banged up . . .'

I winced at his words. Why did it sound as though I was the one who should be guilty? Right then, I wished I'd never been involved in the whole mess at Leicester races. It had changed a lot of people's lives. But I'd had no choice. Not with Silvie being a target.

I walked out of the changing room and went to find Mike down in the racecourse stables.

He was still on a high from the two wins for his stable. I filled him in on the unpleasant news. Whether he realized the implications the news heralded was doubtful. But I wasn't going to spell it out.

'I don't want to run the risk of bumping into Dunston if he's in the horsebox park right now. So, I'm driving straight home, OK? See you at the stables in the morning.'

I changed my mind. Over a light supper of steamed plaice, which had Leo sensuously winding in and out of my legs whilst it cooked, I realized time was fast running out. The events of yesterday had precipitated everything. Tomorrow afternoon, I was riding at Fakenham racecourse and in the evening it was Uncle George's party.

I didn't have time to ride out for Mike; there was someone I needed to see urgently.

Finishing my meal, I washed the dishes and rang Mike.

'About tomorrow morning: no can do. Forgot, there's something I must do that can't wait, OK?'

'Is it dangerous?'

I had to smile. Mike was far from stupid; he knew I had my nose down on scent.

'Could be.' We'd been here before. And how thankful I'd been to have his help that time.

'My back-up's here, you know that.'

'I know, Mike, and thanks. Later when I see the whites of his eyes, possibly, but not tomorrow.'

I switched off my mobile. I needed no distractions.

Reaching for a notepad, I made a graph of the murders and

locations, principal suspects, times and places they'd been; clues I'd uncovered, only half suspected, some only guessed at. A lot of information had still to be uncovered, so it wasn't entirely comprehensive, but gaps could be jumped.

I poured a whisky and sat down on the settee, put my feet up and relaxed. Leo immediately jumped up on to my stomach, curled into a ball and made himself comfortable, purring contentedly. Half closing my eyes, I ran all the available data through my mind.

The human brain is said to be millions of times more efficient and sophisticated than any computer. The HOLMES police computer is a massive help in analyzing data. But if the brain is so incredibly superior, I was happy to put in all the information and relax whilst, hopefully, it did the hard work of linking up and sorting out for me.

My method, lying on a settee with a whisky and a purring cat, certainly beat developing square eyes, mouse clicking and typing.

It was probably on a par with the proven method of using water as a medium for getting the mind to provide illumination. When writing her detective fiction, Dame Agatha Christie had lain in the bath to help develop her plots, and the master thriller writer, Dick Francis, had walked down the beach and stood up to his middle in the ocean for inspiration. They hadn't been disappointed. If the settee version didn't work, I could try my own bath.

A trail was slowly becoming apparent, but I needed to force the pace before anyone else was injured.

It crossed my mind that Lilly Dunston could possibly have been pushed down the stairs. But almost immediately I dismissed the theory. Having Lilly alive was certainly much more beneficial to the man behind the scenes. It kept John Dunston on a short lead and obedient. He was only responding because of Lilly's needs. Without her dependency, the hold over him was gone.

I spent a couple of hours letting half-formed theories run through my mind, but with nothing concrete coming to the surface, I gave my brain a rest and went off to bed.

Perhaps tomorrow morning's meeting would supply another piece of jigsaw and fill in one of the gaps that would enable me to see a lot more of the picture.

Next morning, when the clock got round to an acceptable time to make a house visit, I pointed the Mazda north towards Newark.

Twenty minutes' driving saw me parking up in Wellington Street. I locked the car and walked up to number twenty-nine.

As I lifted a hand to knock, there was a shadowed movement behind the curtains. So, my visit hadn't been a waste. An older version of Jake opened the door all of six inches and eyed me up and down.

'Yes?'

'Mr Fred Smith?'

'Yes.'

'My name's Harry Radcliffe.'

'I knows that. Seen you on television, racin'.'

'May I have a word?'

'About what?'

'The events that led to Carl's death.'

It was a toss-up whether he would cooperate or not, and I could only hope. If he denied me access, there was nothing I could do about it, and it was crucial to ask him some questions – and get answers.

Very slowly, the door eased open.

'Can't see what good it'll do. Won't bring him back . . . or our Jo-Jo.' But he jerked his head, indicating I was to step inside.

Fred Smith himself posed little in the way of a physical threat. I could give him thirty years, and bodily he looked in poor shape – thin as a stick and with a week's growth he hadn't bothered to shave off. However, I needed to know if the real danger was some-where in the house.

'Is Jake here?'

'Nah.'

I edged in through the half-opened door. It was immediately closed behind me. An unpleasant smell of unwashed bodies and old, lingering cooking overlaid by a distinct fug of cigarette smoke pervaded the house.

Smith led me through to the lounge. It hadn't seen a vacuum cleaner in a long, long time and every surface was cluttered with accumulated junk and newspapers all covered in a good layer of dust. In the centre of the room was a coffee table ringed by numerous mugs and beer cans, and an ashtray that was trying very hard to hold all the cigarette butts stubbed out in it, but losing the fight.

'You're the bloke who found out who killed Carl, ain't you? Our Jake reckons you're helping to find Jo-Jo's killer an' all. That right?'

'Yes.'

'So, what do you want from me?' His eyes bored into my face.

'Mr Smith, if I could alter things, believe me, I wouldn't hesitate.'

'Nothin's going to bring my kids back.' He sat down on a sagging settee and lit a cigarette with trembling fingers.

'It was certainly my fault I clouted Carl when we both came off at Huntingdon racecourse back in March, although it was an accident. But it still knocked his teeth out.'

'Ah, it did. He had to have a set of false ones made.'

'Mr Smith, do you know the name of the dentist who made those teeth?' I waited with barely held-down anticipation. If I could find out, the trail would be red-hot.

'Wait here. I'll fetch it.' He heaved himself out of the chair.

I didn't have time to ask him what he was talking about. He disappeared and I heard him climbing the stairs.

Minutes later, he was back holding a small box. It looked for all the world like a child's very small shoebox in plain brown cardboard. He lifted off the lid and showed me.

Inside, it was empty except for a bedding of tissue paper and a folded sheet of paper that looked like an invoice.

'They came in this 'ere box. 'Course, they was only the plaster cast, like – the first impression, Carl called them. His real ones was buried with him.' He took a deep drag from the cigarette wobbling dangerously in his trembling hand. 'These 'ere plaster 'uns was stolen. Reckon it must have been done at Carl's wake. Nobody else has been to the house.' He shook his head. 'Don't know who it was. All I knows is everybody who came to the wake was racin' folk.'

'Can I ask you: was John Dunston one of the people at the wake?'

He peered suspiciously at me. 'You reckon it was him?'

'Was he at the wake?' I persisted.

'Aye, he was.'

'Thank you. And the invoice . . .' I pointed to the folded paper inside the little box. 'Could I see the name of the dentist who supplied them?'

In answer, he took the sheet of paper and unfolded it.

Across the top was the name of the firm: White, Hubbard and Brownley.

TWENTY-SEVEN

When I'd gone up to bed last night, I'd left out the graph of suspects and events on my desk. Now, there was one more piece of jigsaw to add in. Even as I wrote down what I'd learned from Fred Smith, I could see the connections being formed. To complete this particular portion of the picture, I needed to make a phone call to Paul Wentworth. If what I suspected proved correct, it would really bring the investigation to life.

A phone call to Jake Smith was also on the cards. I didn't hold great hopes that he could answer the one question I needed to ask, but it was worth a phone call to find out.

I went into the kitchen, made a strong coffee and took it back to my desk. In between taking slurps, I mentally rearranged this latest line of approach. At last, there were links forming; not chain-links maybe – more tenuous, gossamer ones – but still they were there, and the more I played about with the 'what ifs' the more I could see which way the trail was leading. A surge of excitement was building inside me as one name kept flashing like a neon sign in my mind's eye.

Finishing my drink, I reached for the phone and dialled Paul Wentworth's number. There was no way of disguising what I needed to know. The only way was to ask him straight out. But if he hedged around and wanted to know why, he was going to be disappointed. Right now, I needed to hold all the aces. The slightest hint of what my investigation had uncovered would be disastrous.

'Hello, Paul. Harry Radcliffe here.' We exchanged small talk for a minute or two and then I pitched my question.

'Do you remember I was asking about the dentist you recommended to Barbara Maguire?' He did. 'I meant to ask you how you found out about him. I mean, you and Pen are relative newcomers to the area. Was it the case that you had a different dentist before you moved to Boxton?'

He confirmed that yes, he had used a different one where he'd lived before.

'So how did you find out about White, Hubbard and Brownley?'

Then I waited. His reply brought a wide smile to my face. His answer confirmed my suspicions. Lying on the settee had worked magnificently. I had a hard time holding myself in check, but I thanked him and replaced the receiver.

Then I bellowed 'Yes!' and punched a triumphant fist in the air. The chase was on.

The journey to Fakenham proved frustratingly slow. It wasn't like a straightforward trip up or down the country. Going across took much longer. Jockeys were well used to a toe-down approach when travelling to racecourses, but it wasn't always possible and the racecourses located in the east of the country were notoriously slower journeys, prone to hold-ups. Today, however, it helped that the one race I was booked to ride in was the last one on the card.

The horse, Grey Shadow, wasn't one from Mike's stable. It was a ride I'd been fortunate to pick up when the jockey who was due to ride him got dropped the previous day at Ludlow. I'd ridden two winners and as a result was high profile at the meeting. The injured jockey's trainer had approached me, offered the ride at Fakenham and I'd gratefully accepted.

When I arrived, I left my car in the owners, trainers and jockeys' car park and went straight to the weighing room, but during the journey I'd used the time to run over Paul Wentworth's answer and where it fitted the jigsaw. His answer had been the one I'd been desperately hoping for.

All I needed now was for Jake Smith's answer to one more question. His mobile phone had been switched off this morning and I was loath to try Fred Smith's landline. The state of the man spelled out he wasn't coping with his double bereavement. Jo-Jo's death had undoubtedly brought back all the trauma and grief of losing Carl. Two deaths were too heavy a burden to bear. But I had to speak to Jake. Just that one question to ask. If I got the right answer, the killer was in my sights.

Providing proof, though . . . now that would be something else.

Unable to contain my impatience any longer, I left the weighing room and threaded my way through the crowd of racegoers to the pre-parade ring. Standing by the rail, I dialled Jake's number. This time his phone was switched on and he answered straight away.

'Hello, Jake. Been trying to get you earlier.'

'Yeah. Stayed over last night at Alice's. Didn't want distracting. Know what I mean, Harry?' He chuckled softly.

His words threw me for a minute. I'd gained the impression Alice had been wary of him. However . . .

'I went to see your father this morning. He showed me the box that Carl kept his false teeth in – the ones made of plaster.'

'The old man's taking it bad.'

'Yes, I could see that. I'm sorry. Losing family is bloody hard.'

'You can say that again.' The menacing edge in his voice was chilling.

'I just need to ask you something. How come Carl used that particular dentist? Was it his usual one?'

'No. Never went near 'em, did he? Except this time – well, with a mouthful of teeth gone, like, he'd got to do something. A man needs to eat.'

'Yes,' I said, well aware that, accident or not, it had been my fault. 'So, do you know why he went to that particular firm?'

'Someone recommended them.'

'Who was it, do you know?' I waited in suspense for his answer. He did know – and he told me.

If I hadn't been surrounded by racegoers, I'd have whooped out loud in triumph and punched the air again.

The surge of adrenalin lasted until my race. It added an extra super-charge of energy that carried me along with it. I rode an inspired, punching finish and Grey Shadow flew past the post five lengths ahead of the field.

It was a great feeling to ride into the number-one spot in the winners' enclosure. To know everyone was rooting for me. It gave me a tremendous lift.

After every race now, I gratefully gave thanks to the man upstairs for letting me have my racing back. Life itself was precious, but for me, racing made life worth living. And because of that, I needed to give back too.

Amongst the crowd ringing the enclosure, I noticed Edward Frame and Samuel. Holding aloft betting slips, they waved enthusiastically. I touched my cap in acknowledgement of the applause, dismounted, undid the girths and went to weigh in.

Later, back in the jockeys' changing room, I stripped off and gave the silks to the valet. I couldn't wait to get back home and follow the trail unwinding before me. And then I realized what day it was – Thursday. I was due at Uncle George's party tonight. There was nothing further I could do until tomorrow. Except perhaps one thing. As I dressed in my normal clothes, I gave it serious thought.

Far too late now to help Lilly Dunston, but I could face John Dunston, offer my sympathy for his loss. Tell him I knew he'd stolen the plaster cast from Fred Smith at Carl's wake, left it on the cottage doorstep to get at me. Tell him I knew why he'd engineered the deaths of Louis Frame and Jo-Jo Smith. That I knew he was over a barrel because of Lilly's condition, and I understood. I didn't condone his actions – but I understood where he was coming from.

Lilly had been his wife and had relied on him to look after her. He'd needed money badly. Fully aware of that fact, the vindictive bastard behind the murders had deliberately exploited him, made him an offer he couldn't refuse. Nothing like using the love between husband and wife as a lever. Love was the strongest force in the world.

I came to a decision. Robson had a runner in the same race as my own. If Dunston was working, and it was highly likely he would be – no Lilly to look after now and a funeral to pay for – he could be in the box park right now, preparing to load up.

Collecting my saddle and grip, I made my way to the jockeys' car park. Visibility had worsened during the last half-hour and heavy, pewter-coloured storm clouds were rolling in from the west. I unlocked the boot of the Mazda, tossed my grip inside and relocked it. Then I walked back across the car park.

By the time I reached the horsebox park, it was practically dusk. Rain had begun spitting sporadically. It was going to be a wipers-and-lights-on, slow and miserable journey home. I quartered the field like a springer flushing game. By the time I found Robson's horsebox, the rain was torrential.

The ramp was down but the horse hadn't been loaded yet. I went to have a quick look in the cab, but Dunston wasn't there. Walking to the back of the box again, I heard a strange noise coming from inside.

To begin with, I thought he might have been sobbing – very likely in the present circumstances – and I hesitated. Grief was a private thing. But the sound was more of a gurgle than a sob. I climbed up on to the ridged ramp and went inside a little way.

In the gloom at the rear of the driver's compartment, I saw a figure on the floor. Edging closer, still unsure of my reception, I could now make out an unpleasant smell, one familiar to all jump jockeys – one that made the back of my neck prickle with apprehension.

Moving closer now, I could hear the noises were certainly not sobs. My eyes were becoming accustomed to the deep gloom inside the box and I could tell the figure lying down was a man.

I went up to him. It was Dunston all right. But he was most definitely not all right. Shock hit me like getting double-barrelled by a horse – right in the solar plexus.

He was lying in a pool of blood. A knife slash had almost severed his right ear, which lay across his cheekbone, the diagonal, gaping wound running on down the back of his neck, a knife protruding from his chest. Just how much blood he'd lost was impossible to judge – a hell of a lot. He was, miraculously, still alive. I saw the white flash as his eyes moved when I bent over him. Reassuring him that he was going to be OK, I phoned for the on-course doctor.

Then I quickly pulled down the cuff of my white shirt and ripped it free. Placing the makeshift pad firmly on top of the neck wound, I applied pressure, trying to staunch the flow. Although the cotton became saturated, the blood was no longer pouring out. If the killer had hit the carotid artery, further to the side, the man would be dead now. Maybe the killer had been aiming for that and Dunston had swung round at the last moment. It would explain the shape of the wound and the severed ear.

The knife could stay where it was. Buried in his chest, it was preventing blood loss. Once removed, death would follow quickly unless medical help was on hand.

Dunston made a gurgling sound as he tried to get words out.

'Don't talk, mate. Save all your strength. Just hang on. The doctor will be here in a minute or two.'

'Too late . . .' I could just hear the whisper.

'No, no, don't try talking. Hang on, that's all, hang on.'

'Lost Lilly . . .' He choked, coughed up blood.

'I know, I'm so sorry.'

'I . . . killed . . .' He struggled for words.

I realized Dunston, believing he was about to die, was trying to confess, absolve himself before he went.

'I know. You killed Louis Frame and Jo-Jo, but the bastard had you over a barrel, I understand.'

His eyes stared up at me as he fought to breathe.

'You didn't kill Lucinda, though, did you?' I was talking fast now. I wanted his confirmation, but I also wanted his attention, to keep him conscious until the doctor got here. Dunston was very close to death, but there might just be a chance if he could hold on. The knife hadn't gone into his heart – it was too far to the right – but I was pretty sure it had punctured a lung.

'You didn't kill her?'

'Nooo . . . told me to . . .' He was dragging the words out.

'The bastard wanted you to kill Lucinda as well as Louis and Jo-Jo?'

'Ye . . . es.'

'Tell me, who was it?' I didn't want to mention the name, didn't want to put words in his mouth.

But his strength, what little he had left, wasn't enough. His mouth was working, but the blood continued to trickle out and he was barely breathing.

Outside, there was a bright splash of light from a lamp, voices and flurried activity.

'You're OK. The doctor's here. You're going to be OK.'

His eyes stared up at me glassily, despairingly. I knew it was probably too late, as he'd said, but I also knew he didn't want to take the secret with him.

'If you can't talk, can you blink? Twice for yes,' I said urgently.

He blinked twice.

I bent close to his good ear so no one else could hear, and as the doctor came up the ramp, I whispered the name of the killer.

'Give me space . . .' The doctor came between us.

I backed away, desperately watching Dunston's face. There was a blaze of light now inside the box and I could see him quite clearly.

He blinked twice.

TWENTY-EIGHT

I was late getting to Uncle George's party – very late.

'Harry, thought you weren't coming.' As he opened the door, Uncle George's face broke into a wide smile. 'Come on in, lad.'

I took a deep breath, then stepped inside. Right now, the last thing I wanted to do was party.

I'd seen Dunston screamed off by ambulance to the nearest hospital. His life was only holding between one fought-for breath and the next. For all I knew, he was dead now. But I didn't know. I'd been banged up at the police station, being asked a million questions and having a statement taken. They were really, really interested in me.

'You were the gentleman who found Carl Smith's body when he was murdered at Leicester races, I understand. And you were first on the scene to find Lucinda Frame's body on North Shore golf course. Now, it seems, you've discovered an attempted murder at Fakenham racecourse.'

I'd groaned. 'I'm never going to live this down now, am I? How is Dunston? Is he still alive?'

They wouldn't tell me. I'm not sure whether they even knew.

I was the first person on the scene, covered in Dunston's blood. I'd been the person to discover Carl Smith, head first down a lavatory at the races, and then poor Lucinda, stabbed and bloodstained. Was I making a habit of it? Going for the treble?

I could possibly be the prime suspect.

Any information the police knew, they were keeping to themselves. I had been there for hours before they relented and I was free to go to Uncle George's party.

The party was already into the later stages, everybody well oiled and enjoying themselves hugely. Amongst the throng, I noticed quite a few of Uncle George's cronies from the fishing club, but the majority of people I didn't know.

As if sensing my thoughts, Aunt Rachel homed in on me, busily doing her hostess bit, giving introductions, holding out a beer. I reached out for the glass, my arm now clothed in a shirt complete with clean cuff. 'Thanks, I could do with this.' I could have done with a double whisky.

'Busy day?' she said brightly.

'You could say that.'

'Evening, Harry.' Victor Maudsley, looking very sharp in a beautifully cut suit, came up to us and took over where she left off. 'A happy day.'

'Er . . . er, yes.' I had to think quickly what he was referring to. All that came into my mind when he said it was *not if you've just had your throat cut*. Fortunately, I stopped myself from saying the words out loud just in time. Of course, he meant the celebration of thirty years of married life. All the same, I looked at him sideways. He alone amongst the guests would know the real truth about George and Rachel's marriage.

His silence had been the one thing that had caused the caustic waste of most of their years together. If he'd had the guts to speak up at the time, a lot of people's lives would have been played out differently. George and Victor had been great golfing friends for years before the rift, and it crossed my mind that I had been the catalyst. I had had to expose the truth. Without the exposure, there wouldn't have been a party tonight, no celebration and no mending of the rift between the two men.

And George and Rachel would still be living in marital hell.

I took a long pull of beer. I'd stay for a bit – an hour maybe, for decency's sake – then I'd make my excuses, plead an early start tomorrow morning and get back to the cottage. I was not in a celebratory mood.

And then, across the room raising her drink to me, I saw Annabel.

Sod, Uncle George!

Knowing I wasn't going to bring her, he'd steamed on, arranged for her to be at the party himself. I knew why: it was for Aunt Rachel's sake.

But it was too much. After discovering the murderous attack on Dunston, my emotions were still reeling. Coming into Annabel's orbit without full control was asking for it. If I'd known she was going to be here, I'd have stayed at the cottage when I stopped off to change my ripped and bloodied gear.

Annabel was now weaving her way through the crush.

'Harry, how're things? I'm so glad you made it. Uncle George said you might not.' She smiled up at me but the smile started to fade almost immediately. 'There's something wrong, isn't there?'

'No, no.' I brushed off her query.

'Oh, yes. Your face is really pale under the top tan. You can't fool me.'

'Nonsense, I'm fine.'

'OK, if you're playing it that way. We are at a party, but I'll see you afterwards.'

'No, my love, you won't. I'm not planning on being here for more than an hour.'

'And why's that?' She raised an eyebrow at me.

'Because I'm not in a party mood.'

'Because . . .?' she persisted.

'For God's sake, Annabel, leave it.'

She drew back, hurt showing in her face. 'I expect you've had another bloody fall,' she said coldly.

The words hurt. It was the elephant in the room between us and she knew that. She'd said it to hurt.

I shrugged. If she thought that the reason, fair enough. It was a good deal better than attempted murder.

Rachel's sister, Lucy, came up carrying a tray of wine glasses. 'Hello, Harry. I know it's been a difficult year for you, but how are things now? Getting better?'

I wish. I waved a hand to show I didn't want a drink from the tray. Told her what she wanted to hear.

'Yeah, things are getting better, thanks.'

'Good, good,' she nodded. 'But please do take a glass. We're about to drink a toast to George and Rachel.'

'Oh, yes, sure.' Annabel immediately took two from the tray and handed one to me. 'They deserve to be toasted. Thirty years being married is a marvellous achievement.'

Her gaze challenged mine until I looked away first.

Lucy tapped a teaspoon against a glass. 'Has everyone got a drink?' she called above the laughter and chatter filling the room. There were murmurs of assent.

'Then I'd like to propose a toast to George and Rachel. Tonight's a celebration of their enduring love. Only love can survive all the hardships of married life. And they are both survivors. Thirty years

– that's wonderful. May you have many, many more anniversaries to celebrate. Everyone – George and Rachel.'

We all raised glasses, drank the toast and clapped.

'Speech, George,' Victor called out.

Flushed with pride, Uncle George held up a hand.

'First of all, thank you, everybody, for coming tonight. Rachel and I appreciate your company and your good wishes. But I specially wish to thank Harry. He did a damn fine job of sorting out the truth for us a few months ago. I know I speak for Rachel as well when I say our life together now is a far cry from what it was, and we are blessed to still be together and more in love now than we ever were before. So, thank you for our second chance, Harry.'

I felt the biggest heel. In acute embarrassment, I raised my glass. 'No need to thank me, Uncle George. You deserve happiness. I'm glad, for you both. Very glad.'

Spontaneous clapping broke out again amidst cheers and whistles.

'You can't leave now, Harry,' Annabel murmured.

She was right. I was ashamed of my earlier attitude. It was very small-minded of me. No way did I want to spoil their special evening.

Early the next morning, I switched on Sky television to check on the breaking news. Nothing indicated Dunston had died. It was mentioned as an attempted murder, an attack that had taken place inside a horsebox at Fakenham racecourse in the early evening yesterday. The victim had been transported to hospital.

So Dunston must still be alive.

Did that mean that his attacker would risk another go? I hoped the police had provided a guard at his bedside. If he lived, and he'd seen the man – recognized him – Dunston was in a very dangerous position.

Over a strong coffee, I pondered the last few moments I'd been alone beside him in the horsebox. He'd heard what I whispered in his ear and the name. I was certain of that.

What I'd been asking myself over and over ever since was: did Dunston blink twice in confirmation of the murderer's name? Or had he simply blinked because, at that precise moment, the interior of the box had been suddenly flooded with bright light?

The only way would be to ask Dunston again. And I couldn't do that. The police already thought it very odd I'd been the first person at the scene on all three occasions *and* had links to the victims. It would be very unwise to risk a visit. But until I could prove otherwise, my money was on the double blink being an affirmation of the murderer's name.

The police could follow up what leads and forensic evidence was available; I was following a different trail. If the two trails converged at the end, that would be excellent. If not, and I could provide concrete proof, I'd simply have to come clean and hand my findings over to them to finish the job. If I kept anything to myself, I would certainly be charged with withholding information. No way did I want to join Darren Goode.

I drank my coffee, locked up and drove over to Mike's stables. He was in the kitchen as usual, preparing for the working day. He greeted me with a beaming smile. Although normally of an amiable nature, his effusiveness was unexpected.

'Harry.' He banged the kettle back on to the Aga ring. 'Let me make you a drink.'

'What's with the five-star treatment?'

'I'm in a happy mood, that's all.'

I twigged. 'Would it have anything to do with a certain lady reciprocating your feelings?'

He clapped me on the shoulder. 'Now, there you have it.'

'Well, whilst I'm glad for you, Mike, there's some pretty disturbing news I need to share.'

By the time I'd finished filling him in, the smile was long gone, replaced by a shocked expression.

'Good God, Harry . . . I reckon you did well to get out of that police station.'

'It is getting a bit regular, I must say.'

'And you were covered in the poor man's blood?'

'Of course I was, trying to stop it pumping out.'

'Has he died?'

'I don't know. It wasn't on the early news, except to say he'd been attacked.'

'So he could still be alive?'

'Yes.'

'Have you thought, Harry, that if he was one of the loose ends Darren Goode was talking about, he's still a threat to them?'

'Yes, I have. But I can't go steaming in and tell the police. I'm just hoping they've placed a guard by his bedside.'

'I'm pretty sure they will have. The police aren't stupid. They'll know if the murderer wanted Dunston dead, he'll have another go.'

'Yes.'

'So, what's your next move?'

'Later this afternoon, I'll get myself over to North Shore Hotel. I'm supposed to be meeting Tom. Says he's got something important to tell me.'

'The wine waiter, on Saturday night, at the wedding?'

'That's him.'

'Who are we talking about?' Fleur walked in, kitted out in jodhpurs and padded jacket.

'Not someone you know, love,' Mike said.

'Morning, Fleur.' I deliberately tried to break the ice.

In acknowledgement, she cast an indifferent, casual glance at me that clearly said I was barely above frog-spawn level.

'After second lot, Uncle Mike, I'm off with Mum to have a final viewing of the cottage, OK?'

'Oh, yes, sure,' he said hastily. 'You don't have to ride out at all, Fleur, if you'd rather not.'

She shook her head decisively. 'I'd rather. Got to think of my race fitness.'

'You're riding in a race?' I feigned interest – anything to lighten the atmosphere she'd brought into the kitchen.

'Didn't Mike tell you?' She turned and stared at me. 'I'm off back on a flight to Italy tonight.'

'Oh . . . right,' I said, taken aback.

'Her trainer's rung,' Mike explained quickly. 'Lost one of his other jockeys in a shockingly bad fall yesterday. So he rang to see if Fleur wanted back in.'

'And I do,' Fleur said emphatically, walking to the back door leading to the stable yard. 'Just two lots, then.' She closed the door behind her.

I looked at Mike and raised an eyebrow.

'Best thing, I reckon,' he said comfortably. 'She has her own path to tread.

'And your sister?'

'Maria's going to take a six-month rental on a cottage in the village. They both went to view it yesterday, after the trainer's call. Says three's a crowd, y'know,' he smirked.

'Don't tell me . . . Pen's moving in, yes?'

He nodded. 'Bloody marvellous, isn't it?' He was like a schoolboy with a first date.

'All these years older,' I laughed, shaking my head at him, 'and a whole lot dafter.'

'I know. Great, isn't it?'

TWENTY-NINE

I'd taken my Blackberry with me to the stables and done a quick hourly check for any news about Dunston. There was no news.

I had to assume he was still holding on and the hospital was monitoring him closely. The longer he lasted now, the better his chances, it seemed. It also increased the risk of the killer trying again. Once Dunston was well enough to talk, that would be it. So, if another attempt was going to be made, it would be in the next few hours, maybe running over until tomorrow at the latest.

The irony was I couldn't warn the police. I had no proof. Whilst Dunston remained the only threat to the killer's identity, he was also my only sure way of proving who the man was. And that only applied to the attack on Dunston himself.

I'd no proof the same man had killed Lucinda. I knew he had, but I couldn't prove it.

Another unpleasant thought crossed my mind. Maybe if Dunston did pull through after all, he could refuse to divulge the killer's name. It would make sense. Once he'd blown the whistle, he'd have to admit he'd taken money from the man to see off Louis Frame. Even as my thought pattern threw up this scenario, I knew it was the most likely.

Dunston wasn't going to shoot himself in the foot by confessing. All that would get him would be a custodial with Darren Goode. The tiny hope I'd fanned into a flame every time I checked the

Blackberry for further news on Dunston's condition now flickered and went out. Even if he survived, Dunston wasn't going to back me up.

I was in this on my own.

In sombre mood, when evening stables were over, I nosed the car through Mike's gates and headed east, to the coast.

The first person I saw on entering the North Shore Hotel bar was Dan.

'Good to see you again, Harry.' He put down the glass he'd been polishing.

I perched on one of the tall stools near the wall-mounted television.

'Just a mineral water with ice, thanks. Need my brain working tonight.'

'Why's that?'

'Not sure, to be honest. Know why when it happens.'

'Like that, is it?'

'Oh, yes.'

He pushed a misted glass across the bar.

'You the only barman on duty tonight?'

'No, young Danny's on, too.'

'Not Tom?'

'No.'

'How did he get on in the baby stakes?'

He grinned and ran a hand upward through his gelled hair. 'Got a girl.'

'He was pleased?' I didn't mention he'd said his wife would have liked a baby boy.

'Oh, crikey, yes. Never stops talking about his little Alice – that's what they're calling her.'

'Uh-huh. And how's the murder enquiry going? Nothing seems to be getting reported in the news. Have you heard anything, possibly even on the grapevine? Any progress at all?'

'Nah, the killer vanished off the face of the golf course, didn't he?'

'Were any of the guests absent, do you know, at the time the murder was taking place? Say, any of the major players, like Edward Frame, Brandon himself – anybody you may have served who asked for a drink and then left it untouched. Did you happen to notice?'

'The police never stopped grilling me about that. On and on at me, they were, but it was useless. I just wish I had. I'd tell them straight away if I knew anything.'

Dan looked troubled. I could understand why: weddings were his special baby. He liked them happy, with a big H.

'What about Edward Frame?'

'Yeah, he was there, and Richard, the best man – they were drinking together a lot of the time. Richard had a load on board from earlier on. And Edward was really knocking it back.'

'What about Brandon?'

'Well, Brandon and Lucinda went upstairs to . . . to . . .' He was struggling to put it delicately. I understood. He was working, and respect and discretion for guests was paramount in his job.

'Consummate their marriage?' I helped him out.

'Yeah. But Brandon came down to the party again a bit later, until the alarm was given.'

'And the bridesmaids were there all the time?'

'Yeah, leading the dancing, they were.'

'Do you think they might have noticed anyone possibly?'

'Don't think they would have noticed, not in that crush. Reckon the police would have asked that.'

I sighed. 'Yes, yes, of course they would.'

'The police found a footprint in the bunker, but you know that.'

'Yes. Did they find the shoe that made it?'

He shook his head, 'Not that I heard. Except . . .'

'Yes?'

'It was a trainer that made the footprint, they reckoned.'

'And the murder weapon – any news on that?'

'Nothing.' He waved an expressive hand. 'There's the whole of the North Sea out there. The killer could have chucked it in. Gone for ever, then.'

'Hmmm . . . best hiding place in the world.'

'Wish they could get the bastard.' He returned to vigorously polishing glasses.

'Have any of the guests who attended the wedding been back since, Dan? You know, as golfers or in the restaurant, perhaps?'

'No, I'd have seen them probably. And if I wasn't on shift, one of the others would have told me. Everybody on the staff's on red alert still. No, I'm sure no one has been back.'

I glanced to my right at the clock by the main door: two minutes to eight o'clock. As I did so, I saw Tom walk in. Our eyes met and he gave the faintest tip of his head and went out again. I glanced at Dan. He was intent on replacing the polished glasses and hadn't noticed.

Sliding off the bar stool, I left my drink and followed Tom. Dan would no doubt assume I'd gone for a leak. Which, as I followed Tom through the reception hall and down the stairs leading to the billiard room and toilets, was exactly where he was headed. The whole scenario had played out so smoothly, and so unnoticed by anyone else, it could have been scripted and rehearsed.

Partway down the stairs, I hesitated, giving him time to enter the toilets, check if anyone else was in there. He'd been practically paranoid when I'd spoken to him on the phone. The need to keep what he had to tell me too private to risk a third party overhearing. I knew he would be certain to ensure the toilets were empty. I gave him a couple of minutes then followed.

'Thanks for coming, Harry.' He was standing by the washbasins, waiting for me.

'Sorry I couldn't make it any sooner.'

'You're here now.'

'So, what do you want to tell me?'

'I need to confess.' His words startled me. Never, in all my searching and digging for the truth of who the killer was, had I remotely considered Tom.

'I should have said at the time of the murder but I was too scared.'

'Now, just hang on; what exactly are you confessing to?'

'To seeing the murderer.'

I stared at him. 'You witnessed Lucinda's murder?'

'No, no,' he said agitatedly, 'but it must have been the man I saw that night. I should have told the police . . . but I didn't.'

'Whoa, let's have it straight, right? Tell me what you saw, in the order you saw it.'

He licked his lips and cast a quick glance at the door.

'I'll make it quick; don't want anybody else knowing.'

'So, why tell me?'

'Because you're the detective.'

'Give over. I'm a jump jockey, OK? One who just happens to have got caught up in this foul mess.'

'I'm caught up in it, too. God, I'd give anything not to be.'

'Sounds like you're in it up to your neck. But if you don't hurry up—'

'I know, I know.' Sweat stood out on his forehead. 'I was in here, on the night of the murder. I'd come in the toilet to have a slash and a quick fag. Yeah, I know, it's against the rules, but I was worried sick about my wife.'

I nodded. 'Yes, I could see you were. Go on.'

'So, I'm in the cubicle, like, having a drag, and I hear this scrabbling noise, see. Well, I couldn't risk being found, so I stood on the toilet seat.'

'No feet showing under the door.'

'That's right. But then I could just see over the top, and I saw this man coming through the window, feet first – bare feet. He'd got a hell of a bunion on one foot. Dressed all in black, he was, an' all.'

A picture came into my mind. Expensive, black patent shoes – the left one misshapen on the medial side. It shook me. I had painstakingly assembled the pieces of jigsaw, made a clear picture of the killer – now they simply didn't fit.

'Which foot was the bunion on?'

He considered. 'Reckon it was the left . . . yes, it was.'

'Go on.'

'He was tall, reckon he needed to be – that window's a good six feet or more above the floor.'

'And he dropped in?'

'Yes.'

'What happened next?'

'He rushed over to the washbasin, ran the water and washed his hands. They'd got blood on them.'

Tom was starting to shake, his face paper-white as he relived the experience. 'But don't you see? Right then, I *didn't* know' – he pushed his face close to mine – 'I didn't know there'd been a murder.'

'I do see. I was out on the course chasing a shadow, whilst the bastard had made it back here to the hotel. That's why the police couldn't find anyone outside.'

'What am I going to do, Harry? If I go to the police I'll cop a charge of withholding information, won't I? I'll get banged up.'

'Not sure. As you said, at the time, you didn't know a murder had been committed.'

'But afterwards – I did afterwards.'

'So what stopped you coming clean when you knew they'd found a body?'

'I couldn't afford to lose my job. If management knew I'd skived in here for a fag, I'd be out. And they'd be within their rights. They've got to obey the law like the rest of us. Emma had given up her job to have the baby. We were relying on my wages to get by.'

'I can see that, but what's changed? Why have you decided to tell me now?'

'Like I say, you're the detective. I can't tell the police and I've got to tell somebody. I'm going mad keeping it to myself.'

'You'll still lose your job if it comes out.'

'Don't much matter now, though.'

'How's that?'

'I've been offered the management of a pub up in Newcastle. It's near the wife's mother. I've accepted. Emma will be able to help me run the place whilst her mother looks after our Alice.'

'I see.'

'It's my big chance to make a go of things. But . . .'

'But you need to confess.'

'I need you to tell the police for me.'

'Sorry, Tom.' I shook my head. 'Right now, they've got their beady eye on me. What we need is proof of the killer's identity. Do you know who this man is?'

'I'm not sure – too busy trying to stay hidden myself. I only caught sight of his face from the side. I know who I *think* it is . . . but I couldn't swear in a court of law it definitely was him. And I'm not going to perjure myself. No way.'

I asked him if it could have been the person I'd seen wearing the black patents. He was quiet for a minute, thinking about the possibility – like me, not wanting to believe what he already knew. Then, finally, he nodded.

'Yes – yes, I think it was him. Bloody hell . . .'

'Was he still wearing a balaclava?'

'A what?' He looked blank.

'I take it he wasn't.'

'Oh, I see what you mean, over his head and face . . . with just eye slits. No, he wasn't.'

'So,' I persisted, 'that means he must have taken it off just before he dropped through the sky-light window.'

'Could have taken it off after he'd murdered the woman.'

'No, he couldn't, Tom. Because he needed to keep his face covered. Bare faces show up in the dark. With a balaclava on, you're practically invisible. He'd keep it on all right until he felt safe. That means to the very last minute. Did you see if he had a knife with him?'

Tom shook his head. 'No, I'm sure he hadn't. I didn't even know about the murder. Didn't know why he'd got blood all over his hands.'

'So that means he ditched both items before he scrambled through the window.'

'Looks that way.'

We suddenly looked upwards. There was the noise of faint voices coming along the hall above. We made for the door and ran up the stairs.

'Go out the front door, meet me outside, in the car park,' I hissed and, turning left at the top of the stairs, I headed for the back door.

It would take Tom at least a couple of minutes more to leave by the main entrance, come round past the side kitchen and the Pro's shop before he reached the entrance to the car park.

It gave me time to get to my car and lift the boot. I took out a large screwdriver and the heavy rubber flashlight I kept for emergencies. I had a damn good idea where I should start looking. As I dropped the boot, Tom came running up.

'What're we doing?'

'Looking for a balaclava and the murder weapon.'

He gaped at me. 'Could be anywhere.'

I shook my head. 'Uh-huh. Unless I'm well out on my reckoning, we should find them just a few yards away.'

'You serious?'

'Deadly.'

I led the way over the gravel, past the golf buggies drawn up into line and securely chained for the night to the east side of the hotel. We followed the wall round to the left and came level with a tiny window only a foot above ground level.

'That's the one.' Tom pointed. 'It leads to the men's toilet.'

'Yes, I know, and look here . . .' I showed him the deep gully running around like a dry mini moat beneath the conservatory where the wedding was held. It was gravel-based and had a three or four feet high wall surrounding it.

'I'm sure the killer came off the links, down the steps at the other end of the moat, then climbed up and out at this end.'

'There's no steps to get out here.'

'No, but it's doable if you hang on to the top of the wall and scramble over.'

'Yeah,' he said, beginning to get excited, 'and it brings you straight to the toilet window.'

'Exactly. Now, at this point, I reckon our man snatched off his balaclava and ditched it before going back inside the hotel. A balaclava's something that would stand out immediately if anybody spotted him. Don't forget, he couldn't take it off before because that would drastically reduce his chances of escaping. But once he got to this point, he could stay down in the gully and get rid of it before coming in through the window.'

'You think it's down there now, in the gully?'

'Yes. If anybody had already found it, the police would be investigating who it belonged to, and they aren't.'

'Wow! It's concrete evidence, isn't it?'

'I'm hoping it's the proof I need to get the killer sent to trial and convicted for the murder.' As I spoke, I lowered myself over the supporting wall and stepped down on to the deep gravel.

I shone the torch around. There was no sign of anything lying on the ground. Holding the torch out to Tom, I asked him to play the beam where I needed it. Then, taking the screwdriver and working methodically every six inches, I gently prodded through the layers of pale yellow gravel. It took several minutes before the tip of the screwdriver met a spongy resistance.

'Here, Tom, shine the torch directly on to this spot.'

I moved the gravel away as carefully as I could without touching anything with my fingers. In the bright glare of the light, the gravel appeared even paler, but buried below the surface a piece of black woollen fabric could clearly be seen. I let the gravel roll back to cover all traces. And then, telling Tom to wait, I made my way along to the far side of the gully where a short flight of ten steps rose up to join the path on the west side of the hotel. Walking quickly round along the path, I rejoined Tom.

'Didn't want to scramble up the wall to get out.' I explained. 'There may still be traces of the killer's DNA clinging to the rough brickwork because it's protected from the elements by the building above it.'

'Right,' he nodded. 'We've found that balaclava, haven't we? You've literally dug up the evidence.'

'I think so. Now, we have to bite the bullet and call in the police.'

He looked apprehensive.

'It's got to be done, Tom,' I said gently. 'You know that; so do I. And we're staying here on guard until the police get here. This is incontrovertible proof of the killer's identity. There'll be saliva no doubt, plus skin sloughs, maybe even hairs, inside that balaclava. Should be enough to nail him. And if I'm not mistaken, I saw a glint of steel. I think he wrapped up the murder weapon inside.'

'Bloody hell!'

'Exactly.' I grinned at him. 'Brace yourself.' I reached into my pocket, took out my mobile and dialled the Skegness police. 'Bloody hell's about to break out.'

THIRTY

They didn't hang about. Descending on North Shore Hotel, the police sealed off the area, rigged up lighting and then the SOCOs went to work.

Tom and I found ourselves down at the police station. We were interviewed separately. It didn't take long for them to find the black woollen balaclava. It was wrapped around a five-inch kitchen knife. The hotel chef had reported his five-inch knife missing from the magnetic rail in the kitchen on Saturday evening. Both balaclava and knife had been buried beneath layers of gravel. And not only those: the SOCOs also uncovered a pair of trainers – black, size nine and spattered with blood. The left one badly misshapen around the area of the hallux base.

I'd wanted proof – now I'd handed it to the police.

Despite being questioned at length and in depth, having statements taken and signed, there was undoubtedly barely suppressed elation in the air.

Tom, under close questioning, told them the man's name: Richard Lutens.

The proof was incontrovertible, or would be after the necessary DNA had been established, and the identity of the killer would be confirmed.

I thought back to the night of the wedding. As best man, he'd stood up to give a speech. He'd been wearing black patent shoes. And his left shoe had been contorted out of shape in exactly the same place as the left trainer.

Richard Lutens had been traced and picked up straight away – he'd been at home, watching television – and arrested on suspicion of murder. Right now, the police were busy grilling him in yet another interview room.

My car was still where I'd left it many hours ago in the far corner near the gateway to the garden in North Shore Hotel car park. I unlocked it and slid in behind the wheel. There was an hour and a half's journey in front of me before I reached home. And home right now was the one place I wanted to be. I had to be alone to think. A reassessment was desperately needed.

OK, the evidence I'd found tonight would prove, beyond doubt, the killer was Richard Lutens. His DNA would be all over it and place him securely in the frame.

But except for John Dunston – and he might already be dead – I was the only person who knew that the real killer was someone else. Without a shred of proof, it would have been pointless to tell the police. They would have laughed in my face. I'd just presented them with all the evidence they needed to put Richard Lutens away. Their case was as good as closed.

Unless I could work a miracle, the real killer – the brains behind it – was going to get away with murder.

I switched on the engine, engaged first gear, and then my mobile bleeped. I dropped the gear back to neutral, checked what had come through on the phone. There was a horrific, graphic picture and some text. It took me a minute or two to tear my gaze away from the picture and read what the message said. Icy fear froze me to the seat.

If you want to see her alive again, get yourself to the hospital and finish Dunston off. Got it? It's Dunston's life or hers. Your choice. You've got three hours.

No signature. None needed.

It was from the real killer.

The picture showed Annabel – trussed and gagged. Her hands were tied to an empty hayrack and the bonds securing her wound around her body. One under her breasts, another cutting in viciously just above her pubic bone, emphasizing the bump of her unborn baby.

I felt the punch of shock like a physical blow in my stomach.

The picture danced and retreated before my eyes. Bile rose in my mouth. I flung open the car door, dropped forward and hung out. Taking huge gulps of cold sea air helped. The nausea backed off. I took a last shuddering gasp and sat back in the driver's seat, trembling violently.

If I drove off now, I would probably crash. I desperately needed to get a grip on my shot nerves. But in which direction did I need to drive? To Norfolk and Dunston? Or to try to find Annabel? But where was she?

Forcing myself to look at the ghastly picture objectively, I analyzed what I saw.

The stable was not a working one – there was no bedding, no horse. It was obviously being used as a store. The floor space was taken up by numerous bulky paper sacks. The manger, a heavy cast-iron job, was a very old type, battered and misshapen. Securely fixed to the brick wall, it was going nowhere. Which also meant neither was Annabel.

However, that type had been manufactured before I was born, at least forty years ago. By the state of it, the manger had seen a lot of use – and abuse – by a lot of horses.

Higher up on the wall, cemented in between courses of brick, was a massive butcher's hook. A strange thing to be found in a stable. What had it been used for originally?

Even as I questioned, a memory opened up in my mind. As a small boy, I had often accompanied my father on his various jobs. His trade was bricklaying – not on building sites, but on small individual jobs, contracts for farmers and householders. Mostly, he specialized in repair work and that had encompassed a wide range of differing jobs. If it was what he deemed a suitable job, he took me along. I liked to go with him, hand him tools, help hold the measuring tape and spirit level.

In particular, I loved it when he had work to do on stables. The horses, even at an early age, exerted a tremendous attraction for me. He knew this and would ask permission to bring me along.

A strangely familiar yet horrified excitement stirred inside me as I stared at the iron hook high up on the wall. I'd seen it before! And I knew what it had been used for.

As that young child, I'd asked my father the reason for the hook and, without thinking of the effect his words might have, he told me.

Nearly a century earlier, before the building was converted to use as a stable, it had housed pigs. The hook had been used to support the weight of a pig after it was slaughtered.

Now, at thirty-four years old, I felt again that disturbing horror created by the image my young mind had conjured up. But I was no longer a child. The feeling of horror dissolved and turned into potent anger. I knew where the hook and the manger were.

Switching on the Mazda's engine, I spun the wheel and flung up gravel in a wide arc as I floored the accelerator out of the car park and down on to Roman Bank Road. I wasn't going to see Dunston in the Norfolk and Norwich hospital; instead, I was headed seventy-five miles west to Harby in Leicestershire, to Barbara Maguire's stables.

At the time I'd first seen that frightening hook, the stables had been run by Barbara's grandparents. They had two daughters. The elder one was called Barbara and the younger one was Jane. Jane had married very young, whilst her elder sister had remained a spinster. Tragedy had occurred when Barbara died from cancer. It must have been a very bittersweet time for the family because, on the very day she died, Jane gave birth to a baby daughter. Jane and her husband had called their new baby Barbara in remembrance.

Many years later, following the death of her grandparents, Barbara had returned with her husband, Sean, and made a fantastic job of running the racing stables.

The killer had given me three hours. It would take me an hour and a half or more to get to Barbara's stables. I thought wildly of ringing her, sending her off the half-mile down the back lane to where the old stable block stood, isolated from the main stable complex. Then I realized if Barbara was on her own, she'd simply be running into acute danger. The killer was almost certainly waiting in the stable. When the three hours were up, without news of Dunston's death, he wouldn't hesitate. He'd kill Annabel.

This was my fight. I couldn't place anyone else in the line of fire. And it was pointless to ring the police. Even I couldn't be a hundred per cent sure that I was right in assuming it was Barbara's stable where Annabel was being held hostage. There was always the possibility that, somewhere in the thousands of old buildings dotted around the country, another one would house a battered manger with a hook high above it.

The police had got their man. To try to convince them otherwise would take time, too much precious time.

So I simply drove – fast.

The bastard hadn't even let Annabel have a chair to sit on. Apart from the terror she must be feeling, she would also be in extreme discomfort with the rope biting into her belly and distended womb. Pray God the baby was being protected from damage by the ambiotic fluid surrounding him. As I thought about the innocent life at great risk, fury raged through me, increasingly pressing my right foot down hard.

The man had said three hours, but for all I knew he might have killed her already. With four deaths to his tally, and Dunston running a close fifth, the bastard wasn't going to hold back. And if I got myself killed before I could release Annabel, her end would be swift, too.

The only weapons I had in the car were the screwdriver and torch. They weren't going to protect me at all. When I reached the stable, I needed to find something like a broom handle before I went barging in. I didn't know if he had a gun. But since none of his victims had been shot, it was odds-on that he didn't. The most likely weapon would be a knife – an effective murder weapon and, above all, a silent one.

As my mind ranged over what lay ahead, the road sped away beneath my car tyres. Cutting through villages and avoiding potential town traffic, I came off the A52 at Bingham and roared up the hill to Langar. I had made it back in an unbelievable hour and twenty minutes. Harby was the next village ahead and I spun the Mazda's wheel and turned off down what was little more than a narrow farm track. It led over a cattle grid, wound through the fields, then ended by the defunct stable block. Part way down, out of sight around a bend, a car was parked up close by the hedge, undoubtedly ready for a swift getaway.

Before rounding the last bend, I dowsed the lights and lowered my speed to a crawl before coming to a silent halt. My best hope was to take him unawares, but first I needed to find a weapon.

Walking the last few yards, I fetched up by a corner of the stables. Tiptoeing carefully, I went all around the four sides of the building. It was in darkness, and yet from the side farthest from where Barbara's working stables were sited was a window. It had what looked like a hessian sack nailed up, and through the thick weave I could just make out a dim yellow glow. It was ten-to-one Annabel would be in there.

Going round to the opposite side of the stable block, I eased open a door and inched myself round the doorjamb. The stable was pitch-black and numbingly cold. An overpowering smell of animal feed filled my nostrils and I knew at least one of the big sacks must have split, allowing the contents to spill out. If they were horse nuts, it would be like trying to walk on ball bearings and the floor would be as treacherous as ice.

Covering the head of my torch with my jacket, I switched it on. Luck was running my way. Along the wall to my left was an array of disused old tools left over from the days when the stables were used to house horses. I walked very quietly along and picked out a dusty pitchfork. Rusty it might be, but it still had the capacity to penetrate and kill if jabbed hard enough into someone's chest. Even the thought of having to do so made my hands sweaty and slippery. Then I thought of Annabel – and the baby – and gripped the handle firmly. Whatever it took to save them . . .

If the killer was watching out for anyone coming, his eyes would be focused at normal head height. Bending double, I moved along the centre walkway. Under one of the doors, I could see a very faint crack of light. The door itself was the usual style, comprised of two parts. Both were closed. But the woodwork was so old, the doorjamb had been eaten away by woodworm and there was a vertical gap running up by the top half where the door no longer fitted snugly. I drew myself up flat against the brickwork and angled my head. Barely an inch wide, the gap nevertheless afforded me all the inside view I needed.

The man was sitting with his back half turned away from me, oblivious to my presence. In his hands, he repeatedly weighed a knife. The steel glinted brightly in the light from two flickering candles. So, I'd been right in guessing he didn't possess a gun. It certainly evened up my chances.

Then I looked past him to the far wall. The hook was there, just as I remembered it. So was the manger – and firmly tied to it was Annabel.

My guts and body heaved in a spasm of anguished empathy. Her knees had buckled as far as they could go. Leaving her almost hanging by her hands. The gag was still in place, preventing her from crying out. But her face was contorted with pain and fear. And her loss of dignity was pitifully completed when I saw, running down her skirt, a long wet stain of urine. I hoped to God it was only urine, and wasn't a sign that her waters had broken. The viciously tight rope was still bound beneath her breasts and cutting into her belly above her pubic bone. I could have wept for her pain and humiliation.

Fury roared through me, but whilst all my instincts screamed at me to charge in and cut her free, it was too dangerous. Not for me, but for *her.*

She was facing me, and for a split second I thought she had glimpsed the involuntary jerk I'd made because she began to make a despairing rolling motion with her head. I drew back instantly. Right now, I needed to get back outside the building and ring for help before tackling the evil bastard. If I could get the knife away from him, hold him there until help arrived, Annabel would have a chance. If I tackled him on my own and he stabbed me, it was an odds-on certainty he would stab Annabel.

Silently, I eased my way back outside, leaving the pitchfork ready by the doorway but taking my torch and mobile. Time was still on my side. There must be at least an hour to go to the deadline.

With trembling fingers, I punched in Barbara's number so she could ring for the police and ambulance. If she told them to come straight away because a woman was being held hostage at knifepoint, they couldn't refuse.

Then I rang Mike's number and, almost an afterthought, Sir Jeffrey's. I still regarded Annabel as my responsibility, but she wasn't. I had to tell myself she belonged to him now, not me. And right now, he needed to know.

With back-up in place, I forced myself to wait a long, long five minutes. Ten would have been better, give them time to get here in case I cocked up, but images of Annabel burned my mind.

I turned and went back inside to face the killer.

THIRTY-ONE

I felt the rasp of the rusty pitchfork prongs as they ran down either side of my throat and then I was knocked back by the force of the blow. The prongs penetrated the woodwork behind my head and I found myself pinioned to the stable door. When Mike had said if ever my back was up against a stable door, he couldn't have known how true that would turn out to be.

The killer had known I was there, had seized the pitchfork from where I'd left it and waited his chance. I'd walked straight into the trap. Now, I was pinned as helplessly as a butterfly to the stable door facing the one where Annabel was being held. He kicked that door open so I could see her.

'So, top jock,' he sneered, 'what're you going to do about it?'

Annabel struggled ineffectively against her bonds, blood now running down her wrists where the rope had bitten in through skin and flesh.

'Cut her free. You can do what you want with me, you sadist.'

'Oh, I will, when it suits me. What about Dunston? You haven't had time to finish him.'

I thought rapidly. My only chance now was to rely on my wits.

'No need to go.'

'Why?' He narrowed his eyes.

'Rang the hospital, didn't I?'

'Well?'

I shrugged my shoulders. I needed to keep him talking, play for time. 'He's already left.'

'Left? What the fucking hell are you on about?' He lunged at
me with the knife and I felt the blade razor into the top of my left
arm. 'You've got five seconds . . .' He twisted the knife savagely
before pulling it out.

Pain streaked through my nervous system like molten lava.

'He's dead.' I forced the words through clenched teeth.

At the edge of my vision, I could see Annabel battering herself
back and forth against the manger, but I knew it was useless.

'Don't, don't, Annabel, for God's sake . . .'

At my words, she sagged and crumpled, hanging now by her
wrists that were pouring with blood. I was bleeding myself. My left
arm was saturated, the blood dripping off my fingers on to the floor.
How long did I have before the blood loss rendered me unconscious?
I didn't know. The wound was not only deep but jagged from where
he'd twisted the knife. I began to pray somebody would turn up in
the next few minutes or it would be too late for us.

'How do you know he's dead?' He jabbed the knife at my face.

The skin down the side of my cheek split and blood gushed out.

'I told you. I phoned the hospital.'

For one glorious moment, I saw the uncertainty in his eyes.
Dunston dead meant he was in the clear. OK, he'd then go ahead
and kill us. But he wasn't going to finish us off until he'd made
sure.

He took his eyes off me, laid down the knife and fished out his
mobile phone. I knew he couldn't have the number, would have to
ask directory enquiries first.

Whilst his attention was taken up, I hunched my shoulders as
high as I could, stiffened my neck sinews and rocked from side to
side. Then I grasped each of the prongs of the pitchfork and flung
myself forward. For an agonizing moment, I thought I'd failed, then
the wood groaned and I felt it give where the woodworm had weakened it and I was catapulted into the stable beside Annabel.

He gave a bellow of rage, dropped his mobile, made a grab for
the knife and came at me.

Sprawled on the floor, I did the one thing left to me. Drawing
my knees high to my chest, I let him have a double barrel straight
in the crotch. His bellow of rage turned to a high-pitched animal
shriek of agony. The knife flew from his hand as, bent double, he
clutched his genitals.

I launched myself at him. It was a bizarre contest, I with one arm useless and pouring blood, he in extreme agony, unable to straighten up. Locked together, we rolled around, mauling and kicking each other without either of us gaining an advantage. But the thrashing around brought us to where the knife had landed.

Too late, I saw him make a grab for it.

He dragged himself to his feet, waving it in triumph. In the guttering candlelight, the steel glittered evilly as he raised the knife ready to strike. But as his arm reached the highest point before he plunged the steel down into me, we both heard cars racing down the lane, complete with wailing sirens. He hesitated, arm still high in the air. A smirk crossed his face.

'Too fucking late,' he crowed and brought his arm down.

Despairingly, I gave a thrusting roll, kicking out with my feet and hitting one of the paper sacks. His hand brought the knife down, but instead of finding me as target, it ripped through the sack, spilling thousands of horse nuts that bounced, rolled and cascaded everywhere.

Already prostrate on the ground, I was OK. But for him, up on his feet, the nuts were lethal. He took just one step towards me. It was all that was needed. His feet skidded on the equivalent of thousands of ice cubes and he came down with a sickening crash. Just as the police and Mike burst into the stable.

'Watch out underfoot,' I shouted.

But the powerful beams from many torches illuminated the stable, clearly showing the danger. It also illuminated the man.

He was lying motionless, his right arm twisted underneath his back. A bright red pool of blood spread out beneath him. He had fallen back on his own knife. The point was sticking up grotesquely through his chest. His eyes were wide open but they weren't seeing anything.

Brandon Lutens was dead.

EPILOGUE

Sir Jeffrey answered my ring on his doorbell. He was wearing a butcher's apron, navy-and-white striped, over expensive trousers.

'Very good to see you, Harry. How's the arm?' He indicated the sling supporting my left arm.

'Healing, thanks. How's the girl?'

'*Our* girl, you mean.' He gave me an amused, knowing look. I tried a nonchalant shrug with one shoulder and grinned.

'Possibly.'

'Come on,' he said, 'come and see her. She's lying in state in the lounge.'

Annabel was indeed laid out on a sumptuously squashy four-seater settee, a rug covering her legs and precious bump. I went over to her, took a hand and squeezed it.

'I've been to Janine's flower shop.' I held out a large bunch of highly perfumed white freesias. 'How're you doing?'

'Darling Harry, my favourites.' She lifted her face for a kiss. 'Thank you.' Having received her kiss and still holding my hand, she turned to Sir Jeffrey, 'Jeffrey, dear, would you mind rustling up three coffees?'

'Of course.' He smiled indulgently down at her and disappeared towards the kitchen. I gave Annabel a wry look.

'He's so civilized. In his position, I don't think I would be.'

'Nonsense,' she laughed. 'He *knows* he has nothing to worry about – as regards you.'

I inclined my head. It was true. He was the man she'd chosen to share her life with, bear his children. Involuntarily, my gaze dropped to the baby bump.

'He's still fine in there?'

'Oh, yes. Knows a safe place when he sees one.'

And again, it was true. Annabel also knew she was safe with Sir Jeffrey. Whereas life with me, well . . . my life continued to grow less and less safe.

We had ended up in the same hospital last week, although not in the same ward, and been kept in for observation. They'd stitched my arm back into one piece again, repaired my face and brought Annabel and bump safely through her traumatic ordeal.

We'd been ordered to rest with absolutely no undue exertion.

However, having had my discharge pass signed, that hadn't prevented me from going over to the Norfolk and Norwich hospital. The police had, of course, hastened to inform Dunston that his would-be killer was dead and that meant he was safe from any further attack. It must have given him peace of mind. But I felt I owed it to Dunston to go and visit him in person.

I'd walked in and sat down beside his bed.

'I was sure Brandon Lutens was the killer,' I'd said. 'He was the man who recommended other people to use White, Hubbard and Brownley, the dentists. He was the one person who linked everything together. But when I asked you to confirm he was the man who knifed you – actually tried to kill you – I couldn't be sure if you blinked twice for yes, or whether it was because of the sudden lights inside the horsebox.'

'Ah, yes, I see what you mean.' He'd rolled his head on the pillow to ease it. The whole of the right side of his cheek and around his ear was a complex network of stitches. 'Nay, it weren't the lights. I wanted to tell you t'was him. Thought I was off to join Lilly, y'see. An' I didn't want him getting away with it.'

'Yes, I do see.'

I'd reached across and placed a bag of grapes on the locker at the side of his bed.

'I've had time to think, lyin' here. An' I want to thank you, Harry, for saving my life, 'cos you did.'

'Get away. I'm just so sorry about your Lilly.'

'An' I am, believe me. But what's happened has happened; it's all you can say. I'm just glad you got the swine. He's paid for it now.'

'Indeed he has.'

'An' that young woman – the one expectin' – is she all right?'

'Yes, thanks, John. Yes, she and the baby are OK.'

'Good, good . . .'

He'd closed his eyes and gone off to sleep.

*　　*　　*

'So, Harry,' Sir Jeffrey said and poured fresh coffee as the three of us sat relaxing in front of a blazing log fire in the lounge after a most acceptable dinner of steak and salad, no chips, 'give us the full SP.'

I smiled at his phrasing. Despite him sharing the same bed as the woman I still thought of as my wife and who I was still hopelessly in love with, I liked the man, damn it. The irony of life!

I'd already filled Mike in with the details – he'd been co-opted as Leo's carer whilst I'd been in hospital – now I needed to relay them again.

'It all started with the false teeth on the doorstep, didn't it?' Annabel smiled at me.

'Yes. John Dunston was gunning for me because I'd found out the truth regarding the Leicester races murder. He had stolen Carl Smith's replica pair of teeth at the wake following Carl's funeral. As you know, he left them on my doorstep. But, in turn, Dunston was being held over a barrel by Brandon Lutens. With the money he was being paid by Brandon, Dunston could afford to provide the nursing care his sick wife needed. It was Brandon who paid him to engineer the car crash that killed Louis Frame and the pregnant Jo-Jo.'

Annabel drew in a sharp breath. 'She was *pregnant*?'

'Afraid so.'

'Three lives were lost in that crash.' Sir Jeffrey shook his head sadly.

'And when Jo-Jo died, Jake Smith decided to put me over a barrel with threats against Chloe so that I'd agree to find Jo-Jo's killer. What escalated things, of course, was when Lucinda was murdered on the golf course.'

'That's what I don't understand, Harry.' Annabel frowned. 'What motive did Richard Lutens have to kill her?'

'Apparently, when Richard learned of Brandon's death, he told the whole sordid tale to the police to try to save himself.

'He and Brandon were in business selling horse feed. But the business was shaky. They needed to expand. Brandon deliberately set out to seduce Lucinda in order to get her father's fortune – that's why he had Louis killed.

'When Louis died, Lucinda was the sole beneficiary to his vast fortune. Of course, if Jo-Jo had lived, the family line would have gone on, but when she died, everything went to Lucinda. And when Lucinda was murdered, everything went to Brandon.

'But he was clever. To avoid suspicion, he knew he had to be seen by the wedding guests in the St Andrew's Suite at the time Lucinda was murdered. So the two men hatched it between them. And no doubt Richard would have been given a sizeable chunk of Louis' money for his services.'

'How wicked!' Annabel clenched her fists.

'Hmmm, it was. And then poor Lilly fell downstairs and died, which meant Brandon's hold over Dunston was ended and Brandon tried to kill Dunston to prevent him talking.'

'Why was I taken hostage in that old stable, though?'

'When Barbara's stables expanded, she ordered extra feed from Lutens. He was told to store the bags down in the old block until they were needed. That's how he knew about it being isolated. I guess when he panicked about Dunston still being alive, he thought it would be safe to use it to hold you hostage. I was supposed to kill Dunston and he used you as the lever to make me do it.'

'Well, it's all over now,' Sir Jeffrey said. 'You can relax, Harry – go back to being a jockey.'

'What about Jake Smith? Have you told him?' Annabel queried. 'Is he off your back, too?'

'He knows Jo-Jo's death was a horrible accident – she wasn't the target.'

'So you've solved the Golf Course Murder.' Annabel deliberately gave the words capital letters.

I groaned and drained the last of my coffee. 'I expect that's what will haunt me now, along with the Leicester races murder.'

'I think you'll live it down in the end, Harry.'

'I sincerely hope so, Jeffrey.'

'As long as there isn't a third case, of course.'

'God forbid . . . I couldn't stand a third.'

We were all laughing as I stood up to go.

'Best get back. Leo's seen so little of me he's starting to think he's an orphan.'

'Come and see us again.'

'Yes, of course.'

*   *   *

I took my leave and turned the car towards home. But halfway there, mulling over the events of the evening, I realized there was one other person who needed to know the facts about Jo-Jo's death. And I had promised to tell her – Alice.

It wasn't too late to call on my way back.

Half an hour later, I parked outside Alice's house in Newark, walked up to the door and rang the bell. No one answered. I tried a knock. The door swung inwards a little. It wasn't fully shut. Hesitating a moment, I called her name. Silence.

Feeling uneasy, I pushed the door open and stepped inside. Calling her name, I walked down the hall to the kitchen. The street lamp outside shone a glow through the window. The light wasn't bright but it was enough for me to see her.

Alice lay on the kitchen floor, face down. She was dead. Must have been dead for some days, judging by the smell emanating from her body, the blood congealed and black. The back of her head had been smashed in.

In shocked horror, I stood and stared down at her. I'd liked Alice. Brash and common, she might have been, but underneath she was good-hearted, had cared a lot about Jo-Jo. I'd thought her a survivor in a harsh world. I was wrong.

And then it really hit me. I knew who'd killed her. I could hear again his words as he'd sat opposite me in the pub.

If Jo-Jo hadn't met him, she'd still be alive . . .

It had been Alice who had introduced Jo-Jo to Louis Frame.

Later, Jake Smith had said he'd spent the night with Alice.

What he hadn't said was that he'd killed her.

Looking down at her lifeless body, I also knew I was the only person who could identify her killer.

I'd been here before.

What the hell did I do now?

Lightning Source UK Ltd.
Milton Keynes UK
UKHW042345170119
335781UK00001B/22/P